"WHAT ARE YOU DOING, PATRICK?"

Pam frowned, uneasy under his gaze.

"I enjoy looking at you. Life is for enjoying, Pam, and I enjoy you."

"Is life for enjoying, Patrick?"

He nodded. "I decided that it was some years ago, when I had to reevaluate my life after a big disappointment."

So he, too, had known disappointment. Pam was curious, but she decided to keep the discussion impersonal. "Disappointments that change our lives stay with us. At least, the lingering effects do."

"Right now, I don't want to think about past disappointments. It's Friday night, I'm out with the loveliest woman in town, and all's right with my world. How about yours?"

She warmed under his heated gaze. "My world's pretty fine right now, too."

He nodded toward the crowded room. "What do you say we blow this joint? I'd like to be alone with you."

That sent her blood racing, but not with fright. With anticipation. Taking his hand in hers, she pulled him up and headed toward the door.

Special thanks and acknowledgment to Pat Warren for her contribution to this work.

Special thanks and acknowledgment to Joanna Kosloff for her contribution to the concept for the Tyler series.

Published April 1992

ISBN 0-373-82502-1

BRIGHT HOPES

Printed in U.S.A.

BRIGHT
HOPES

PAT WARREN

Harlequin Books

TORONTO • NEW YORK • LONDON
AMSTERDAM • PARIS • SYDNEY • HAMBURG
STOCKHOLM • ATHENS • TOKYO • MILAN
MADRID • WARSAW • BUDAPEST • AUCKLAND

TYLER

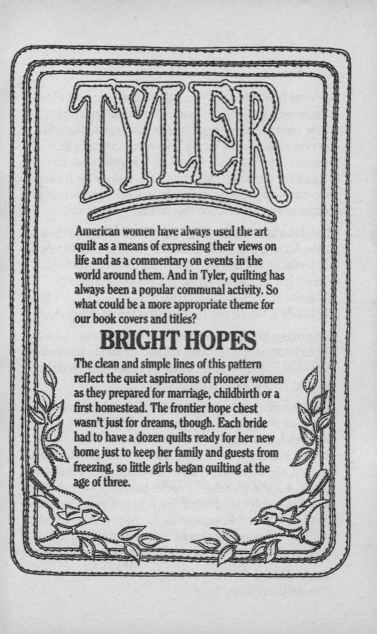

TYLER

American women have always used the art quilt as a means of expressing their views on life and as a commentary on events in the world around them. And in Tyler, quilting has always been a popular communal activity. So what could be a more appropriate theme for our book covers and titles?

BRIGHT HOPES

The clean and simple lines of this pattern reflect the quiet aspirations of pioneer women as they prepared for marriage, childbirth or a first homestead. The frontier hope chest wasn't just for dreams, though. Each bride had to have a dozen quilts ready for her new home just to keep her family and guests from freezing, so little girls began quilting at the age of three.

Dear Reader,

Welcome to Harlequin's Tyler, a small Wisconsin town whose citizens we hope you'll soon come to know and love. Like many of the innovative publishing concepts Harlequin has launched over the years, the idea for the Tyler series originated in response to our readers' preferences. Your enthusiasm for sequels and continuing characters within many of the Harlequin lines has prompted us to create a twelve-book series of individual romances whose characters' lives inevitably intertwine.

Tyler faces many challenges typical of small towns, but the fabric of this fictional community created by Harlequin will be torn by the revelation of a long-ago murder, the details of which will evolve right through the series. This intriguing crime will culminate in an emotional trial that profoundly affects the lives of the Ingallses, the Barons, the Forresters and the Wochecks.

Renovations have begun on the old Timberlake resort lodge as the series opens, and the lodge will also attract the attention of a prominent Chicago hotelier, a man with a personal interest in showing Tyler folks his financial clout.

Marge is waiting with some home-baked pie at her diner, and policeman Brick Bauer might direct you down Elm Street if it's patriarch Judson Ingalls you're after. The Kelseys run the loveliest boardinghouse in town, and you'll find everything you need at Gates Department Store. Pam Casals gives hometown favorite son, Patrick Kelsey, a run for his money when she hires on as Tyler High's new football coach. So join us in Tyler, once a month, for the next eleven months, for a slice of small-town life that's not as innocent or as quiet as you might expect, and for a sense of community that will capture your mind and your heart.

Marsha Zinberg
Editorial Coordinator, Tyler

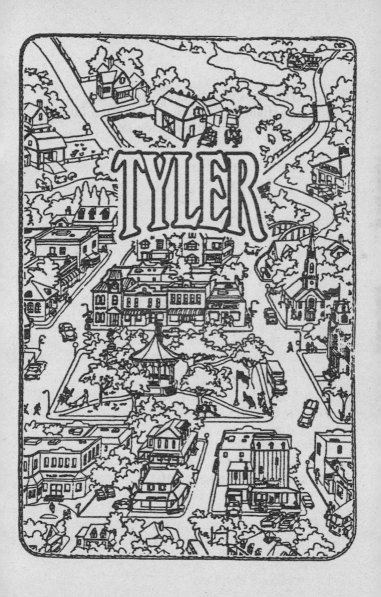

This book is dedicated to Lynn Soriano,
whose strength, determination and zest for life
inspire all who know her.

CHAPTER ONE

"A WOMAN FOOTBALL COACH?" Patrick Kelsey laughed out loud. "Come on, Miss Mackie. You've got to be kidding!"

Josephine Mackie sat back in her desk chair, adjusted her round, rimless glasses on her long, thin nose and looked up at the tall gym teacher. "Why, Patrick, don't tell me you're a chauvinist. Not with that superachiever mother of yours and three charming sisters."

Patrick ran a hand through his short, dark hair. That was the one drawback to growing up and living in a small town like Tyler, Wisconsin. Everyone knew you, your family and most of your business. Miss Mackie had been principal of Tyler High School when he was a freshman twenty years ago. She wasn't meddlesome so much as knowledgeable—about everyone. He flashed her what he hoped was a disarming smile.

"Not me. It's just that... well, these are guys, Miss Mackie. Young men, really. There'll be problems, like the locker room, for instance. They're going to hate having a female around when they're changing."

"I don't imagine she'll shower with the boys, do you?"

Patrick reached for patience, never his strong suit. "How about the game itself? I never heard of a woman who knows football inside and out."

"Really? Ever hear of Phyllis George, to name one? I thought she did a highly commendable job, and on national television at that. And now there's Pam Casals. Have you read her credentials?"

Patrick felt his irritation grow as he paced her small office. "I know she was a runner in the Olympics."

"A little more than a mere runner. She won a silver medal when she was seventeen, then returned and won a gold medal at twenty-one."

"Okay, so she can run. But does she know football?"

Disappointed in his reaction, Miss Mackie nevertheless continued unruffled. "She went on to become an exhibition performer, earned a degree in phys ed, was head coach at a college in the east and an Olympic coach for a year in Seoul. For a young woman who's just turned thirty, I would call that an impressive list of accomplishments."

Stopping in front of her desk, Patrick braced his hands on the edge and leaned forward. "I repeat, does she know football?"

"I would think so, having coached football at the college level. Surely she can manage high school boys." Josephine Mackie felt her gaze soften as she studied Patrick's stubborn features. She thought she knew exactly why he was so upset, and chose her words carefully.

"I realize that when I asked you to join our coaching staff ten years ago, Patrick, your dream was to one day be football coach here at your alma mater. I believe you took on coaching basketball temporarily, thinking that when Dale McCormick retired, you'd shift over to football. But you've done such a tremendous job—guiding the basketball team from class B to class A status and giving us a championship season for the past two years. We don't want to lose you in that capacity.''

Patrick's blue eyes were serious as he straightened. He'd figured that was what she'd thought, and the rest of the town, too. But they were wrong.

He'd been a star quarterback during his years at Tyler, and at the small Midwestern college he'd attended while earning his teaching degree. Then there'd been problems—serious problems—and he'd had to rearrange his dreams. When he returned to his hometown, he'd been pleased to be asked to coach basketball and assist Coach McCormick occasionally in football. Even now, what he really wanted was what was best for the Tyler High boys. But he knew that changing the thinking of a whole group of people who had their minds made up wasn't something he could do without revealing more than he felt comfortable doing.

''Miss Mackie, I'm perfectly happy coaching basketball. You're aware, I'm sure, that many of the boys on the football team also play basketball. I know these guys, and they aren't going to accept a woman coach.''

She narrowed her pale gray eyes and zeroed in. ''They will if you encourage them to accept her.''

Settling into the old wooden chair facing her desk, Patrick scowled. "I don't know if I can do that, in good conscience."

Propping her elbows on her desk, Miss Mackie leaned forward. "Patrick, I don't have to tell you that this town gets greatly involved in our school athletics. And the football team's been on a long losing streak. Dale McCormick was a good coach once, back when you were playing for him. But for some time now, he's been merely coasting along, counting the days to retirement."

"I agree," Patrick admitted.

"The school board felt we needed new blood, someone to get the boys all stirred up. Of our six applicants, Pam Casals is by far the most qualified. I've talked with her on the phone and she's personable and intelligent. I've hired her on a one-season trial basis and she's arriving next week. Won't you open your mind and give her a chance?"

Miss Mackie was a good administrator, her judgment usually on target, Patrick felt. This time, though, she was wrong. "I have nothing against this particular woman, you understand. I just don't feel *any* woman can coach football. It's too rugged a game, too physical." He picked up Pam Casals' file and flipped it open, to where her picture was clipped to the inside front cover. "See how small she looks? She could get hurt out there."

Josephine Mackie sighed. Patrick Kelsey was an instructor who seldom gave her problems. He was making up for lost time today. Glancing at her watch, she stood, realizing she could debate this issue with Patrick all day and neither would bend. "It's only the first of August. We have several weeks before classes start. During that time, we'll be observing Pam and her training and practice methods closely."

Picking up her purse, she walked around the desk. The school was deserted; she'd come in to get a head start on some paperwork and had been somewhat surprised when Patrick cornered her. "Why don't you study her file a bit more and then leave it on my desk? I have an appointment."

The gentleman in him had Patrick rising and smiling at the slim principal. "I don't mean to give you a hard time. But you know what these guys mean to me."

She smiled back at him. "They mean a great deal to me, too."

Patrick nodded. "You off to a board meeting?"

Josephine found herself blushing as she patted her sparse gray hair. "No, actually I have an appointment at the Hair Affair."

He grinned at her. "Big date tonight, Miss Mackie?"

Girlishly, she pursed her lips, turned from him and opened the door, choosing to ignore his question. "Please lock up when you leave," she said, then hurried down the hallway.

Chuckling, Patrick sat back down, wondering why Miss Mackie had never married. Too wrapped up in her job, he supposed. Few women could juggle work and children, and still maintain a happy marriage. His mother, Anna Kelsey, was about the only one he knew of. But she was one of a kind.

He opened the file again. Pam Casals did not look like his idea of a football coach. From the picture, she appeared to be of medium height and quite slender, with the muscular legs of a runner. Her shoulder-length brown hair, wind-tossed, framed an oval face, and her large brown eyes gazed directly into the camera. She didn't appear aggressive or arrogant, but there was a hint of determination to the angle of her chin. Still, if this woman could handle that rowdy group of high school boys, then he was the Easter Bunny, Patrick thought with a frown.

Quickly he read through her file. Like millions of people, he was always drawn to watch the Olympics. He'd heard countless stories of the dedication, perseverance, sacrifices and sheer guts it took to win a medal. She was a winner, he'd give her that. But could she make the Tyler boys into winners?

Doubtful, he thought, closing the file. He knew these boys better than anyone, certainly better than an outsider. And a woman at that. He would give her a chance, but he would remain in the picture. He'd keep an eye on her, check out her methods, look out for his boys. He'd mention to a couple of the guys—Ricky and B.J. and Moose—that he'd be interested in knowing what Coach Casals did during their training sessions.

It wasn't really spying, Patrick told himself as he placed Pam's file on the principal's desk. It was protecting.

Digging in the pocket of his jeans for his keys, Patrick left the office whistling.

A RAINBOW. Pam Casals glanced to the right as she drove along the country road, and smiled. Slowing, she pulled to a stop by a wooden fence bordering pastureland. Shifting into park, she slid out of her sporty white convertible and went to lean on the weathered fence.

It had been raining that morning when she set out from Chicago, a light drizzling summer rain. Wisconsin being north of Illinois, it wasn't quite as warm here. Fall would be along all too soon.

The rainbow shimmered in the sky, where the last of the clouds were moving off to the east. Rainbows were a sign of good luck—Pam remembered reading that somewhere. She certainly hoped so. It was time for a bit of luck.

On an impulse, she made a wish. "I wish that I might find happiness in Tyler," she said aloud.

A small herd of cows grazing nearby, brown shapes on a field of still-damp green grass, didn't even glance her way. She breathed in deeply, air so fresh it almost hurt to inhale. No automobile fumes, no pollution or even smoke. On the drive she'd passed dairy farms, many with large wooden barns, as well as cornfields, orchards and several horse farms. She'd taken the scenic route instead of the highway, enjoying the twisting rural roads and the lakes tucked in among rolling green hills. The clean country atmosphere was a welcome change from the city she'd left behind.

She'd left a lot of things behind, or so she hoped. Pain and confusion and doubt. Frustration and anger and broken dreams. And a shattered love affair. A few good things, too, like her father, Julian Casals, still living in the family home in a suburb of Chicago. And her two married brothers, Don and Ramon, who'd taught her so much more than football.

Pam swung around, leaning her elbows on the fence. She was only a short distance from Tyler, and she hoped there were more two-lane roads like this one around. It was a perfect place to run—smooth blacktop, very little traffic. And run she must, while she could. For her health and her mental well-being and the sheer, physical pleasure of it.

A low-throated bark drew her attention to her car, and she grinned. Her old, white, long-haired English sheepdog sat in the back seat, his head cocked in her direction, his pink tongue hanging low. "All right, Samson," she said, slipping behind the wheel again. "I know you're impatient to get going." With another glance at the rainbow, Pam shifted into drive. "I'm anxious to check out our new home, too."

Flipping on the radio as she pulled away, she heard Willie Nelson's unmistakable voice ring out. "On the road again . . ."

Pam glanced back at Samson, whose ears were blowing in the breeze. "That's us, pal. On the road again." Laughing for no apparent reason except a sudden happy sense of anticipation, she headed for Tyler.

IT WAS EXACTLY two o'clock when she arrived in the middle of town. There was a central square—an open, grassy area with huge old oak trees and well-maintained flower beds. The downtown business section consisted of a few blocks of two-story brick buildings, predictably lining Main Street. The small-town atmosphere pleased Pam as she pulled up in front of the post office. High on its pole, the flag rippled in the wind, but the building had a Saturday-afternoon-deserted look. Stretching, she got out of the car.

According to the map Rosemary Dusold had sent her, she was only a couple of blocks from her friend's house. But there was no time like the present to get oriented. Across the way, she spotted the Tyler library and the brick town hall. On the opposite corner was a beauty shop, the sign heralding it as the Hair Affair. Cute, Pam thought.

Around a corner, she saw a sign for Marge's Diner. She patted Samson's shaggy head. "I'll be right back, fella," she said as she headed for the square.

A bank on another corner featured a tower clock. The usual array of grocery store, drugstore, cleaners and so on filled out that side of the block. She walked on.

A couple of older ladies seated on a park bench smiled up at Pam as she approached, giving her a feeling of friendly welcome. A handful of youngsters were playing tag on the far side. In the center of the green, she spotted several adults involved in a loosely organized game of touch football. Her interest heightened, Pam stepped closer.

Watching took her back in time to her early teens, when she and her father and two brothers would spend many an autumn afternoon tossing the pigskin. Soon, playing catch hadn't been enough for Pam, so she'd organized a group of neighbors and divided them into two teams. Then she'd mapped out strategies for her side, trying to make up for her size by outwitting the opponents. Much to her brothers' surprise, her maneuvers worked more often than they failed. Their respect had spurred her on to try even harder.

She'd already been running then, her dreams focusing on the future Olympics. But her love of football had never died. She'd learned the game first by playing, then by watching the college teams on television, as well as the pros. Fun times, Pam thought. Times that had bonded their small family closer after the devastation of her mother's early death. Shoving her hands into the pockets of her white slacks, she leaned against a tree.

There was one big guy, a solid wall of muscle, who wasn't much on speed but nearly impossible to get past due to his size. She noticed a woman about her age with dark hair, a tall rugged outdoor-type man with black curly hair and, to Pam's surprise, her friend and new roommate, Rosemary Dusold, leaping high to catch a pass, her blond ponytail bobbing. Smiling, Pam stepped out of the shade, hoping Rosemary would notice her.

As she stood on the edge of the green, she saw a wild throw coming her way. No player was out this far. Forgetting herself, she ran a few steps, jumped up and caught the ball. Acting instinctively, Pam began to run toward the makeshift goal line, hotly pursued by two or three players she heard running behind her.

Exhilarated, the ball tucked close to her body, she picked up speed. *Almost there,* she thought. Then she felt the hit. Strong arms settled around her waist, sliding lower to her knees, taking her down. Her tackler rolled, cushioning the fall with his lean, hard body, letting her land on him rather than on the unforgiving ground.

"Touchdown!" someone called out from behind as thundering feet arrived.

"She fell short," yelled a dissident.

Still clutching the ball, Pam eased from the grip that held her and scrambled to her feet. Her opponent rose, too, and she found herself looking up into the bluest eyes she'd ever seen. Unexpectedly, her heart missed a beat and she found herself swallowing on a dry throat.

He was several inches over six feet, with curly black hair falling onto a lean face etched with laugh lines at the corners of those incredible eyes. He smiled then, his features softening as he reached out to brush leaves and grass from her shoulder. Pam's reaction to his light touch was on a parallel with the way she'd felt when her gaze had locked with his. Dizzying. She took a step backward.

"I hope I didn't hurt you," he said. She was lovely, with warm brown eyes and skin the color of a pale peach. Who was she? Patrick wondered.

"No, I'm fine."

She had on baggy white slacks and a comfortably faded green-and-white Jets football jersey with the number 12 on the back. "I see you're a Joe Namath fan."

"I was." She couldn't seem to stop staring into his eyes.

Strangers in Tyler—especially strangers who joined in impromptu games—were uncommon. There was something familiar about her, Patrick thought, but he couldn't put his finger on what it was. "That was a great catch."

"Thanks," Pam said, giving him the football.

"I'm Patrick Kelsey." He offered his hand.

Politely she slid her own hand into his grip, feeling the calluses on his roughened skin—and the warmth. "Hello," she replied. Before she could say more, Rosemary came alongside.

"Pam," Rosemary greeted her. "Glad you're here at last."

Pam withdrew her hand and turned to smile at her friend. "Me, too."

"Hey, everyone," Rosemary went on, "this is Pam Casals, a friend of mine from Chicago who's come to stay with me for a while. Pam, this is Kathleen Kelsey and Terry Williams and Al Broderick. The big guy's Brick Bauer. Watch out for him—he's going to be our next police chief. That's Nick over there and you've already met Patrick."

Patrick frowned. "You're Pam Casals?"

As Pam nodded, Rosemary chimed in again. "She's going to be working at Tyler High with you, Patrick. Pam's the new football coach."

"So I've heard. Welcome to Tyler."

Though his words were welcoming, his tone had cooled considerably. Pam couldn't help wondering why. "Thanks. Are you one of the teachers?"

"Gym teacher. Also basketball coach." Glancing at his watch, he tossed the ball to Rosemary. "Sorry to break this up, but I've got to run. See you all later."

"Nice to meet you, Patrick," Pam called to his retreating back.

"Yeah, you, too," he said over his shoulder.

"Don't let Patrick worry you," Kathleen said as she smiled at Pam. "He's my brother and I know he's a little moody, but he's a great guy. Glad you're with us, Pam."

"Thanks," Pam said quietly. So she would have the pleasure of working with the moody Patrick Kelsey. Terrific.

Calling their goodbyes, the others left to go their separate ways. Rosemary fell into step with Pam. "Come on. My place is only a couple of blocks from here," she said. Impulsively, she slid an arm around Pam's shoulders and squeezed. "I think you're going to like Tyler."

Pam heard the squeal of tires and looked toward Main Street as Patrick's truck zoomed out of sight. "I hope so," she answered.

THE WHITE FRAME HOUSE was on Morgan Avenue, two stories high with a wraparound porch and green shuttered windows. There was a Victorian elegance to the old building, Pam thought as she parked her car in the side drive. She watched Rosemary hurry out of the car. Five foot eight, Rosemary was bigger than Pam and incredibly strong, yet she moved with a style and grace that Pam envied.

"You want to put old slobbering Samson in the backyard for now?" Rosemary asked with an affectionate pat on the dog's head.

Pam nodded, and slipped on the dog's leash as she opened the car door. Settling Samson inside the fenced enclosure, she returned to the front and climbed the wooden steps with Rosemary. A swing, painted red, hung from two chains at the far end of the porch. Very inviting, she thought.

"About five years ago," Rosemary said, opening the screen door for her, "after the owner died, the heirs renovated the house, turning it into four apartments. They're all very roomy and comfortable. Mrs. Tibbs, a sweet but somewhat nosy widow, lives on the right, a young married couple upstairs on one side and a piano teacher across the hall from them. Mine's this one on the lower left." She paused in the neat hallway, glancing at mail spread on a small mahogany table. "Nothing for me." Pulling out a key, she unlocked the door.

Charming was the word, Pam thought as she looked about. A rich carved mantel above a huge stone fireplace, highly polished floors with gently faded area rugs in floral designs, and furniture you could no longer buy. Running a hand along an overstuffed rose couch, Pam smiled. "Are these your things?"

"No, not a single piece. I arrived with only my clothes." Rosemary went through the arch into the dining room and past into the spacious kitchen. "It even came with dishes and pots. Don't you just love it?"

Strolling past the drop-leaf table and an antique Singer sewing machine, Pam agreed. "Who owns this place now?"

Rosemary poured lemonade into two glasses tinted pale gold. "I don't know. Relatives of one of the original families of Tyler, I think. When you get to meeting people around here, you'll learn that half the town's related in some way to the other half." Handing Pam her drink, she tilted up her own glass and drank thirstily.

Sipping, Pam wandered back into the living room. Lace curtains billowed at the front bay window, dancing in a lively late-afternoon breeze. A large maple tree just outside shaded the whole front yard. She saw a squirrel with bulging cheeks scamper busily up into thick limbs and get lost in the leafy top. Turning, she sat down on the comfortably sagging sofa with starched doilies pinned to each armrest and sighed.

"It's like time has stood still in this house. I feel like I walked into a fifties movie."

Rosemary flung herself into the chair opposite Pam. "Maybe the forties, even. I was lucky to find this apartment."

"Are you sure you don't mind my moving in with you?" Pam asked with a worried look.

"I told you back in Chicago that I'd love the company. There're two large bedrooms and a big bath with this marvelous claw-footed tub. And I'm not even here much, what with working at Tyler General Hospital, my commitment to the Davis Rehab Center in Chicago and my backpacking trips."

"I'll pay half the rent, of course. I can't believe how low it is compared to Chicago apartments."

"Isn't it great?" Rosemary finished her drink and set the glass aside. "So tell me, how are you feeling?"

"Fine."

"Honestly? No pain, no numbness, no tingling? Don't lie to me now. I'm your therapist, remember."

"I remember. I truly feel great. No symptoms at all. I think I'm solidly in remission."

"Good." Rosemary nodded. "If you have any problems—I mean *any*—let me know. Therapy works best if we catch the problem early. You know how sneaky MS is. One day you notice a little blurry vision, next day your big toe goes numb, and the third day you try to stand and you can't feel anything from the knees down."

Pam stared into the cloudy remains of her drink. "I know. Believe me, I don't want that happening. I'll tell you at the first sign."

"This job at the school, do you think you'll have a lot of stress with it? Stress can aggravate your condition, you know."

Pam shrugged. "No more than anyone else starting in a new position in a new town." She looked up, remembering the man who'd tackled her, the warm way he'd looked at her, then the way his eyes had frosted over when he learned who she was. "What do you know about Patrick Kelsey?"

Rosemary swung both legs over the fat arm of the easy chair, scrunching down comfortably. "His family goes way back. He's a descendant of one of the first families. His parents own and operate Kelsey Boardinghouse on Gunther Street not far from here. Plus his father works at the Ingalls plant and his mother is receptionist for Dr. Phelps. Anna's real personable. I want you to meet George Phelps, too. He's a good man in case you need a doctor.''

This wasn't what Pam wanted to hear. "Why would Patrick have turned so moody back there in the square, when before he heard my name, he was smiling?''

''Maybe he wanted the job you got. He teaches gym and coaches varsity basketball. He's some kind of hero around here, dating back to his high school football days.''

''Sounds like the people of Tyler take high school sports seriously—and have long memories.''

''You got that right. Fierce loyalty around here. They give newcomers a hearty welcome, then sit back and wait for them to prove themselves. They accepted me, so don't worry.''

''But you've been here three years. It seems I was here three minutes and managed to offend one of their favorite sons.''

''Patrick will come around. He's really a great guy, always helping people, very family oriented. I've often wondered why he's never married.'' Rosemary eyed Pam as she slipped out of her running shoes. ''Maybe he's been waiting for the right woman to come along.''

Pam shook her head. ''Don't look at me. Besides, he seems a bit touchy. If he's lived here all his life, it can't be my fault I got the job and he didn't. Or is it having a woman coach he's against, possibly?''

"I don't know. I wouldn't worry about it. Don't add to your own stress level."

"Good idea." Pam stretched and yawned. "I should unpack, go get some groceries and turn in early tonight. I want to look around tomorrow, and Monday morning I meet with the principal."

"Oh, she's nice. Everyone likes Miss Mackie. And she'll understand about your limitations with MS."

Pam leaned forward, her eyes serious. "I don't plan to tell Miss Mackie or anyone else that I have multiple sclerosis. And I don't want you to say anything, either."

Slowly, Rosemary raised a questioning brow. "Do you think that's wise?"

"I don't know. I do know I need to prove myself, and I can't do that if everyone's waiting for me to fall over from fatigue or show up one day in a wheelchair."

"But if they know, they can—"

"No. Please, Rosemary." She had to make her friend see. "This is my life and my decision. When we first started working out together at the rehab center, I was going through the aftermath of depression, really feeling sorry for myself. Well, I've spent all the time doing that that I plan to. You're the one who challenged me to learn to live with MS, and I'm honestly trying to. I realize that remissions are temporary, but I feel good and I don't want constant reminders that I could slip back again any day."

"Remission periods can last for months, even years."

"I'm hopeful that's the case with me. But I want no quarter given because I've got a problem here. I want to earn people's respect, not their pity. Listen as my friend, Rosemary, not my therapist, and try to understand."

Gracefully Rosemary untangled herself from the chair and walked over to Pam, hugging her as she sat down on the couch. "I do understand. I just don't want to see you hurt. Over the past two years, I've grown to care about you a lot."

Pam blinked back a quick rush of emotion. "Me, too. I just have to do this my way, okay?"

"Sure." Rosemary stood. "Now, let me get your bag, so you can unpack while I start dinner. You can shop tomorrow. Tonight I'm cooking my specialty. Chicken chow mein."

"Sounds great." Pam searched for her keys. "I hope you'll make enough so Samson can have dinner, too. He loves Chinese."

"Not dog food?"

Pam grinned at her friend's surprised look. "He never touches the stuff. And he likes a wedge of lemon in his water dish."

"Of course he does." Rosemary smiled at her friend. "I'm really glad you're here." Glancing down, she pointed. "Grass stains. I hope they come out of your slacks."

Pam considered the green stain on her pantleg. "Think I could get Patrick Kelsey to clean them for me?"

"You really should get acquainted with him. He knows the boys at Tyler High better than anyone else. They trust him."

Pam tossed her keys in the air and caught them in her fist. "Then I guess it'll be my job to get them to trust me. Why haven't you gotten to know him better, since you think he's so swell?"

Rosemary shook her head. "I've been divorced five years and I intend to stay that way. Once burned is twice shy." She sobered, studying Pam's face. "Do you ever hear from Bob?"

"No, never. It's best this way, really. When something's over, it should stay over."

"Amen," Rosemary agreed.

CHAPTER TWO

"YOU LOOK even younger than your picture," Josephine Mackie said, rising and offering her hand to her new football coach.

Pam smiled as she shook hands with the principal. "I know. It sometimes keeps people from taking me seriously."

"Not after they hear about all you've accomplished," Miss Mackie said, resuming her seat and indicating the chair across from her desk. "I'm very impressed with your credentials."

"Thank you." Despite her somewhat austere looks, there was a warmth about Josephine Mackie that had Pam relaxing.

"It must have been thrilling, being in the Olympics."

"An unbelievable experience, yes."

"You won your gold medal when you were only twenty-one. I'm surprised you didn't try again the next time. You were only twenty-five."

"I'd planned to. I'd even begun training. But younger women were my competition, and although I hated to admit it, the body doesn't respond at twenty-five as it does at seventeen no matter how hard you try.

And the old-timers have more difficulty getting sponsorship money. I decided to turn professional.''

Miss Mackie smiled. She had no trouble understanding the body's limitations. She glanced down at Pam's file, then back up. "I hope you'll understand that I need to ask these questions. Although the college where you coached spoke highly of you, you wrote on your application that they fired you. Why was that?''

"I have no problem answering that question." Pam crossed her legs and adjusted her cotton skirt. "In training for the Olympics, I learned that an athlete must try to be the best he can be, to push as hard as physically possible and to keep a positive attitude about winning. When I began coaching, I approached the team with the same no-excuses, hardwork strategy. The college administration didn't agree with my perfectionist methods, even though we'd gone from last place to second in our division. They thought I expected too much from the boys.''

Honesty, even at her own expense. Miss Mackie liked that. "Our Titans aren't in last place, but we haven't had a championship team since 1972, the third consecutive year they won the title.''

"That's impressive. Who was your coach then?''

"Dale McCormick, the man who just retired. He was a real fireball back then, but he seemed to run out of steam." She watched Pam's crossed leg rock rhythmically as she sat. Not nerves, she decided, but rather Pam seemed to have trouble remaining idle. "You look as if you have a lot of energy.''

"I do. And a great deal of enthusiasm and love of football."

Josephine crossed her hands over the closed file. She had no regrets about hiring this young woman, yet it wouldn't hurt to bring up the concerns voiced by Patrick Kelsey last week. They were apprehensions shared by several others on the school board, she was certain. "Tell me, do you run into any problems as a female coaching young men in an almost exclusively male sport?"

Pam nodded. "A few. I find as I go in that the boys have their reservations. Many think that women don't even understand football, much less how to coach the game. I usually let them make their jokes, get it out of their systems, and then we get down to work. Once they see that my methods work, they forget I'm a woman. The same theory applies to the school board."

Miss Mackie found it difficult to believe that young men would forget Pam was a woman, but she let it go. "You certainly have a great deal of confidence."

If only you knew, Pam thought, but she smiled. "I've found that focusing on your strong points and learning to compensate for your weak points builds confidence. And going into a game—or a new job—with confidence is half the battle."

Leaning back in her chair, the principal studied the young woman seated across from her a long moment, then nodded. "I like your attitude, Pam. I believe you can put the Tyler Titans back into the running for the championship."

"Thank you. I appreciate that."

"So now, are you settled in? You mentioned you'd be sharing a friend's apartment."

"Yes. Rosemary Dusold. She's a physical therapist and she has a lovely place on Morgan Avenue."

"I know the house. Beautifully refurbished a while back. Marge Peterson lives on Morgan Avenue. She runs Marge's Diner right off the town square."

"Oh, yes. I drove around town yesterday, getting oriented. Is the food pretty good?"

"I don't eat out much, but they tell me it is. The diner is sort of a gathering spot for folks around here."

"I noticed it was crowded when I passed by. You've lived here all your life?"

"Yes. Tyler has its drawbacks, but I'm comfortable here. It's a nice, quiet way of life."

"Coming from Chicago, I like the country atmosphere. I drove out to a lake yesterday and saw this beautiful old place they're evidently renovating. I believe the sign said Timberlake. I'm glad it's being redone instead of torn down. These old buildings have such charm. Tyler might attract even more visitors when they finish."

Miss Mackie pressed her lips together tightly. She'd heard some disturbing things at the Hair Affair last week—that a long-buried body had been found on the grounds of the lodge. However, she hated gossip and wasn't about to pass any on to this newcomer. "I'm not sure Tyler wants tourism. We kind of enjoy being a sleepy little community."

"Who owns Timberlake, do you know?"

"Judson Ingalls. His family goes just about as far back as the founding of Tyler. The Ingalls family also owns Ingalls Farm and Machinery and a variety of other holdings."

"I believe Rosemary and I drove past his home on Elm Street. A beautiful Victorian house."

"You'll undoubtedly meet Mr. Ingalls at the games. He's a member of the Booster Club and a big supporter of our athletic program." Leaning forward, she changed the subject. "Do you have any questions about your position?"

"Well, I'd hoped you might have some films I could watch on last year's games. Some of those players are probably on this year's team as well, and it would give me some idea of their capabilities. Naturally, I'd also like to see the boys' school records so I can get to know them a bit before we meet next week."

"I believe our gym teacher, Patrick Kelsey, can help you with all that. Dale McCormick turned over all records to Patrick when he left. I can arrange an introduction or give you his number."

Pam felt herself stiffen a bit and hoped the astute woman hadn't noticed. "We've met, in the town square last Saturday. I have to ask you. Did Patrick Kelsey want to be football coach?"

So they hadn't hit it off, Miss Mackie thought. She wasn't surprised, after her last conversation with Patrick, although she'd hoped he would keep an open mind. "I suspect he did. Patrick played football here at Tyler when he was in high school, and he was an outstanding athlete. He'd been out of college a couple of years before he moved back. Dale McCormick was still doing well with our football teams, but we badly needed a basketball coach. I called Patrick and persuaded him to take over that spot. He's made those boys into winners, and I think he's happy in basketball now."

Pam folded and refolded the edge of her skirt thoughtfully. "I got the impression he wasn't pleased at my arrival. I could be mistaken, of course, but..."

Josephine sighed. "You've been honest with me, so I'll return the favor. Although he's only thirty-four, Patrick's from the old school. He's not really a chauvinist—after all, he works for a woman and he's always shown me a great deal of respect. Also, his mother manages two jobs and he adores her. Maybe he's in the habit of protecting women because he has three younger sisters. At any rate, Patrick doesn't feel women belong in football."

That sounded pretty chauvinistic despite Miss Mackie's explanation, Pam thought. "Is he going to be interfering with my coaching?" she asked quietly. Better to find out now than later.

"Absolutely not."

"Are you giving me carte blanche, the authority to coach this team *my* way then?"

The wording was a little strong for her liking, but the principal had to let Pam know she was behind her. "Yes, I am. For one trial season."

"I understand."

Miss Mackie's fingers drummed on the desk top. "Patrick has been told to give you every assistance. He may try to push his ideas on you, as he's quite opinionated when it comes to sports. And he used to assist Coach McCormick. But you needn't listen to him. The methods Dale and Patrick used obviously haven't worked in recent years. I'm anxious to see what you can do. Patrick will back off, you'll see."

Pam seriously doubted that. In her mind's eye, she pictured those intense blue eyes, the solid bulk of his shoulders, the confident stance. Back off? Not Patrick Kelsey. But despite his formidable good looks and his past football glory, he would soon learn that Pam Casals was no pushover.

"I'm sure we'll manage to keep from coming to blows." With a smile, she stood. "Thank you, Miss Mackie, for your time. And your confidence."

"You're very welcome. I look forward to seeing more of you."

Leaving the principal's office, Pam walked down the main-floor corridor, glancing into open classrooms. Curiosity leading the way, she made her way around back to the gymnasium and paused to look it over. Then she moved toward the locker rooms and sports office.

The locker rooms, one for boys and the other smaller one for girls, looked the same as they did in most schools, as did the connecting showers. From there, she walked up a ramp to the football field. It was well maintained, with lights for night games and a fairly new digital scoreboard. The extensive wooden bleachers on both sides were freshly painted, and there was an enclosed announcer's box. Impressive, Pam thought, remembering she'd been told the Tyler Booster Club actively sponsored improvements.

Retracing her steps, she again passed the gymnasium with its polished floor and headed down a hallway. At the first door, she looked up and read the nameplate. Coach Kelsey. Above it was an empty slot where Coach McCormick's name had evidently been and where her nameplate would likely go. So she was to share an office with Patrick. Interesting.

She tried the knob but found it locked. Not unusual, since there were probably files inside and possibly equipment. She could go back to Miss Mackie and ask for a key, but she decided to wait.

Staring at the door, she wondered if Coach Kelsey would allow her nameplate to be put into the top slot. With a smile she turned. She would bet her silver medal he wouldn't.

Pam stood at the far end of the bleachers, watching the football players arrive for the first day of practice. She wore running shoes and gray sweats, and had her hair tied back in a ponytail. Holding her clipboard, she studied the boys, trying to match them to the players in the game videos she'd been scrutinizing for days now. These were the young men who'd successfully tried out in the spring. Most of them had learned the ropes on the junior varsity team.

She'd gotten a key to the office from Miss Mackie and pored over their scholastic records as well. Some were impressive; others were not. She'd found the films neatly boxed and carefully labeled and taken them home to view, leaving Patrick Kelsey a note explaining their absence. She had yet to run into the man himself again.

It was a lovely day, a sunshiny August afternoon, and she was anxious to get started. Around her neck, she wore a yellow whistle dangling from a chain.

Putting it to her lips, she gave three long blasts and motioned the boys over.

"Take a seat on the bleachers, fellas," she invited as they straggled over. Most wore wary expressions and she couldn't blame them. The unknown always made a person hesitant.

The Wednesday edition of the *Tyler Citizen* had featured a story about her as the newest addition to the high school staff. They'd run her picture, played up her Olympic achievements and done a commendable job in extolling her coaching experience. The boys and their parents had likely read the article. By the looks on their faces, none of it had removed their skepticism as to her ability to coach them.

Uphill all the way, Pam thought with a familiar tug. When had anything ever come easily to her? Dad had always told her that victories hard won were the sweetest. She believed her father.

Moving to stand in front of the seated group, she looked up at them and smiled. "I'm Pam Casals, your new football coach. I..."

Whistles, nervous giggles and veiled comments followed the announcement as the boys elbowed one another, laughed and stared. Pam patiently waited for them to resettle.

In the back, a heavyset boy wearing a shirt with Italian Stallion emblazoned across the chest stood to be heard. "Hey, you're a girl!" More guffaws and laughter.

Shifting her feet, Pam smiled indulgently. "Thank you for noticing. Now, I'd like you to forget that I am."

That announcement was greeted with whoops and hollers and more rib-tickling laughter. Pam banked her annoyance, trying to remember that these were young boys ranging from fifteen to nearly eighteen, feeling the need to assert their masculinity. And feeling safe within their familiar group. But enough was enough.

"Let me ask you a question. Are you proud of the Titans' record last year, winding up sixth in an eight-team league?" She saw a few faces lose their grins, others look a bit chagrined. "Would you like to play on a winning team, to walk proud, to be the best there is? Would you like to be Class A champions?"

There was a hushed silence for a moment, then a couple of them shouted out.

"Yeah."

"Sure."

"You bet."

"Good," she said, nodding. "Because I want to work with champions." More cheers and punches of agreement. "I've spent a lot of hours lately studying your game films from last year. And I want to tell you all something." She paused, waiting until she was certain she had their complete attention. "I think you guys have the potential to beat any team in the league."

The grins were wide now, the affirmative nods and comments that followed rousing. They were beginning to picture themselves as champions, Pam noted with satisfaction. The first step.

When they quieted, she continued. "We're going to learn three things before our first game. One is conditioning. You have to get in shape and stay in shape. Two, we're going to learn to play football.''

A blond boy shouted out, "We already know how to play football."

"Perhaps you do. But we're going to learn to work together as a team. I want no superstars here. I want team effort. There are no unimportant positions in football. It's one for all and all for one, straight across the board. And three, we're going to learn how to win."

They were strangely subdued as they studied her. Moving her eyes from face to face, she saw the beginning of a reluctant respect forming on a couple. Uphill, but not impossible, she decided. Now if only she could deliver.

"As your coach, I have only two rules. One is that if you don't pass your classes, you don't play. Rule number two is that if you don't come to practice, you don't play. There are no exceptions to either rule. Other than that—'' she paused to flash a big smile ''—we're here to play ball, to have fun and to win.''

"Yea, coach!" a redheaded boy yelled out, followed by several other shouts of agreement.

"Okay, now. Grab your helmets and pads and get out on the field. I want to see what kind of training exercises you've done in the past, and I want to watch you run through a few plays so I can see what we need to work on."

Some whispering together, some openly discussing her talk, they filed off the bleachers and disappeared toward the locker room. Several paused to say a few words to someone seated on the bottom bench at the opposite end. It was only as the last of the boys walked out of sight that she recognized Patrick Kelsey. Unwinding his long legs, he started toward her.

Instinctively, Pam braced herself. He was wearing jeans, a cutoff football jersey and sneakers. Lord, but he was big, she thought as he stopped in front of her.

"Do I call you Coach, Miss Casals or what?" he asked, wrinkling his face as if he'd been pondering the question for some time.

"Pam will do nicely." She could play this game. "And you? Do you prefer Coach Kelsey, Mr. Kelsey, Patrick or Pat?"

He gave her an engaging grin. "The fellas call me Coach, the newspaper boy calls me Mr. Kelsey, my grandmother calls me Paddy, short for the Gaelic version of my name. I hear my history students call me Napoleon. My friends call me Patrick."

The sun was in her eyes as she squinted up at him, holding her clipboard to her chest in what she recognized as a protective gesture. "Well, I'm not the fellas, nor the newsboy. And I'm not your grandmother. I also don't think we're friends, at least not yet. That leaves me stymied."

Kill the enemy with kindness, Patrick thought as he rocked on the balls of his feet and watched her. "Honeybuns is open."

She laughed. "I think I'll pass on that one, too."

He watched her sit down on the bench and shift her attention to her notes. She looked young enough to be a high school senior. No wonder the boys had whistled and stared. The sun brought out the red in her brown hair. There was some red on her cheeks, too, and he wondered if it was from weather exposure or from hassling with him. He sat down beside her.

"I heard most of your pep talk. Not bad."

Why was it she could almost hear him add the rest: *for a woman.* Keeping her features even, Pam looked up. "Thanks."

"What'd you learn from the game films?"

"Too early to tell."

She had to be the least chatty female he'd met in a while, Patrick thought as he leaned his elbows back on the seat behind. "I saw you and Rosemary riding around yesterday. Checking out the town?"

"Mmm-hmm."

"Where'd you go?"

Pushy, friendly or just plain nosy? Pam asked herself. She put on a polite smile. "Here and there. Rosemary showed me the hospital where she works and we drove past some beautiful old mansions on Elm Street. Then we went out toward the lake and saw the lodge, Timberlake. Seems like it'll be really something when they finish the renovations."

"Did you hear about the body they found there while they were inspecting some plumbing pipes?" That caught her interest, Patrick thought as he saw her eyes widen.

"No, really? Who was it?"

He shrugged. "They're not sure yet. Some old-timers around town think it might be Margaret Ingalls."

Pam frowned, trying to sort through the many names she'd heard over the past few days. "I don't think I've heard of her. There's a Judson Ingalls...."

Patrick nodded. "Margaret was his wife. Disappeared one day some years before I was born. Rumor has it that she got bored with her marriage and left with a lover."

Pam shook her head. "And I thought this was a sleepy little town."

Patrick straightened, shifting closer. "It is. Small towns are not immune to love affairs or even murder. My mother told me the story of Margaret Ingalls' disappearance years ago. She's always suspected something more happened than the woman just up and left. Margaret's daughter, Alyssa, went to school with my mother. Mom can't imagine a woman turning her back on a child, even for a lover."

"Your mother's a romantic."

"She certainly is."

Pam found herself looking into those compelling blue eyes. "But you're a cynic, aren't you?"

"I wouldn't say that." Patrick lifted her hand from where it had been resting on her knee. "Which are you, Pam?"

She felt herself drowning suddenly, in fathomless blue water. Without conscious effort, her hand tightened in his. "You know, I've never seen eyes as blue as yours. Never."

"And I've never been this close to a football coach who smelled as good as you. What are you wearing?"

"Jasmine. I..."

Thundering footsteps heralded the arrival of the team. They rushed onto the field, carrying helmets and equipment, suited in practice gear. Pam snatched her hand back and jumped up guiltily, flushing as she did.

What was the matter with her, sitting here discussing cologne and eye color when she had a job to do?

Clearing her throat, she grabbed her clipboard and started toward the field.

"Hey, you didn't answer my question," Patrick called after her. "Are you a cynic or a romantic?"

Over her shoulder, she frowned at him. "Somewhere in between. Now, if you'll excuse me, I have work to do."

She hurried off to watch her boys.

THE FIRST PRACTICE did not go well. Of course, they were rusty after the long summer, but that wasn't all. Two hours after they'd begun, Pam blew her whistle and motioned the boys back to the bleacher area.

Some time ago she'd seen Patrick leave, and she'd felt relieved to be left alone with her team. Strolling from group to group, she'd taken notes, given short instructions, requested demonstrations of various plays. Now she felt more confident about the things they needed to work on.

"Okay, fellas, there's some good news and some bad news." She paused to let the groaners have their say. "The good news is I wasn't mistaken. You have amazing potential, many strengths and much going for you, both individually and as a team. The bad news is we have a lot of work ahead of us. Sit down, please."

Pam glanced at her notes as the sweaty players sprawled on the benches. "The summer's taken it's toll and some of you are badly out of shape. I've looked at your weigh-in figures, and a couple of guys are going on a diet, starting tonight." She ignored the gripes this time. "I'm posting a weight-requirements chart in the locker room. We'll weight in every Monday." She tossed meaningful looks toward the heavier boys.

"Coach, you're sadistic," the kid named Moose complained.

"You're defense, Moose, so we need you strong. But we don't need you flabby. Twenty pounds have to come off, starting today."

"There go my Twinkies," Moose moaned, then laughed.

"Tomorrow morning, practice starts at nine sharp. I've arranged for tires to be brought in. Your footwork is sloppy. A man running the ball has to be able to pivot and swivel on a dime. You also need to learn how to fall with the ball. A few of you are going to break an arm or dislocate a shoulder if you don't master falling. That means falling *without* letting go of the ball."

"Sounds like we won't be through before noon," someone grumbled.

"More like three or four," Pam explained. "You'll have an hour for lunch and then back to work. Our first preseason game is in two weeks. We can't get in shape on a couple hours a day. We'll be doing push-ups, sit-ups, running exercises, and in the afternoon, we'll scrimmage."

"It's still pretty hot to work that hard," B.J. threw out.

"So come in shorts. But come prepared to work." She stepped back and gave them an encouraging smile.

"It'll be worth it. You'll see. Picture us on Thanksgiving Day walking off the field with the trophy."

"Yeah, man!" Moose called out.

"That's it, fellas. See you in the morning."

Pam stood aside, watching them file off, catching a few fragmented phrases.

"Not as bad as I'd thought she'd be."

"Tougher than McCormick, can you believe it?"

"Wait'll Coach Kelsey hears what she's got us doing."

Shaking her head, Pam picked up a forgotten helmet. Coach Kelsey again. It would seem she'd have less trouble winning over the boys than the man whose amused blue eyes seemed to hint that she wouldn't last.

Walking toward her office, she vowed to prove him wrong.

AT SIX IN THE MORNING, dew was heavy on the grass in the pastures and the air was fresh and clean. Pacing herself, Pam ran along the edge of the two-lane road, enjoying the slip-slap sound of her running shoes as they briefly hit the asphalt. She wore a blue cotton shirt and shorts, and had scarcely worked up a sweat though she'd been at it for about twenty minutes.

Loping along beside her, Samson kept up somewhat grumpily, his tongue hanging out, his breathing huffy. Though quite large, sheepdogs had great stamina, and Pam knew he dropped back occasionally not from fatigue but to investigate a tree or some creepy-crawly he'd spotted. For years a morning run had been part of their routine—until Pam's illness had put a halt to most physical activity.

Those months confined to a wheelchair, when the debilitating numbness made it difficult and sometimes impossible to do even the smallest of chores for herself, had been the worst weeks of her life. Pam followed a bend in the road, letting herself remember back four years ago, when she'd returned to her father's house in Chicago from her coaching stint with the Olympic team in Seoul. She'd been happy, in love, planning for a limitless future.

Bob Conti had coached with her, a tall blond giant of a man who'd never been sick a day in his life, or so he'd said. They'd met in Seoul, two athletes in the prime of life, attractive and attracted, with mutual interests and goals. Love had hit like a thunderbolt and life had taken on a rosy hue.

When Pam developed flu symptoms after their return, she'd naturally thought them temporary. When two weeks later she'd still felt tired and weak, sometimes having such difficulty with dizziness that she couldn't walk straight, Bob had insisted she see a doctor.

Even during the battery of tests, Pam hadn't really worried. After all, she was young and healthy, an athlete who'd always taken extraordinary care of herself. By the time a neurologist had been called in, her hands were plagued with needlelike tingling and she couldn't trust her legs, for they would often go numb from the knees down. Finally, the doctors met with her to discuss the diagnosis—multiple sclerosis.

Feeling warmer now, Pam slowed down, slipped her sweatband around her forehead, then resumed her pace. She'd learned she was a prime candidate for MS. The disease struck mostly young adults under thirty, seventy-five percent of the patients female, thirty-five percent white women from upper middle class homes, a good many of whom had had scarlet fever. Unfortunately, Pam fit the profile to a tee.

Shock more than anything had slowed her return to health, her movement into the remission state. The doctors had been very helpful, very informative, but she'd been so devastated that no one had seemed able to reach her. Not her family nor her friends. Not even Bob. No one, until therapist Rosemary Dusolt had come into her life.

Working with Pam's weak limbs, Rosemary not only pumped life back into her body, she tapped into Pam's strong will and taught her to learn to live with her disease as well. She convinced her that she could still live a full and vital life by coming to terms with MS. As she grew stronger, Pam slowly came to realize that Bob was unable to deal with her situation, that he didn't want to be committed to someone for whom life at times would become a daily struggle. Though the hurt and disappointment ate at her, she broke off with him.

Just as Rosemary had predicted, she was eventually able to leave her wheelchair, to rebuild her body, to heal her mind. Pam knew what to avoid now—extremes of temperature as in saunas and very hot showers; humid places, like the seashore; getting stressed out or overtired. She also knew that she'd

move in and out of remission, and that bad times
would come again. Perhaps that was why the good
periods were so sweet, so much to be savored.

Needing to work, to keep busy, she'd started looking for a job only recently, answering ads and sending
out résumés. The Tyler High position, necessitating a
move, had been ideal. She'd be close to Rosemary and
away from her well-intentioned but hovering family.
She needed to prove to herself that she could go it
alone.

Smiling down at Samson as he came galloping up to
her from behind, Pam stretched out her arms and
slowed to hug the shaggy dog. Life was good if you
didn't expect too much, if you took each day as it
came and counted your blessings. Learning to live one
day at a time had been a hard lesson, but she'd mas-
tered it.

When life tosses you lemons, Dad had often said,
you have to learn to make lemonade. Pausing under
the shade of an overhanging tree to catch her breath,
Pam realized again how right her father was. He'd
been wonderfully supportive about her new job,
maintaining that she could make the Titans into winners, that she could conquer MS in the same way she'd
overcome adversities on the way to her gold medal.
Too bad Bob couldn't have had that kind of faith in
her.

Pam started to run back to her car. Bob was no
longer a sharp ache inside her, but rather a dull disappointment. Though Rosemary and her doctors had
told her that marriage and children were not things an
MS patient would have to do without, Pam wasn't so

sure. It would take a special man—patient, caring, tolerant—to live with and love her. She knew it wouldn't be easy, for either of them.

Limitations at the outset of a relationship were difficult to face. And her future would always be cloudy. She no longer counted on finding a man she could love who would return her feelings, without pity, without regret. Pam looked up at the climbing sun. She had today, and today she felt wonderful. Perhaps that would have to do.

"Come on, Samson," she shouted over her shoulder at the lagging dog, "race you to the car."

PAM STOOD on the sidelines of Tyler High's football field watching the boys returning from lunch. She'd finished her own yogurt and apple juice a while ago and was ready to set up some scrimmages.

She'd had them exercising fiercely this morning, as they had the past six mornings—push-ups, rope climbing, running through tires for foot coordination, tossing the pigskin through hanging tires to improve aim. She'd given them Sunday off, then had them back on Monday. Now, a week after they'd begun, she could see improvement—in performance and in pride.

Stepping out onto the field, she blew her whistle and waited for them to join her. "Okay, fellas. I want to see you divide into teams and practice the plays we worked on yesterday." She frowned as she looked through the crowd. "Where's Ricky Travis?"

"He had work to do on his father's farm this afternoon, Coach," B.J. said. "Said to tell you he'll be here in the morning."

She leveled her gaze. "I'll talk to Ricky. If any of you see him before morning, you might remind him of rule number two. If you don't come to practice, you don't play in the games. There are no exceptions."

"Come on, Coach," Moose said, "Ricky's our quarterback."

"He is if he comes to practice. He won't be if he misses. B.J., you play quarterback this afternoon. And fellas, remember what we went over yesterday. Be aware of each man around you, and of your opponent. You've got to protect the quarterback, not let him take hits. Especially since we're down to one today. Okay, let's go."

She jogged back to the sidelines and put on her sunglasses. Hunkering down near the fifty-yard line, she scribbled on her clipboard as the boys went into position.

SHE WAS WEARING pink today. Patrick couldn't believe it. Did she have sweats in every color? he wondered as he stood at the far end of the bleachers. The boys were all in abbreviated uniforms and protective gear, mostly in drab colors. Pam stood out like a pink beacon across the field, her dark hair tied back with a piece of pink yarn. Damnedest sight he'd ever seen on a football grid.

Why would a woman want to coach football? he asked himself, not for the first time since hearing of Pam Casals. She was attractive and talented. She could travel, do promotional work, put on running exhibitions, coach women's basketball—any number of things. Why football?

Was it the challenge, a climb-the-mountain-because-it's-there type of thinking? She'd conquered running, now she wanted to conquer a man's domain. Was she hoping to make the Titans into winners, thereby luring another college coaching offer? Or—God forbid—did she have her sights set on the pros? Was Tyler merely a stepping-stone to Pam Casals?

Patrick ran a hand through his windblown hair. She was a hard one to call. She looked so feminine, so young. Yet watching the boys, he had to admit they were listening to her, following her instructions. The smart remarks and clowning had stopped. For nearly a week now, he'd come by for a few minutes every day, just to check on her methods and the team's progress. It wasn't sensational, but it wasn't shabby, either.

He'd stayed mostly out of sight, seeing that she was too occupied to notice his brief visits. A couple of the guys had glanced up, but they hadn't come over. He'd noted that she was tough on discipline, something he tried to instill in his basketball team as well. He'd checked with several of the fellows off campus about how they were getting along, and except for the usual grumblings about workouts and diet, none had really complained about Pam specifically.

Patrick watched her toss down her clipboard and leap into the air to catch a stray ball, her movements clean and sure, yet gracefully feminine. She was cute rather than beautiful. Not that he was here because of Pam as a woman. He owed it to his boys to keep an eye on their new coach, that was all. Leaning against the back bleacher, he saw her call them into a loose huddle and wondered what she was saying.

"THAT LAST PLAY was lousy," Pam said, hands on her hips, eyes on her players. "Where'd you learn to hand off like that, B.J.?"

"From Coach McCormick."

Pam turned aside thoughtfully. This had come up before and she'd ignored it. No more, she decided as she paced a short distance and returned to address them. "I told you from the start that we would learn to play football all over and that we'd be winners. I want you to forget everything else you've been told—no matter who told it to you—and do things *my* way. I'm not saying I'm always right. But doing plays the old way, you wound up near the cellar in the standings. Let's try the new way and see if it works. If it doesn't, I'll bow out. Is that fair?"

Exchanging uneasy and skeptical glances, the boys nodded.

"Okay, then. Let's run that play over again. On three, B.J., and I want to see some blocking, defense." She jogged off the field and turned to watch them move into formation.

Pam was hunched down observing, so deeply absorbed she didn't hear anyone approach. The play went off beautifully, and B.J.'s receiver, Todd, caught the throw and ran clear. "That's more like it," she shouted out.

"Where'd you learn that play?" Patrick asked from behind her.

Startled, she nearly fell over from her awkward position. Rising, she glared at him. "What are you doing, sneaking up on me?"

"I didn't sneak. I walked around the field in plain view. I repeat, where'd you learn that play?"

Pam wiped her damp palms on her sweatpants. "What difference does it make? It works and that's what's important."

"The plays Dale and I taught them last year worked, too, and most of the team know them backward and forward."

"If they worked so well, why did the team wind up in sixth place in a field of eight?"

Patrick made a dismissing gesture. "Couldn't be helped. We had a lot of injuries, our best running back moved out of town halfway through the season, and our kicker contracted mono and we didn't have a backup man."

She shook her head. "Tough luck. Each position should have a backup and every team has injuries. Let's face it, McCormick's methods were outdated and unimaginative." She didn't add that she lumped Patrick's routines in with the retired coach's, but she could see by his stormy expression that he got the message.

Becoming aware that the boys, waiting for the next call, were moving closer and enjoying their heated exchange, Pam turned to them. "Take a water break, guys," she yelled out.

As the players strolled off the field, Patrick got hold of his temper. "Listen, there's no guarantee your new ways will work when these guys face other, more experienced teams, so don't be so damn cocky. And don't you be undermining my methods to them. I coach quite a few of the boys in basketball, and I don't want you messing up their thinking."

"I haven't said one word against you to those boys. Which is more than I can say about you and the way you've just *happened* to run into several of them and pump them for information."

Patrick felt his face flush and could have cheerfully popped the kid who'd blabbed to her. "I've never talked detrimentally about you."

Pam picked up her clipboard. "Maybe not, but you haven't exactly spoken up on my behalf, either. Listen, we're supposed to be on the same side, working for the same school. You could have encouraged them to give me a chance, to try things my way. But you chose not to. All right. I'll win them over without you. It's just a damn shame your ego's so monumentally big you can't accept that there are several ways to build a winning team and that yours might not be the *only* way."

Turning on her heel, she started across the field.

"Wait a minute," Patrick called after her. "I want to talk to you."

"Well, I don't want to talk to *you*," Pam shouted over her shoulder as she walked toward the drinking fountain. What she really would have liked was to pour a pitcher of cold water over the arrogant Patrick Kelsey's head.

CHAPTER THREE

SHE ALWAYS HAD the most voracious appetite when she was nervous, Pam acknowledged as she poured melted butter over a huge bowl of popcorn. She also had a craving for sweets, so she popped the lid on a can of cola and took both into the living room.

Tomorrow night at this time her team would be playing its first preseason game. Miss Mackie had happily reported that it would be in front of a sellout crowd. Everyone in town, it seemed, was curious as to what the new woman coach had done with their high school football team. Pam closed her eyes and prayed she wouldn't bomb the first time out.

Grabbing a handful of popcorn, she dug in. No negative thinking, she ordered herself. The boys had come a long way, their spirits were high and, blessedly, there'd been no serious injuries so far. They were revved up and ready to go. Winning this one was important to their self-esteem. And maybe to hers.

Samson loped over and laid his big chin on her knee, his eyes begging to share in her treat. "Did I forget about you, Sam?" Quickly she got his bowl, tossed in several generous handfuls and placed it on the floor alongside the couch. "Go to it." He wasted no time in doing so.

The two of them were home alone tonight, Rosemary having gone backpacking for several days with a couple of friends. The weather was definitely cooling, the very first leaves starting to change color. Soon she wouldn't be able to camp out, Rosemary had explained.

Pam took a long drink of her cold soda. She felt restless and a bit jumpy. Too fidgety to read, and she'd never been one to watch much television. Maybe what she needed was a boost to her own morale. Rising, she went to her room, found the right cassette and returned to shove it into the VCR.

Watching herself on tape—the pageantry of the Olympics, the winning run itself and the moment of glory as she'd stood in the winner's circle—smacked of living in the past, of wishing for things that were no longer possible. Pam had rarely done so before MS had struck. Yet occasionally now, it seemed necessary for her to remind herself that she'd excelled once, and could do so again, albeit in another capacity.

Almost forgetting to eat, Pam watched the grandeur of the torch-lighting ceremony, remembering what it had felt like to stand among her fellow Americans, proudly wearing the red, white and blue. She remembered the lump in her throat as the final runner had stretched to ignite the flame. Her father and brothers had been in the audience, and it had been such a glorious time. Dad had asked a friend and neighbor to tape the event both years, and then he'd had copies made for all of them.

The next scene showed an interviewer asking her questions about her training, her motivation, her expectations. The time had flashed by in the wink of an eye, it had seemed back then. She remembered now only the excitement, the anticipation, the anxiety of wanting so badly to win.

Samson had finished his bowl and cocked his head, then ambled toward the door. Sniffing first, he soon gave a short series of barks. The knock that followed didn't surprise Pam, since Sam had keen hearing. She pushed the hold button on the cassette and went to answer.

PATRICK HADN'T INTENDED to drop by. He stood in the hallway, a thoughtful frown on his face. Pam Casals was, after all, one of his fellow faculty members. It would be only polite to wish her well on the eve of the first football game. And Patrick had been brought up with the burden of good manners.

He'd stopped by to watch the boys practice even after he and Pam had had those rather heated words. But he hadn't lingered, and he hadn't walked over to talk with Pam again. He also hadn't sought out any of the boys to ask how things were going. She'd made him feel small about that, despite his good intentions in doing it in the first place.

Basically, he wanted to be friends with Pam. They would be brushing shoulders at Tyler High and around town for months, perhaps years, to come. He was a friendly kind of guy; everyone said so. There was no reason for him to keep chipping away at her or vice versa. So he'd decided to come over, to mend this particular fence, to offer a truce.

Shuffling his feet, he swore under his breath. That wasn't exactly it. The honesty his mother had instilled in him years ago had him facing an uncomfortable truth. He wanted to see Pam Casals, to be with her, to get to know her.

What was so terribly wrong with that? Patrick asked himself. She was attractive, personable, interesting. And like it or not, she seemed to invade his thoughts with increasing frequency. It was time to see if there was something between them. He raised his hand to knock again.

The door swung open and the smile slid from his face. How could a woman wear such ordinary clothes—faded jeans that hugged her slender legs and a short-sleeved blue sweatshirt—and still be extraordinarily feminine down to the pink-painted toes of her bare feet? Her hair wasn't tied back, either, but rather hung to her shoulders, softly framing her face. And she wore lipstick, also pale pink. Patrick felt like a high school freshman calling on his first girl.

Clearing his throat, he met her wary eyes and found a smile. "Hi. I was . . . in the neighborhood, taking a walk. Just thought I'd stop in and wish you good luck for tomorrow's game."

Nervous. He was actually nervous. Pam couldn't imagine why. However, she'd never been one to hold a grudge. But she would still proceed with caution. "Thanks. I appreciate that."

Samson shoved past her and came out to sniff at their visitor.

"That's a big dog," Patrick commented unnecessarily. "What's his name?"

"Samson."

Leaning down, he patted the dog's shaggy head.
"He needs a haircut."

"Can't cut Samson's hair. It'll remove all his
strength, remember?" She smiled at his questioning
look. "Like in the Bible."

Patrick grinned. "Right. We wouldn't want that."
He straightened. "I hope I'm not interrupting anything."

Pam debated for a heartbeat, then stepped back.
"No, you're not. Would you like to come in?"

"Thanks." Samson at his heels, he strolled in, his
gaze taking in the attractive room. "I haven't been
inside since they redid this place. Very nice."

"I think so." Closing the door, she moved back to
the couch. "Samson and I were just sharing a snack.
Would you like some popcorn?"

He took a handful from the bowl she held out and
sat down at the opposite end of the couch. The television, caught in a freeze-frame, captured his eye.
"Were you watching something?"

"Nothing important." Pam popped a few kernels of
corn into her mouth.

"What was it?"

He was persistent. But she already knew that about
him. She let out a sigh, feeling foolish. "My Olympic
tapes. I watch them when I need a shot of confidence."

"You worried about tomorrow?"

"Not exactly worried. But not wildly confident, either."

Patrick nodded. He'd experienced the same feelings with his own teams. "You've worked really hard, and so have the boys. They'll do all right."

She hadn't expected that, not from him. "I hope so."

He nodded toward the television. "Could I see the tape?"

She'd never watched it with anyone outside her own family and teammates. Yet she could think of no way to refuse. Trying to look nonchalant, she pushed the play button on the remote control. She chewed popcorn nervously as the camera zeroed in on the twenty-one-year-old Pam and her competitors warming up just before the run. The announcer's voice was almost breathy in his excitement, preparing the viewing audience for the actual event.

"You haven't changed very much," Patrick commented as he moved closer to her for another handful of popcorn.

"I prefer to think I look older."

"Not much." He turned to her. "Prettier, though."

She felt a flush of pleasure as the gun went off and the women on screen began their run. The action saved her from responding to his compliment.

Silently, Patrick watched the event; saw Pam sprint ahead of her competitors easily and early, and never relinquish her lead. He thought her quite beautiful as she burst across the finish line, a look of giddy triumph on her face. He swung back to her. "Your finest hour, right?"

"So far," Pam said, feeling a shade embarrassed as she snapped off the cassette.

Patrick stretched his arm along the couch back, studying her. "What could beat winning the gold?"

Setting down the nearly empty bowl, Pam shrugged. "I've always thought having a baby would be the ultimate achievement." She sent him a quick, shy look. "At least for me."

Her answer surprised him and shifted his opinion of her ever so slightly. Yet seeing her quiet beauty tonight, he had no difficulty thinking of her as very much a woman and not merely a football coach. "Do you have someone special in your life?" He watched her shake her head and wondered why her answer pleased him. "I'm surprised."

She wouldn't dwell on the past two empty years. Instead, she'd go way back. "I spent most of my teens and early twenties training, then more years traveling and competing. That kind of commitment takes time and leaves very little energy for building relationships."

"You've never had a serious relationship?"

She was growing annoyed with the slant of their conversation and frowned in his direction. "I didn't say that. I did have a relationship, but it didn't last."

"A fellow athlete?" He no longer asked himself why he wanted to know.

"Yes."

"Did you break up because he couldn't handle your success?"

He couldn't know how far off he was. "No. We broke up because we wanted different things out of life." Time to shift the focus. "What about you? Mid-thirties and still footloose and fancy-free. How come?"

Leaning back, he gazed toward the empty fireplace. "I came close once, about two years ago."

"What happened?"

It was what *hadn't* happened more than what had. "Kelly was nice enough, worked as a buyer for Gates Department Store in town. We got along quite well. But there just wasn't enough between us. No fire, no enthusiasm. I think I was considering marriage to please my folks more than to please me."

Pam nodded, understanding perfectly. Her father had often urged her to think about settling down.

Patrick smiled as he remembered something else. "I did go steady all through high school, with Hayley Ingalls. But after graduation, Hayley left to attend this elitist college out east. That wasn't my cup of tea. Neither was she, I guess."

"Another Ingalls. Related to Judson?"

"Yes, his great-niece. Judson's brother, Herbert, and his family live in Milwaukee. At any rate, since Kelly I haven't had a relationship that lasted more than a few weeks. Maybe I'm looking for the kind of woman who doesn't exist anymore. Someone like my mother. She's such a terrific lady. Raised four of us, ran the boardinghouse, and she's been Dr. Phelps's receptionist for years. Plus she supports my dad in whatever he wants to do."

"You're right. They don't make women like that anymore." She looked at him and they both laughed. "Actually, my mother was like that, too. She raised three of us, my two brothers and an overactive tomboy like me. And she worked in real estate, yet she was always there for my dad, as well. She died when I was thirteen, and I still miss her.''

''She never got to see you win the gold. What a shame.''

That thought always sobered Pam. It was her one regret about the Olympics, that her mother hadn't been there to share the joy.

Patrick saw the sadness come and go on her face, and decided to lighten things. ''Could I see your medals?'' He watched her slowly turn to him, a frown on her face. ''What's the matter?''

''Nothing. I'm trying to remember where I put them.''

Could she really be as ego-free as she sounded? Patrick wondered as he shook his head.

''Why are you so surprised? Do you think I should display them on the mantel or perhaps hang them around my neck?''

''I probably would.''

''Oh, you would not.'' She jumped to her feet. ''I remember now. They're in my sock drawer. I'll get them.'' She was back in a flash and found him as she'd left him, looking toward her rather incredulously. She handed him the two cases.

Patrick flipped open one, then the other. He studied the dull silver medal, then the gleaming gold. Running his thumb over the hard surfaces, he found himself impressed. ''Really something. Don't you think you ought to have them framed and hung on your wall?''

Pam curled up in the corner of the couch, drawing her feet up under her. "Maybe I will one day, when I settle down somewhere permanently. It's a little ostentatious to display them openly, though, don't you think?"

"No, I don't. I think they should be a source of great pride to you."

"They can be that in my sock drawer as well as on the wall. I know they're there even if people who come to my home don't see them."

He closed the cases and handed them to her. "I suppose so. I just think something so outstanding should be shared."

"I'll take it under advisement," she said, knowing full well she wouldn't.

"I'll bet the guys on your team would love to see those medals."

She set the cases on the table. That was the last thing she'd do. "I don't believe in dwelling too much on the past—or the future. I believe in living for today."

Patrick crossed his legs and leaned forward, wanting to make his point. "Of course, those boys aren't going for the gold right now. They're young and spirited and need understanding. They should be having fun."

So there'd been a hidden agenda to his casual visit, Pam thought. She leaned her elbow on the back of the couch and toyed with her hair as she narrowed her eyes. "And you don't think that I understand them, or that they're having fun?"

She'd never worked with teenagers, didn't really know them. Patrick tried to keep his tone level. "I didn't say that. However, I think you push a bit harder than is good for young boys."

"And you've come to this conclusion by dropping in on our practices for ten minutes a day? You should be scouting for pro teams or something more in keeping with your wonderful powers of observation and interpretation."

"I don't mean to offend you."

"Really?" No, he'd meant to rile her enough to quit. "I'm not offended, Patrick. Actually, you're behaving exactly as I'd have predicted. Like a know-it-all *male* who has his mind made up on every situation before he even encounters it."

Why did it always come to this with Pam Casals? Patrick tried to appear reasonable. "I have an open mind. I—"

"Oh! You wouldn't know an open mind if you fell into one. I thought, since the last time we shouted at each other, that maybe you'd come around. That perhaps you were going to, at the very least, reserve judgment until we were into the full season."

"I'm here, aren't I? I came to wish you well."

"Did you?" What was there about this man that sent her emotions into overdrive every time they were together?

Patrick was fighting his churning emotions, too. But they'd not been fueled by temper. He was sitting close enough that he had only to move his hand slightly to touch her hair, and he couldn't resist doing so. Incredibly soft, like silk. "Maybe not. Maybe I came for an altogether different reason, one that has nothing to do with football."

Pam could feel her pulse suddenly pounding in her throat. "What reason is that?" Her voice sounded oddly thick.

A car horn blasted twice out on the street, and they both looked out the window. The car passed on by.

Pam turned back and found herself gazing into those fascinating blue eyes mere inches from hers. He was so close she could feel his warm breath on her cheeks. Instantly, she forgot the car, the subject they'd been discussing, everything.

Mesmerized by his gaze, she was helpless to pull back, nor did she really wish to. His hand moved to her cheek, his strong fingers warm against her skin as he traced the contours of her face. Until then, she hadn't known she'd wanted his touch, hadn't admitted she needed the simple human contact.

Patrick shifted his gaze to her lips and saw them tremble open. She was as nervous as he, and oddly enough, the thought relaxed him. He'd wanted to discover if there was anything between them. Even before he lowered his mouth to hers, he knew there was.

He'd been afraid she might pull back, but she didn't. Just a taste, he told himself. Just a sample to satisfy his curiosity. But even as he dared to lean in, to deepen the kiss, he craved to know more.

Her movements were hesitant, belying his impression of her take-charge personality. Her small hands shifted to his shoulders almost reluctantly, somewhat awkwardly, as if without her conscious permission. Her lips parted in invitation, yet there was a curious shyness to her surrender.

She shouldn't have allowed this to begin, Pam thought through a haze of sensation. She shouldn't want anything resembling an involvement, for it only led to heartbreak. She shouldn't need a man's touch, especially not this man's. Yet even before his lips touched hers, she knew she'd wanted him from the first moment she'd seen him on the village green.

She'd known passion before, had tasted desire in a man's kiss. She'd experienced a demanding lover, the heated madness a man could bring to a woman. But she'd never sampled such patience, such gentleness, such slow seduction. She'd never imagined how captivating tenderness could be.

Yet, as his arms slowly slid around her, bringing her body in closer contact with his, she sensed that deeper needs lay hidden beneath that solid chest. Endlessly, his lips moved over hers, while his heart beat wildly against her own. For Pam, the world suddenly narrowed to this room, to this man and to these incredible feelings he had awakened in her.

He had to stop, Patrick told himself even as his mouth slanted over hers, seeking a better angle. Her scent wrapped itself around him, conjuring up visions over which he had no control. He wanted to pick her up, carry her off and set her down on cool, sweet-smelling sheets, to lie with her and love her all night long.

But his good sense warred with his needs. This wasn't a woman to be treated casually. And Tyler was a small town where people talked. Pam was new here, a teacher with a reputation to protect. And he was the hometown boy, who couldn't violate the trust she'd placed in him by opening her door tonight.

With more reluctance than he'd ever experienced, he lifted his head and drew back. He watched her eyes slowly open and saw the remnants of hazy passion in their brown depths. She blinked, and he opened his mouth to speak, but she quickly raised her fingers to his lips.

"Don't say anything, please. If you apologize, I think I'll cry."

Her trembling admission moved him deeply. Gently he tucked her head under his chin and sat stroking her hair, wondering how one kiss could possibly have affected him so strongly.

Pam held on to him more fiercely than when he'd been kissing her. Bob had been out of her life for many months now, and hadn't held her for some time even before he'd left. How could she have known how badly she needed to be held, to be cherished, if only briefly?

It had been like a raw hunger inside her, one she hadn't admitted even to herself. The very nature of her illness had had her isolating herself from friends and family alike, wanting so desperately to go it alone. She had been handled, probed and examined endlessly by competent medical hands, but all the while she'd been longing for the gentle touch she'd found today. And who'd have thought it would come from such a surprising source as Patrick Kelsey?

Pam sat up, feeling a bit more in control. Forcing herself, she raised her eyes to his and found him looking at her tenderly. It was almost her undoing.

"I wasn't going to apologize," Patrick said. "I've wanted to kiss you since the afternoon I tackled you." He smiled then, somewhat sheepishly. "I was too stubborn to admit it, though."

She wanted to confess that she'd felt the same, but she wasn't prepared for where such an admission might lead. Besides, she wasn't certain if she'd wanted *him* to hold her, or if anyone would have done, and he'd been handy. A troublesome thought. She averted her gaze. "I'm sorry I got a little emotional on you there. I don't usually, but it's been an unsettling couple of weeks."

"I understand."

He didn't of course, but she wasn't about to correct him. Feeling nonplussed, she wished he would go now and leave her to work her way through her tangled feelings alone. But he sat there, calmly studying her. Nervously, she got to her feet, somewhat amazed that she could stand without weaving.

She glanced at the clock on the mantel. "I guess maybe I ought to turn in. Big day tomorrow." It was a weak excuse, especially since it was only eight in the evening, but in her present state she could think of no other.

Patrick needed time to sort out his thoughts, and a bit of distance from Pam wouldn't be a bad idea. She was looking softer, more vulnerable by the minute, and was evoking feelings in him he hadn't counted on. Patrick had always been one to move slowly, methodically. Things were happening too rapidly.

He rose. "I have to be going." He moved toward the door.

Pam stepped aside, but in her distraction, she didn't notice Samson snoozing on the floor. Nearly falling over him, she gave a sharp cry and reached out blindly.

Patrick caught her arms and steadied her as the startled dog jumped up and lumbered off. She gazed up at him and the look held, suspending both of them in a time-halting moment. Such beautiful eyes, he thought, and realized he should never have touched her again. Something happened to him each time he did, something not easy to ignore.

"I didn't expect this to happen tonight," he said, needing to comment on the awareness between them. To pretend it wasn't there seemed ludicrous. "I didn't know I'd feel this much this fast. And I'm damned if I know what to do about it." There, it was out. He'd told her. Why didn't he feel better?

"Neither did I. I never dreamed...." Pam withdrew from his hold, brushing her hair back with a shaky hand. No involvements, she reminded herself. He was on the faculty, a man she worked with. It would be a mistake, for both of them. Squaring her shoulders, she walked to the door and opened it. "We ignore it, that's what we do."

Slowly, Patrick strolled to her. He cupped her chin and tipped it up. "Funny, I thought you were smarter than that." He brushed a quick kiss across her mouth, then walked out and closed the door behind him.

Pam sagged against the door. Yes, she'd thought she was smarter than that, too.

PAM ENTERED the locker room wearing her new gold shirt and blue slacks, the coaching outfit in the school colors given to her this morning by Miss Mackie. The boys, understandably nervous, were clowning around a little as they dressed.

She walked through the aisles of lockers, stopping for a word with her first-string quarterback, Ricky Travis. After she'd talked to him about that one incident of absence, Ricky had shown up every day and seemed in top form, throwing well, running better. She told him so and wished him luck.

Zigzagging around the benches, Pam helped a boy pull down his jersey, stopped to check another player's hands, which had been scraped in yesterday's scrimmage. She spent a few minutes congratulating Moose on losing another two pounds. In a short time, she'd grown very fond of these boys, and she truly wished them every success.

Hearing the loudspeaker announcement that they'd be on the field shortly, she made her way to the door and blew her whistle. The boys gathered around in a huddle, waiting expectantly.

"Okay, fellas, this is it." She saw the nods, heard the affirmative responses. "The Tower City Wolverines are good, right?"

Hesitantly a few admitted their opposing team was pretty powerful.

"At the end of last season, they were in second place." She moved into the inner circle, felt them gather around her. "So they're good. But you're better, right?"

"Yeah," came the collective answer.

"Yes, you're better. You're the best. You're winners. Let me hear it."

"We're better! We're the best! We're winners!"

She waited for the shouts to die down and smiled at them. "Okay, then, let's go out there and show 'em." She turned, and the boys parted to let her lead the way through the door.

Running up the embankment leading to the field, she dropped back as the boys lined up in the formation they'd rehearsed. Clipboard in hand, Pam waited as their names were called, watched each boy run out, give a quick wave to acknowledge the hometown cheers and move to the Titans' bench.

She heard the last name announced, then her own introduction. As she followed her boys onto the field, the cheering was long and loud. She hadn't earned those accolades yet, Pam admitted to herself. But it was heartwarming to hear such a vote of confidence.

Pam stood alongside her team as the national anthem was played. Then the referee's whistle sounded and the coin was flipped into the air. The Titans won the toss, the captain electing to receive. Pam squinted in the harsh floodlights as the players moved into position. The game was under way.

The first quarter revealed nervousness on both sides. Fumbles occurred all too frequently, Pam noted, and the Titans suffered two interceptions. But thanks to kicker Jamie Fields, they scored a field goal, putting them in the lead.

As the teams changed sides, she happened to glance up and see Patrick Kelsey standing by the embankment leading to the locker rooms. Of course, as coaching faculty, he was free to wander the area.

Nevertheless, she'd have been more comfortable to have him up in the bleachers. Way up.

Just seeing his hooded eyes fastened on her, his thoughtful expression, sent a shiver up her spine. She recalled the devastating kiss they'd shared, felt the heat rise as she held his gaze a moment longer. Her heartbeat speeded up as she wondered what he was feeling. Finally, hearing the whistle, she swiveled about, realizing that she couldn't afford to let thoughts of Patrick ruin her concentration. She'd spent enough time thinking about him through a long, restless night.

The second quarter went badly. The Wolverines scored a touchdown early on, and losing the lead seemed to dishearten the Titans. To Pam's dismay, Ricky tossed off a wobbly ball, only to have it handily intercepted. The Wolverines scored again as her boys ran after the receiver in confusion. When the gun sounded and the bands lined up, ready to march onto the field for halftime ceremonies, she followed her dejected team to the locker room.

As she rounded a corner, her heart lurched. Patrick was waiting for her, leaning against the wall.

"Problems?" he asked softly.

"You could say that."

"They'll come around yet."

"First-game jitters, that's all. We'll pull it together during the second half."

"I talked to B.J. earlier. The guys are probably a little confused, trying to remember all the new plays they've had to learn in just a couple of weeks."

So B.J. was his pipeline. "B.J.'s put out because he's second-string quarterback and doesn't get to play unless Ricky's injured. Which, thank goodness, he hasn't been.'' Why did Patrick always make her feel so defensive when they talked about the team?

"I want you to know I wasn't grilling B.J. He cuts the grass at my family's boardinghouse and I just happened to be there. It's natural for him to talk football with me."

She was glad he'd explained. "You can't put much credence in what an envious player says."

She looked nervous, hesitant. Perhaps he should offer his assistance. "Do you want me to go in with you, talk with the guys?"

"No, thanks."

"I just want to help."

"You can. By letting me handle my team my way. Please, Patrick?"

He stared at her a long moment. He'd always admired independence. Was she just asserting herself, or was she trying to shut him out? He would wait and see. Nodding, he crammed his hands in the pockets of his corduroy pants and started back down the hallway.

Pam stood a moment, watching him walk away. There was a little-boy-lost look about Patrick that got to her. He wanted badly to join them, to take over, fix things. And he was still utterly convinced she couldn't coach the team as well as he could.

Well, that was *his* problem, she thought as she opened the door to the locker room. *Her* problem was waiting inside.

Dejection was a mild word to use to describe the boys she saw sitting around, wiping their faces, drinking Gatorade. There was no laughter, no playful punching, no clowning around. They were defeating themselves, Pam realized as she strolled among them.

She didn't say much, only a word here and there as she let the tension build. Finally, she blew her whistle for their attention.

"They're beating us out there," she said, hardly having to raise her voice in the hushed silence. "The Wolverines wound up in second place last year, but that's not the reason. *You're* the reason. You're beating yourselves before they get a chance at you. With your attitude. You don't *feel* you can win, so you can't. You're young and strong, all of you. You're well trained and in top form. But your confidence stinks!"

She swung open the door as she heard the end of the halftime show, then turned back to face them. "*I* think you can win. Too bad you don't." She left the room.

Pam stopped at the edge of the field. In a few minutes, the boys came thundering out of the locker room. No one walked. They all ran. Nearly every one came up to her, overflowing with reassurances.

"It's okay, Coach. We're going to do it."

"We'll show 'em."

"Just keep your eyes on the scoreboard, Coach."

Her smile widening, Pam nodded. Hurrying onto the field with them, she hoped she'd said enough and not too much.

THE SECOND HALF of the game was astounding. There simply was no other word Pam could think of to describe her team's performance. It was as if they'd sleepwalked through the first two quarters and had suddenly woken up. Whatever miracle had happened, she didn't want to question it too closely.

The final score was 34 to 20 in favor of the Titans. As the gun heralding the end of the game sounded, the majority of people in the stadium went wild.

The Tower City Wolverines and their coach looked stunned. Pam felt stunned. And happy. Deliriously happy.

At the bench, there was much butt-patting and hand-smacking among the fellows, with helmets thrown into the air and the sweet sound of victory in everyone's voice. She grinned along with them.

"We didn't let you down, Coach, right?" Moose asked.

"No, you certainly didn't. But then, I *knew* you wouldn't."

"Hey, Bubba, you got a date tonight?" Ricky called out to one of his chums.

"Damn right. We're going to cel-e-brate, man!"

"Right on!"

Excitement reigned as the team drifted toward the passage to the lockers. Pam gathered up her things and turned to find Miss Mackie coming toward her, a smile on her narrow face.

"That was some performance, Pam. You're to be congratulated."

"Thank you, but the boys are the ones who deserve the credit. They've been working tirelessly."

"It shows. The entire Booster Club's elated." The principal leaned closer, lowering her voice. "They're alumni, you know, most of them quite prominent."

She pointed vaguely toward the emptying bleachers. "I'll introduce you to them at the next game."

"I'd like that." Pam picked up her clipboard. "See you Monday." With a wave, she ran toward the lockers.

He was waiting just outside the door in the deserted hallway, wearing a congratulatory smile. "You did it—the impossible," Patrick said. "I'm proud of you."

Why did he have to look so handsome, with that thick, black hair and those disarming blue eyes? she asked herself as she stopped several feet from him. "Thanks, but, as you well know, a coach doesn't win a game. The team does."

He pushed off from the wall he'd been leaning against and shook his head. "Don't be so modest. The coach has a lot to do with a team's performance. I'm impressed."

He sounded sincere, so she took his comments as such, nodding in acknowledgment. She glanced around. "Are you waiting for someone?"

"Yes, you. I'd like to walk you home." He nodded toward the end of the ramp, where a section of sky, filled with winking stars, was visible. "It's a beautiful night."

The school was only half a dozen blocks from her apartment, and she'd jogged over, needing the exercise to release her tension. The thought of strolling along the quiet streets with Patrick held a lot of appeal. And a fair share of apprehension, Pam thought, again recalling that kiss. She was getting in deeper each time she was alone with Patrick.

Yet how could she refuse, since he, her worst critic, had capitulated and even congratulated her? "All right. Just let me change." She turned toward the girls' locker room.

She was halfway there when she heard him call her name. As she looked back, he stepped closer. "Hurry, will you?"

With a nod, she rushed inside and began to undress. What she desperately needed was a cold shower.

CHAPTER FOUR

BY THE TIME Pam changed and stopped to have a few words with the team, nearly everyone else had cleared out of the stadium. Patrick watched her walk toward him, looking fresh and lovely in tan slacks and a black sweater. Then he took her hand and led her toward the street.

He wasn't quite sure why he'd come back to ask if he could walk her home. Perhaps it was because she dominated his thoughts lately, much to his surprise. She wasn't like any woman he'd ever known.

On the field she was spirited, a dynamo in action, passionately involved with her players. Last night, she'd been softly feminine, diffident—almost casual—about her achievements, hesitant about kissing him, then avidly responsive. Afterward he'd glimpsed a vulnerability in her he was certain few had seen. Her temper was quick to flare, yet he could see she was as reluctantly attracted as he.

Undeniably, she intrigued him, which was why he was with her now, indulging in getting-acquainted chatter as they strolled along. She'd just asked him what he'd wanted to be when he was growing up. "A fire chief," he answered promptly.

"Not a fireman, but the *chief*," Pam teased.

"Right. My dad was good friends with Chief Reynolds back then, and he let me ride on the big red engine one day when they took it out for a test drive. That did it. I was hooked."

She smiled at his youthful reminiscences. "And when did you change your mind?"

"When my dad took me to Baraboo to see the Ringling Brothers circus. I decided I wanted to become a trapeze artist." He laced his fingers with hers, distracted by the warmth of her soft skin. "But that career choice ended the day I climbed our cherry tree with a rope I'd rigged up. I fell and broke my arm and decided maybe I wasn't meant for the circus, either."

"I've always wanted to see a circus," Pam said somewhat wistfully. "Somehow, we never got around to going."

"I suppose you spent most of your free time training for the Olympics."

"Yes. And competing with my two brothers. I was a terrible tomboy. I wanted to do everything they did—football, hockey, tennis, baseball."

"I bet you did them, too."

His big hand swallowed hers up, but comfortably so. His arm had hers trapped close to his body, close enough to smell the clean, masculine scent of him. *Look out,* Pam warned herself. She was enjoying his touch altogether too much. Sobering, she walked silently along, the evening breeze gentle on her face.

Patrick glanced down at the soft swell of her breasts through the thin cotton of her sweater. "You outgrew those tomboy days very nicely."

He rarely missed an opportunity to pay her a compliment, leaving her at a loss as to how to respond. "Not altogether. Were any of your sisters tomboys?"

"Yes, the youngest, Kathleen. She still is, I think. You met her that day playing football with us on the green." He shook his head. "Kathleen worries me."

This was more comfortable. "Why is that?"

"She's so unfocused, and she's twenty-eight. She went away to college, but quit after one year. She tried modeling in Chicago and grew impatient with that. She's worked in a department store, spent a year as a meter reader for the gas company, then opened a pet grooming business. She built that up, but sold it just last month because she's bored with it."

"Sounds to me like she's a woman of many interests and talents searching for something she wants to spend the rest of her life doing. What's wrong with that?"

"Nothing, if she'd just zero in on something. I believe you have to make a plan, then work the plan. Sometimes you have to switch gears, but then you set a new goal and work toward that. If you don't plan your future, if you just drift along, letting life happen to you, you wind up with nothing to show for it."

They came to the town square, where the streetlights reflected on his serious face. Pam stopped to study him a moment before responding. "I understand Kathleen. Some people like to live from day to day, finding it too constraining to map out a future that almost always changes on you anyway." Hers certainly had, Pam thought. Her illness had drastically altered her life's plans. Since then, though she had goals, they were short-term and not necessarily written in stone. She was becoming increasingly aware that she and Patrick had opposite philosophies.

"But you had a plan, from early in your youth, to win the gold, to coach the Olympics, and now to coach kids in football. You couldn't have done that without setting goals and working toward them."

They started walking again, past the darkened beauty shop and across the deserted square. "The Olympics was a goal, I admit. But most of the other things I've done came about because of circumstances that made those moves appealing and available at the same time. And a few things happened that made me do an about-face and head in another direction. I try to concentrate on enjoying today and not worrying so much about tomorrow. Maybe Kathleen feels the same."

Patrick was unconvinced. "My sister Laura helps her husband in his construction business, plus has two kids. My other sister, Glenna, just got married and runs a dress shop. I wish Kathleen would settle down, find something and stick with it. There was a C.P.A. in Tyler Kathleen seemed to care for—even got engaged to him. But it didn't last. She's gone through almost as many men as jobs."

"Haven't you heard that a girl has to kiss a lot of frogs before she finds Prince Charming?"

This time it was Patrick who stopped, in the shadows of a large maple tree, and turned to her. "Is that what you were doing last night, trying to determine if I'm a frog or a prince?"

The question brought Pam up short. Though he wore a small smile, she sensed he was serious. "Is that what you think I was doing—experimenting with you?"

"No, I don't."

"Then what did you think?"

"That you wanted to kiss me as much as I wanted to kiss you."

How astute of him. "All right then. Let's not over-think it. After all, it was just a kiss." She knew the minute the words were out that she'd made a mistake. It was almost as if she'd issued him a challenge.

Patrick's arms slipped around her, drawing her closer. As he lowered his head, a car full of teenagers came sailing around the bend, pulling up noisily across the square. The kids jumped out, walking toward Marge's Diner. Despite his need to prove Pam wrong, he stepped back.

"Bad timing," he muttered, then glanced toward the diner. "Would you like something to eat?" When she shook her head, he took her hand and they walked down Main Street, out of the lighted area.

A close call, Pam thought as she strolled along, noticing that he hadn't relinquished her hand. For the life of her, she didn't know if she wanted to avoid another kiss, or experience again that mindless slide into desire. Feeling like a coward, she searched for a change of subject.

"Do you know Cindy Crane, one of our varsity cheerleaders?"

"Yes. She's on the girls' basketball team, a good athlete. Her folks have a farm just outside of town. Nice people."

"Cindy's nice, too, from what I've seen. But she's causing a problem I'm not sure she's aware of. It seems she's B.J.'s neighbor. They've grown up together and have been close friends. Now, suddenly, Arnie Steel has been dating her, and they kind of moon around together during breaks. B.J. has a crush on her, and he's not happy. It's interfering with his performance." As they turned onto Morgan Avenue, she caught Patrick's nostalgic smile under the street lamp.

"Ah, young love. It's not all it's cracked up to be, is it?"

"Probably not. B.J.'s having trouble dealing with his jealousy."

"Want me to talk with him?" he asked as they climbed the steps to her porch.

"No, thanks. Maybe the situation will solve itself." Pam preferred to work out her own problems.

Suddenly a deep-throated bark came from the backyard. "Samson's heard us. I'd better go let him in."

"He can wait another minute." Patrick drew her to the porch swing. "It's too nice to go in just yet." They sat down amid the creaking of the chain support.

Patrick kept them gently moving as he stretched his arm along the back of the swing. Moonlight played through the leafy trees and crickets serenaded nearby. He could smell the roses that trailed up the trellis behind them mingling with the jasmine scent of the woman who sat somewhat tensely beside him. "How do you like rural living compared to all the big cities you've lived in?"

"I like it."

"Could you be happy here, in a small town?"

He seemed to want to project her into a future she could only see as cloudy. "I think most people could be happy in a variety of places," Pam answered carefully.

"Not me." His hand shifted, settling on her shoulder. "I'm a country boy at heart."

"You mean you've never considered living anywhere but Tyler?"

He had once, briefly. But that had been ages ago. "Not for long." He edged closer to her. "Maybe things happen for the best and I wasn't meant to leave at all." His hand touched her hair as she turned to look at him. "Maybe I wouldn't have met you if I had. Think what I might have missed." He watched the wariness leap into her eyes.

He was moving too fast for her again. "I thought we decided last night we were going to ignore these... these feelings?"

"I'm sure I didn't agree to that. Besides, suppressing feelings is bad for you, I hear. It can cause migraines and ulcers, and play havoc with your sciatic nerve." He leaned in to nuzzle her cheek.

She gave him a puzzled look. "Your sciatic nerve?"

"Yeah, from holding yourself so stiffly, like you're doing now. Relax, I'm not going to bite you."

Perhaps a bite would be more easily handled than another of his stunning kisses, Pam couldn't help thinking. She scooted out of reach, groping for a subject change. "Why did you become a teacher?"

Blinking in surprise, Patrick sat up straighter. She had a way of throwing cold water on a heated situation. "What did you say?"

"Well, you mentioned earlier that you wanted to be a fire chief, then a trapeze artist. Yet you're a teacher. I'm just curious how that came about... unless you'd rather not talk about it."

Talking wasn't what he'd had in mind, but she left him little choice. Patrick settled himself more comfortably on the swing and started them in motion again. "I like kids. I discovered I was good with them, so I decided to teach. Why do you want to coach football, when there're so many other less physically dangerous things you could do?"

"Because I feel I'm good at what I do, too. And I've never been hurt coaching football."

"But how long can you keep doing it? Where do you see yourself five years from now, or ten?"

Pam frowned. "I don't think about the future as intensely as you do. I think about tomorrow and not much farther ahead."

"Not even a little? What about marriage, that baby you said you thought of as the ultimate achievement?"

"Male coaches have families. Why can't a woman?"

"Do you think many men would be happy to stay home with babies while you're out on the field coaching football?"

Although certain she was debating a lost cause, she continued. "The kind of man I would love wouldn't categorize the work load into female chores and male chores. We would *share* what had to be done, and if that included baby-sitting during football season, he would do it willingly."

Patrick ran a hand through his hair. "I think most men like to be the main provider. It's a man's responsibility to support his woman."

She laughed, because if she didn't treat this with humor, she'd be tempted to pop him a good one. "*His woman?* Like his sheep or goat, his car or house? His possession? You know, your thinking belongs back in the Dark Ages. I think a man's responsibility is to support a woman—not financially, but support what she needs to do to be happy and fulfilled. And she has the same responsibility to him."

"Most men feel differently. A man has a built-in need to protect his...I mean, *a* woman from things that are too strenuous or dangerous."

"Patrick, this isn't the wild West. A woman doesn't need a man to protect her as much as she needs him to love her. Just love and understand her."

"Maybe you're right." He slid closer, his arm encircling her. But his eye caught a movement and he looked up. The curtains on the window facing the swing had parted, and a round face topped with gray hair was peering at them. He cleared his throat. "I think we've got company. There's a lady looking at us."

Just in the nick of time, Pam thought as she slipped off the swing. "That's our neighbor, Mrs. Tibbs," she said in a low voice. "She's very nice, but a little snoopy." Flashing the widow a quick smile, she walked to the door. "I have to go in anyhow."

Patrick sent Mrs. Tibbs a friendly wave before following Pam. "I didn't mean to get into a heated discussion with you again." He put his hands on her shoulders, marveling at how small she was.

"I'm getting used to it. We seem to be on opposite sides of more issues than not. Maybe it would be best if we limited our time together to school."

"Are you looking for a man who thinks exactly as you do in all things? A yes-man who echoes your every thought?"

Visible in a patch of moonlight, his eyes challenged her. But tonight, she would resist. "The truth is, I'm not looking for any man. Nor am I interested in getting involved with one. Thanks for walking me home. Good night." Quickly she opened the door and closed it behind her.

Patrick took a long breath and turned, shoving his hands into his pants pockets as he stared up at the night sky. It no longer bothered him that he and Pam had divergent opinions. Opposites often attracted. His own parents disagreed often and noisily, but that didn't mean they didn't care. A little friendly disagreement now and then cleared the air and made for an exciting relationship instead of a dull one.

Instincts. He relied regularly on his instincts. Pam's mouth said one thing, but her body language sang out another tune, loud and clear. His instincts told him she was lying to herself.

She could deny her feelings all she wanted. She was interested, all right.

Whistling, Patrick left the porch and headed home.

THINGS WERE a little cool around Tyler High, Patrick realized, and it had nothing to do with the approaching fall weather. In the two weeks since he'd walked Pam home, he'd seen very little of her, busy as she was with her team. And when he did see her, she seemed to be in a hurry. He couldn't decide whether she was really that involved or was trying to avoid him.

Watching the team work out the day before the season opener, he had to admit that in one month, Pam had done wonders with her boys. They'd won all of their preseason games. Around town, people were calling her the "miracle coach." He was happy for her and pleased for the team. But personally he was a bit frustrated at not finding her alone and available more often.

Right now, she was drilling the defense on a particular play, and this was the third time she'd made them repeat the maneuver. Finally satisfied, she praised their work, then stepped back and gazed across the field, her eyes finding his. She studied him thoughtfully for a long moment, then, to Patrick's surprise, she started toward him. Lounging back on the bleachers, he waited.

Pam approached Patrick somewhat hesitantly. "Hi."

"Hi, yourself. How've you been?"

"Fine, and you?"

"Great. I hear your name all over town. You're the woman of the hour." She was wearing a pale yellow warm-up suit today, and her tanned skin looked fresh and young. He all but sat on his hands to keep from reaching out to touch her.

Pam shrugged off his comments as she eased down onto the bench, not terribly near where he was sprawled. "I have a problem and I was wondering if you could help."

Was he hearing correctly? Pam Casals asking him for help? He sat up taller. "I could try."

Pam hated asking anyone for help, always had. But there were times when there were few alternatives. She had to do this, for the good of the team. "It's B.J. again. He wants to quit the team and concentrate next season on basketball."

"Is he having problems on the field or at home?"

"Neither. A problem of the heart. Do you remember my telling you about Cindy Crane?"

"Oh, I see. She's dating another player and B.J.'s jealous. He's tired of watching her hang around drooling over the other guy."

"That's about it. I've tried talking with him, but he gets very defensive. And I need him. He's my reserve quarterback, and I may have to bench my first-stringer."

"Ricky Travis? What's he done?"

"He's missed two practice sessions. I told him, one more and he wouldn't play the next game. He's pretty cocky, though, and doesn't believe I'd do it."

He grinned at her. "I believe you would."

"Good, because I will. Could you see if B.J. would talk with you? He's known you a long time."

"I'd be happy to."

He looked genuinely pleased to be asked, and he'd not made her feel inadequate for asking. She smiled as she stood. "Thanks, I appreciate it."

Leaning forward, Patrick caught her hand as he rose. "Can I buy you a big, fat, gooey chocolate soda tomorrow night at Marge's Diner after the game? A victory-celebration soda?"

"What if we lose?"

"You won't."

She'd missed him, Pam suddenly realized. She'd been able to concentrate on her coaching better without him around, but she had missed him. His fingers played over hers, warm and enticing. At times, the two of them were like oil and water. But some moments, like now, as she stared up into his fascinating eyes, they were like moth to flame. "How can I refuse in the face of such confidence? Okay." She tugged her hand free. "Got to run. See you later."

Returning to the field, Pam found her step lighter and her heart beating faster. Every time she saw him, it got worse. How was she going to fight this deepening attraction?

AFTER PRACTICE, Pam returned to the coaching office just off the gym. Sitting down at her desk to go over some notes, she heard snatches of a nearby conversation and paused. Sounds carried in an empty gymnasium. She didn't mean to eavesdrop, but the connecting door was ajar, and when she recognized the voices, her curiosity kicked in.

"No lie, Coach? That really happened?" B.J. asked.

"The absolute truth," Patrick said firmly. "Nobody gets everything they want. Everyone has to learn to compromise at some time in life."

"I didn't know. You never let on."

"Maybe my strength is in not letting you see my weakness. Maybe you should consider not letting Cindy see how her dating Arnie bothers you. She may look at you differently if she sees you're not upset. If she doesn't . . . well, there're other girls out there, B.J. Focus on another one. You've got a lot to offer. But don't defeat yourself by becoming a quitter."

"I guess maybe you're right. Women aren't easy to understand, are they, Coach?"

Patrick chuckled. "No, they're not. And figuring them out doesn't get any easier as you get older."

At her desk, Pam listened to their retreating footsteps. She'd been wrong not to take Patrick's offer of assistance before. He was more experienced than she. He'd evidently handled a touchy issue and a sensitive boy beautifully.

What, she couldn't help wondering, had Patrick revealed to B.J. that had turned around the boy's thinking? Something about himself, it appeared, something that obviously surprised B.J. and influenced his decision.

She was beginning to realize that there was more to Patrick Kelsey than met the eye.

PATRICK DECIDED to move into the bleachers to watch the second half of the opening game. The Titans were playing the Allentown Angels, and creaming them. At halftime, the score was a comfortable 20–7 in favor of Tyler. The fans were ecstatic.

Noticing Judson Ingalls seated off by himself near the end of a row, Patrick climbed the steps to join him. As a member of the school's Booster Club, Judson attended most games. Reaching him, Patrick held out his hand. "Mr. Ingalls. Good to see you."

Judson shook hands warmly and slid over on the bench. "Patrick, how've you been? Keeping busy?"

"Yes, sir. Quite a game, isn't it?"

"I'd have never believed a woman could do it, but that new coach has sure turned this team around." Shelling peanuts, Judson tossed a couple into his mouth.

The backhanded compliment would probably have had Pam bristling, Patrick thought. "I give her a lot of credit." He watched Judson's eyes scan the crowd as if he were looking for someone. In his mid-seventies, the patriarch of the Ingalls family looked years younger. He was still an imposing figure of a man, more than six feet tall with a full head of very white hair. "Did you come alone?"

"I often do," Judson answered vaguely, watching the band leave the field after halftime ceremonies. He swung back to look at Patrick. "How're your folks? I saw Johnny at the plant last week, but I haven't seen your mother in a while."

"They're both fine, thank you." Patrick looked up to find a tall woman, her red hair artfully arranged beneath a black felt hat, smiling at them from the steps. Her black wool dress was belted and clung to her generous curves. "Tisha," he said, rising. "Hello."

"Hello, Patrick. You're looking as handsome as ever." Her voice was low and husky as her eyes slid to the older man. "Judson, I'm sorry I'm late."

"No problem, my dear." Judson reached to help her step in front of them and sit down on his far side. "Glad you're here."

Patrick hid a grin. Who'd have thought Judson Ingalls would have something in common with Tisha Olsen, the outspoken lady who ran the Hair Affair? Her somewhat shady past lent itself to a variety of rumors around town, but personally, Patrick had always liked Tisha. She had a great sense of humor and she didn't take herself seriously.

"I had a couple of late customers," Tisha explained to Judson. "I almost had to boot them out the door to get here at all." She glanced at the scoreboard. "I see the Titans are murdering them."

Patrick stood along with half the stadium as the teams raced out onto the field. Still seated, Judson cringed, then stared off, a faraway look in his eyes.

"Lighten up, honey," Tisha said. But she touched his hand to soften her words. "I know you're upset about that body they found at Timberlake."

Judson popped another peanut into his mouth. "Of course, I'm upset. I hate the whispering, the rumors and conjectures."

"It's the talk of the shop, I can tell you. They seem fairly certain there was foul play."

Judson sighed deeply. "I may just sell the lodge. Let someone else cope with all of it."

Squeezing his hand, Tisha leaned close as the applause died down and the fans resumed their seats. "Why don't we take a long ride later and talk?" she whispered. "For now, let's just enjoy the game."

"All right." Judson pointed toward the diminutive coach and handed Tisha his binoculars. "There's Pam Casals in the gold shirt and blue slacks. Little bit of a thing to be coaching those strapping boys, isn't she?"

Patrick's eyes were on Pam, too, as she consulted her clipboard. Then the whistle blew and she knelt at the sideline, her eyes on her team. He wished he was down there with her, sharing the excitement, feeling that adrenaline rush that came with each kickoff.

NEAR THE END of the fourth quarter, Pam's adrenaline was pumping. The boys had come back after halftime a shade overconfident. The Angels had sensed it and pushed harder, scoring two touchdowns. The Titans had made a few mistakes, and now, with the two-minute warning sounding, the score was 21–20 in favor of the Angels.

The Titans had the ball on third down with five yards to go for what could be the winning touchdown. Shoulder muscles tense, Pam watched her team go into formation. But the Angels' defense held them down and there was no gain. Hurriedly, Pam signaled for their last time-out, and quarterback Ricky Travis came running over.

Whipping off his helmet, Ricky stood with his hands on his padded hips. "The handoff was slow and I almost dropped the ball on that one. Damn!"

"I want to try something, Ricky," Pam said. "It's fourth down with a minute and a half remaining. I want you to try a dropkick."

"You mean it?"

"Yes. I think we have a better chance with that play than a field goal, especially since Jamie's leg still isn't up to par." Their kicker had missed the extra point and a previous field goal. "Do a power 29 and sweep on one. Got it?"

"Right, Coach." Turning, Ricky secured his helmet as he ran back onto the field.

Hardly hearing the noise of the crowd, Pam moved up along the sideline a bit, straining to watch the play put into motion. Seconds later, the stadium exploded into a collective shout of approval as the dropkick worked. With the additional three points, the Titans were now leading 23–21.

For the fraction of a minute remaining, the Tyler players delayed, shuffling lazily about, falling on the ball until the clock ran out. Everyone could see the shock on the faces of the Angels. They'd been beaten when victory had been near enough to taste. Again, the fans in the stands erupted into wild cheering as the Titans ran triumphantly from the field.

"Hey, Coach, right on," Moose yelled to Pam above the crowd.

"You guys did it!" she yelled back. "I knew you could."

Beaming, slapping one another, the elated players ran toward the locker room amid rousing applause.

Watching them go, Pam beamed, too. As she shifted her gaze to the stands, she caught Patrick's eye. Smiling, he made a thumbs-up gesture and waved to her. Pleased at his approval, she waved back and headed for the showers.

At least she could feel she'd earned the soda he'd promised her.

"CHOCOLATE, of course," Pam said to the smiling waitress at Marge's Diner an hour later.

"Make it two," Patrick added. They were seated in the corner booth in the crowded restaurant. Postgame players, cheerleaders and fans were clustered everywhere, sometimes six to a booth, and overflowing the tables in the center of the cheerful room. As Pam and Patrick entered, everyone had turned to cheer the "miracle coach." Noticing her somewhat shy but pleased smile, Patrick had felt proud of Pam, too. Taking her hand now, he waited till she raised her eyes to his. "You did it, exactly what you said you'd do. You've turned the team around."

"You're still surprised a mere woman could make a difference?" Her voice was low, teasing. She felt a little self-conscious, holding hands with so many people around. After all, she was still new to this town.

"No longer surprised. You could hardly be classified as a *mere woman*."

"Thank you, I guess. I feel as if changing your opinion should be a coup for women's lib. Perhaps I should phone Gloria Steinem or someone."

He toyed with her ringless fingers. "Go ahead, make fun of my old-fashioned views."

"They're not old-fashioned, Patrick. They're archaic."

He sent her a chagrined look. "That bad?"

"Sometimes."

"All right. Next election, I'm campaigning against chastity belts for women, and I might even be in favor of letting them vote."

"Big of you." But she laughed, because very little could upset her tonight, and because he was trying to laugh at himself. Definitely a step in the right direction, Pam thought.

"You took a hell of a chance with that last play. I didn't know you were so daring."

"No guts, no glory, they say. Actually, it's one of those calls that if it works, everyone thinks you're wonderful. If it hadn't, they'd now be asking why I resorted to such a dumb move."

He nodded, knowing she was right.

Marge herself arrived at the table, serving them in person. "On the house tonight, you two," she said as she placed huge chocolate sodas in front of Patrick and Pam.

Patrick thanked her, then introduced Pam.

"Happy to meet you," Marge said. "I hear the game was a real thriller. Congratulations."

"Thanks. The boys have worked really hard."

"A team is only a bunch of boys without a good coach." Marge winked at her and hurried back behind her counter.

Pam studied the woman's retreating back. Average would describe Marge Peterson, she thought. Medium height with medium brown hair. But her eyes were a warm brown and she had a caring smile. "She seems nice," Pam commented before digging into her soda.

"Marge is an institution around here. Her life hasn't been easy, yet she's always got a smile or a good word for everyone, and you never hear her complain."

Silently sipping her soda, Pam overheard a woman in the booth behind her talking about the body found at Timberlake lodge.

"They think it may be the remains of an Indian," the woman said. "The lodge is right next to what some people believe used to be an old Indian burial ground."

"That's possible," her companion agreed. "But the consensus of opinion at the Hair Affair the other morning was that the body is probably an Ingalls. Didn't Margaret Ingalls disappear some years ago?"

"Yes, she did, quite mysteriously."

The lady drank noisily through her straw. "If it is Margaret Ingalls, what do you suppose could have happened to her?"

The other woman grunted. "My mother told me that Margaret was pretty wild, a free spirit. Maybe one of the men she used to have up to the lodge for her parties did her in. Or maybe Judson came home one evening, found her with some man and decided he'd had enough."

"Judson Ingalls, capable of murder?" the companion went on. "I don't believe it."

"You never know about people," the woman said firmly.

Glancing up at Patrick, Pam realized that he'd heard the conversation, too. "Looks like that body's on everyone's mind lately. Must be upsetting to the Ingalls family."

"It is. I sat with Judson for a while at the game and he seemed quite distracted." Finishing, he moved his glass aside, crossed his arms on the table and studied Pam. She was wearing one of her long, full skirts, tan this time, with a brown wool jacket over a yellow blouse. She looked lovely.

Uneasy under his gaze, Pam frowned. "What are you doing?"

"I enjoy looking at you. Life is for enjoying, Pam, and I enjoy you."

"Is life for enjoying, Patrick?" She set her own empty glass aside and blotted her lips. She'd had him pegged as a bit too serious, which was why his comment surprised her.

He nodded. "I decided that it was some years ago, when I had to reevaluate my life after a big disappointment."

So he, too, had known his share of disappointments. But then, what adult hadn't? Pam was curious, wanting to ask more. But knowing Patrick would also probe, she decided to keep the discussion impersonal. "Disappointments that change our lives stay with us. At least the lingering effects do."

"Right now, I don't want to think about past disappointments. I just want to enjoy tonight."

She raised a surprised eyebrow. "You mean, live for today and not worry about tomorrow? I can't believe that came out of Patrick Kelsey, the town worry-wart."

He laughed. "Well, it did. It's Friday night, I'm out with the loveliest woman in town and all's right with my world. How about yours?"

She felt her blood warm under his heated gaze. "My world's pretty fine right now, too."

He nodded toward the crowded room. "What do you say we blow this joint? I'd like to be alone with you."

That set her blood racing, but with anticipation, not with fright. Holding his gaze, she nodded. "I'd like that."

THE NIGHT AIR was cool on her flushed cheeks as they walked toward her apartment. Their leave-taking had generated more handshakes and congratulatory hugs from happy Titan fans. Amid the buzz of excitement, Patrick had finally taken Pam's hand and led her out the door.

"I've never been in a town that cared so much about their high school sports," Pam confessed.

"Most of these people attended Tyler High at one time, so it's alma mater fever. Besides, there're no nearby pro teams, so it's understandable." He smiled down at her, relieved to be out of the noisy crowd at long last.

"If we ever lose, I feel as if I'd have to go to each one and apologize personally."

"Lose?" he asked with mock seriousness. "The miracle coach doesn't lose. What's happened to your confidence?"

"Every team loses some games, Patrick." They turned onto her street and Pam saw from the corner that the only lights on in her house were in Mrs. Tibbs's apartment. She'd seen Rosemary at the game, but her roommate had left with some friends and evidently wasn't home yet.

"No negative thinking, remember?" Patrick reminded her.

"Right." At her door, she turned to him, suddenly hesitant. "I want to thank you for talking to B.J. He's decided not to quit the team after all."

"Any time."

"I really should go in. Samson's been in the backyard for hours and..."

He touched a finger to her lips to stop her excuses. "But first, maybe we should see if how we felt during that kiss we shared was a fluke or the real thing."

She'd been wondering the same thing, wondering if she'd been feeling vulnerable that night and had just wanted a man to hold her, or if she'd wanted *this* man's arms around her. But a sudden movement had Patrick turning to glance at the window.

"Are you going to invite me inside or are we going to give Mrs. Tibbs a performance she'll long remember?" he asked.

Pam turned and unlocked the door. She hadn't particularly wanted to risk the intimacy of her empty apartment and was a bit annoyed at her nosy neighbor for forcing her to do so. In the brightly lighted hallway, she opened her own door and walked in.

Behind her, Patrick sauntered in, bumped the door closed with his hip, removed his jacket and flung it onto a chair. Then he reached out to stop her before she could switch on a lamp. Turning her into the circle of his arms, he nodded toward the window. "I look better by moonlight," he whispered.

As his hands moved to her waist, then crept up her back, Pam tipped her head and looked up at him. Though she was wearing medium heels, he was still so much taller, the breadth of his shoulders making her feel even smaller. His eyes were dark as they locked with hers. In unconscious invitation, her lips opened. It was all the permission he needed.

Patrick leaned down and took her mouth as his arms tightened around her, drawing her closer. He felt her ease up on tiptoe, stretching to meet his kiss, her arms drifting around him. Her taste burst on his tongue as it entered her mouth, and he heard her make a soft sound deep in her throat.

She was kissing him back now, the way he'd dreamed for two weeks that she would. Her body strained closer to his with a giving softness that had his heart hammering in his chest. This was no reluctant female afraid of a man who obviously wanted her. This was a woman eagerly embracing, a woman unafraid to show she wanted, too.

Stunned at her own abandon, Pam savored the thrill of his tongue stroking hers. No, the other evening hadn't been a fluke, nor could just any man have captivated her like this. The first kiss they'd shared had moved her with its tenderness, warming her each time she recalled the sweetness. But this was altogether different. This was that edgy excitement she'd sensed he was capable of bringing to her. This was the passion that had been missing from her life all too long. And she reached out with both hands to gather it closer.

As if to a drumbeat, the blood pounded through her veins, and she felt alive. So alive. She inhaled the clean, outdoorsy scent of him, already recognizing it as familiar and his alone. He angled his lips over hers, taking her deeper, and she was lost. Lost.

His hands roamed over her, sliding through the silken strands of her hair, then down her arms. The bulky blazer she wore frustrated him, and so he slid it from her shoulders. He swallowed her moan of protest as he pulled the jacket free and tossed it aside. His hands touched the soft cotton of her blouse, and as he slid his mouth lower to taste her throat, he still wished she weren't wearing so damn many clothes.

"Patrick," Pam murmured through a fog of desire, "I . . . we should stop. We . . ."

He returned to capture her lips again, because he wanted her kiss as much as he wanted her to stop talking. He'd been right to walk away from Kelly and the others. Right in thinking there was more. This was the uncertain something he'd known someone could bring to him. And that someone was Pam Casals. His hand slipped lower on her back, pressing her to the rigid lines of his body, making her aware of his unmistakable need.

Less shocked than aroused, Pam arched into him, her breasts crushing softly into the firm wall of his chest. Her breathing was labored and the pulse at her throat was pounding as she struggled to keep up with his frantic pace. She closed her eyes as he rained kisses over her face, her throat. A part of her knew she should stop him while she still could, and she would.

In just a moment. Just as soon as she sampled the breathless wonder of one more kiss, as soon as her hands had finished exploring the hard contours of his back, as soon as she no longer trembled for his magical touch. But deep inside, she knew that many moments or minutes, perhaps even hours, would not be enough. Not with this man.

And it scared the hell out of her.

Drawing reluctantly back by inches, she pulled free of his searching mouth at last. "Patrick, wait, please." Her breath came in short bursts as she tried to slow her racing heart. "Slow down, please."

Patrick loosened his hold and straightened, though it was the hardest thing he'd done in a long while. He raised a gentle hand to brush back her hair. "It's all right, honey. Nothing's going to happen that you don't want to happen."

Pam met his eyes, covering his hand, which had wandered to her cheek, with her own. Already, perhaps, he knew her too well. She touched her lips gently into his palm before looking. "I'd be lying if I said I didn't want what we started to continue, and I'm sure you know it." She took a deep, steadying breath. "This is just moving a little fast for me. I have to sort out my feelings."

He trailed his fingers through her hair a final time and kissed her forehead. Pam's presence in his life, in his arms, made him aware of things he hadn't consciously known he'd been missing, of empty places and nebulous dreams. And, as he stared into her huge brown eyes, he knew the feelings he had for this woman far transcended the physical. The knowledge rocked him, which was why he broke the contact and reached for his jacket.

"Maybe we both need a little breathing room," Patrick said at the door. "See you at school next Monday?"

"Yes, and I'm sorry. I didn't mean to lead you on."

"No apology necessary. And no harm done." As quietly as he'd entered, he left.

Without turning on the light, Pam wandered to the bay window and watched Patrick skip down the steps and walk away. No harm done, he'd said.

No harm, if you didn't count the fact that she was learning to care too much for a man whose viewpoint on life differed often and greatly from hers. A man she hadn't been completely honest with. But she had her reasons. Bob hadn't been able to cope with her illness, and he'd known her for more than a year before it started. How could she expect Patrick to handle it?

It would seem she had two choices: break off the relationship before it had really begun and not say a word, or tell him and risk losing him before they even knew each other. As she turned from the window and walked to her bedroom, she realized that both choices filled her with dread.

CHAPTER FIVE

IT HAD TO HAPPEN sometime, Pam thought with a frown as she walked past the gym a week later. The Titans had lost their first game this year last Friday, and the mood around Tyler High was decidedly glum. Of course, it was only mid-September and still early in the season. And the team that had beaten them—the Wildcats—were league champions. Nonetheless, the loss stung.

At the door of the sports office, she paused. Her nameplate had arrived, and it was in place in top position, above Patrick's. She wondered if Miss Mackie had put it up and wondered about Patrick's reaction. Dismissing the thought, she unlocked the door. She had more important worries today.

Settling behind her desk, she got out the notes she'd made over the weekend, some new play ideas and a few changes in the lineup that she was considering. Losing Moose with a pulled hamstring was going to hurt them in next Friday's game. But the doctor had said he'd have to rest for at least two weeks.

Checking her box, she saw that the films of the game had already arrived, and she was anxious to see them. As she looked up the door opened and Patrick strolled in. "Hi. I thought you had a class this hour."

"Not until ten." Patrick set down the files he'd been carrying. "Your nameplate looks good, don't you think?"

Pam studied his face and found his expression sincere. "Yes, it does."

"I see you're about to watch the game films. Thinking of doing a little Monday-morning quarterbacking?" After the loss, he'd joined Pam in the locker room to bolster the morale of the players. He'd been surprised that she'd invited him. Surprised and pleased.

They'd sat around for nearly an hour with the guys, trying to figure out what had gone wrong, discussing failed plays and possible solutions to prevent a repeat. Both of them had felt good about the session. "Do you mind if I watch the film with you?"

"Actually, I'd appreciate it if you would." They'd had an unusual two weeks since their last encounter at her apartment. Pam thought of it as a truce of sorts. They'd talked at school, at the games, in the locker room, and had chatted in their shared office. They'd caught each other in long, thoughtful glances. They'd kept their contacts businesslike and impersonal. But, if she were any judge, the tension between them had been building.

Patrick watched her insert the videotape into the VCR. He moved his chair next to where Pam sat, her pen poised over her ever-present clipboard. For several minutes they watched the filmed game in silence.

"That's the play where Moose got hurt," Pam commented as the boy went down, his face tight with pain.

"Do you remember what he said afterward? 'At least I scored. I didn't get hurt for nothing.'"

"He's a good kid." She leaned forward, watching a punt by Jamie. "It doesn't look like Jamie's leg is up to par yet, either. These injuries are hurting us."

"At least they've been minor so far." He concentrated on the next play. "That's Rob Neff's second fumble. You know, that boy's hands are big and clumsy, but he can run like the wind. Maybe you could use him only on handoffs, where he can grip the ball more easily. Every time he catches a throw, he drops it. See, there he goes again."

"You're right. I never noticed that before."

"Now, look over at Wilson. He can catch even a wobbly throw. But he doesn't run well."

"So we need to use him on the distance plays, close to the goal."

"Right. I used to call it strength versus weaknesses. Figure out a kid's strength and play it up. And compensate for his weakness by using another player's strength."

That sounded like a good strategy to Pam. She bent her head, scribbling several notes.

Patrick was caught up in the film. "Watch Osborn there. See how he always hits a man real high? Now, if the offense player crouches down low, Osborn's got no leverage, right? But if he stands tall, or stretches . . ."

"He'll go down. Yes, I get your drift. I'm going to go over these films with the team this afternoon. I'll point that out to Osborn—that he should tackle when his opponent's on his feet." She glanced over at him. "Thank you. That was a good observation."

Patrick leaned back, meeting her eyes. "I guess I still have a couple of decent ideas." And a few ideas that had nothing to do with football. He raised his hand to touch her hair. "I like your hair longer like this."

Odd how that light touch could warm her. "I was thinking of getting it cut."

"Not too much, I hope." He trailed his fingers through the strands. "I've missed being alone with you, missed touching you." Forgetting himself and where they were, he leaned over and touched his lips to hers.

She didn't pull back. He gave himself up to the velvety softness of her mouth. Ever so gently, she returned the pressure. The kiss was short, but very sweet. He edged back, opening his eyes.

Pam smiled at him. "I guess I've missed being alone with you, too."

"Have we had enough time apart, enough breathing room? Have you sorted out your feelings yet?"

Had she? Pam wondered. Lord knew she'd spent enough time thinking about him, about her feelings. She'd known one day soon he'd be asking. She wished she could explain how she felt. She owed him an attempt, at the very least.

She toyed with the pen she'd been using, her eyes downcast. "I've had a few rough years since the Seoul Olympics," she began, hoping she could tell him enough without revealing too much. "Some things happened and I had major adjustments to make. I thought I was in love and then that fell apart, too. I was a mess for quite a while. I've just recently gotten back some confidence, but I'm far from free yet." She looked up to find him watching her intently. "I'm trying to be very honest with you. I'm not sure I'm ready for another relationship so soon. But if I were, it would be with you."

"Then you do have feelings for me?"

Pam reached to touch his hand, lacing her fingers with his. "You know I do. You're not the kind of man a woman feels lukewarm about. I don't want to mislead you and I don't want to hurt you. But there are things about me you don't know, things I'm not ready to share. I'm in a new town with a new job, and I need to concentrate all my efforts on that. Can you understand?"

Patrick squeezed her hand. "I don't mean to rush you." He sighed. "When I first heard you were coming, I didn't want to like you. I thought we'd be dealing with some prima donna female Olympic champion, medals dangling from her chest, trying to tell us small-town yokels how to play football. I had a chip on my shoulder a mile wide."

Pam smiled at his admission. "I noticed." It had been her experience that a man who could admit he'd been wrong in his thinking was rare indeed.

"But you're not like that at all." His expression sobering, Patrick leaned closer, raised his free hand to trail his fingers along the silk of her cheek. This need to touch a woman each time she was near was something new to him, something as disturbing as it was exciting.

He'd thought a lot about Pam these past few weeks, and realized that he seemed no closer to knowing her—really knowing her—than he'd been when they first met. There was a withdrawn quality to her much of the time, a holding back, a hint of sadness in her eyes that disturbed him. Yet her very private nature prevented him from probing further. He'd have to content himself with waiting until she trusted him enough to open up more.

He was left with only one clear fact. He wanted her. In his life, in his bed. She'd managed to get closer to him than any other woman had, perhaps ever—without trying, without knowing she had. Subconsciously, he found himself including her in his thoughts of the future, his plans. Yet he was a patient man. He would wait her out, win her over. That had always been his strategy—in sports and in life.

He cupped her chin, his fingers drifting down the enticing line of her throat. He saw the color in her face deepen, saw her eyes darken, and knew she was not unaffected. "Now I think of you as a woman who wears her past victories modestly and well. A woman who is talented in what she does and has a genuine concern for her students. A lovely woman I can't seem to stop wanting, or touching."

"Don't stop," Pam said softly. Was she wrong in wanting this to continue? She'd been attracted to Bob—had actually thought herself in love with him. But her feelings for Patrick in far less time were far stronger. Yet, was she being fair to Patrick, not telling him everything about herself? What if he, too, walked away? Already, the thought of that sent chills up her spine. She didn't want to lose him. "Just give me a little time to catch up. If you can be patient for a while..."

"I'm a very patient guy—when the reward's worth it. And you're definitely worth the wait."

"You're very good for me," she told him, her throat oddly clogged with a rush of emotion. Unable to resist, she reached up to touch his face as he'd been stroking hers, marveling at his perfection. How would he feel about accepting less than perfection in a woman?

Her hand moved into his thick hair. He felt so solid, so reassuringly male. She was lost in his eyes, eyes that told her she wasn't alone in what she felt. So lost that she didn't hear the quick knock on the door, or realize they were no longer alone until she heard someone clearing a throat behind her.

Guiltily, Pam dropped her hand and swung about.

Patrick looked up, saw the surprise on Miss Mackie's face, then felt his own flush with embarrassment. It had been a good many years since he'd been caught in this particular predicament. Sliding back his chair, he stood.

"Good morning." He waved somewhat lamely toward the video still flashing on the screen. "We were just reviewing the films, trying to come up with some strategy for the next game."

Struggling to hide a smile, Miss Mackie nodded. "I see. Game strategy." She peered around Patrick and noticed Pam picking up her clipboard with an unsteady hand, not meeting her eyes. "I can catch you later, Pam. Nothing important." At the door, she turned back. "It's nice to see you two are no longer squabbling." She left the room.

Patrick ran a hand through his hair and turned to look at Pam. Slowly, she raised her eyes to his, then burst out laughing. With relief, he joined in.

"Lord, I've never been so embarrassed," Pam muttered. "What must she think of us? We're worse than the kids, necking in the hallways."

Resuming his seat, Patrick shrugged. "Who cares? I'm not ashamed of how I feel about you."

"I'm not ashamed, either. It's just that we might try to find a more appropriate place to... to..."

"Neck?" Grinning, he slid his arms about her. "Your place or mine?"

Pam broke free and reached to turn off the VCR. She was decidedly not in the mood for watching the rest. "I think we both ought to get back to work." Hurriedly, she turned up the lights.

Rising, Patrick stretched. "I guess you're right. Are you free Wednesday evening?"

She regarded him warily. "Why?"

"My mother's having a little bash at the boarding-house. Nothing fancy, just a family dinner. I'd like you to come."

Pam's heart skipped a beat. Was he taking her home for inspection, or was it a friendly invitation? Was she making a mountain out of a molehill? He stood, looking at her expectantly. "If you're sure I won't be intruding, since it's family only."

"No. I've told them about you. They're anxious to meet you."

Deeper and deeper, Pam thought. Once you climbed aboard the roller coaster, it was next to impossible to jump off.

SHE MIGHT HAVE GUESSED that the Kelsey family would be an active bunch. The game of touch football they'd suggested playing on the back lawn of the sprawling boardinghouse was lively and noisy, with every member participating except Patrick's mother.

It was a lovely fall day, the temperature in the seventies, the sun still shining in late afternoon. The Kelseys had been warm and accepting of Pam, and now, as she stood in position at the far end, hands braced on her bent knees, waiting for a dispute to be settled between Patrick and Kathleen, she tried to sort out the names. Johnny Kelsey was definitely the father figure, in his mid-fifties. Tall and still attractive, he was an older version of his son, with his black curly hair showing a light sprinkling of white. But his eyes were gray instead of the deep blue of Patrick's. And, she thought with a grin as Johnny caught the ball and took off, he could run with the best of them.

Laura, the oldest daughter, was slim with a round Irish face, and freckles she probably hated. Her husband, Richard, a lean, trim man with a red beard, seemed nuts about her and their two sons, Timmy, six and Peter, eight. Glenna, newly married to Alan, was a shyer version of her mother, with dark hair and the same blue eyes. And then there was Kathleen, easily the most outspoken. Patrick had told Pam that his cousin, Brick Bauer, also lived with the Kelseys, but tonight he was off on police business. His schedule was so hectic they never knew when to expect him.

"I tagged you, Dad," Kathleen shouted. "You were out of bounds, anyway."

"Not on your life," Johnny Kelsey called back. He turned to Richard for verification. "The oak tree was the boundary, wasn't it, son?"

"I thought so," Richard answered.

"I call for a measurement," Kathleen countered. Everyone laughed. "All right, Dad. You got us this time." She ran back into place and waved her hand at him. "But I'm keeping track of you."

Pam watched the interplay, feeling a mite homesick for her own family. She could sense that the Kelseys, despite their good-natured bickering, were a close-knit group. Healthy, robust, active. She felt a pang of conscience suddenly, as if she were masquerading in front of these good people, passing herself off as something she wasn't. With determination, she shoved the disturbing thought to the back of her mind and returned her attention to the game.

But she was reminded again a short time later, when Patrick threw a high pass in her direction. Running for it, she gauged her time and distance, backed up, caught it easily, then turned toward their makeshift goal line. That was when her left leg gave out on her, with a sudden numbness that had her falling awkwardly to the ground.

She felt no real pain, just the accompanying tingling that set off a warning bell in her head.

Oh, please, God. Not now.

Patrick was beside her in moments, the others close behind. "Are you all right?" Patrick asked, reaching for her arm.

"Yes," Pam said. "Just let me sit for a minute."

"Looked like you twisted your ankle," Johnny commented, crouching beside her. "Which one?"

She'd use the excuse he gave her because she badly wanted to make light of the fall. "The left."

Patrick shoved up her jeans and examined the ankle in question. Gently, his fingers pressed her flesh beneath the sock in a circle. "Does that hurt?"

The tingling was easing and the numbness receding, Pam noticed with gratitude. "No. I'll be okay in a minute. I just stepped wrong when I turned, I think."

"But you've still got the ball," Kathleen said with admiration.

Patrick took the ball and tossed it to his sister. "I think Pam's going to sit out the rest of the game." Sliding his hands under her, he picked her up. "To the infirmary, young lady."

Embarrassed, Pam protested. "I feel fine, really," she said, though she was a little wary of putting her full weight on her leg yet. He carried her as if she were a child and, for a moment, she let herself enjoy the feel of his powerful arms around her.

Anna Kelsey was standing on the back porch, clipping a few flowers for a centerpiece, when Patrick approached. She turned as he placed Pam in the wooden rocker. "What have we here? An injured player?" Anna scowled briefly at her family. "Is this any way to treat a guest?"

"Honestly, it was my fault," Pam said. Rotating her ankle, she realized it felt almost normal again. "The uneven ground. I think I tripped." She looked up into Patrick's frowning face. "I'm all right, really. Go back to your game. I'll just sit here a minute."

"If you're sure..."

"Go, go." Anna shooed him and the others away, then laid her cut flowers on a small table. Pulling up the other padded rocker, she sat down beside Pam. "Are you sure your ankle's okay? I could get an ice bag if you need one."

Pam sent her what she hoped was a reassuring smile. She truly hated to be fussed over. "That won't be necessary, but thank you." In an effort to change the subject, she nodded toward the pale peach roses Anna had gathered. "They're lovely. Such a delicate color."

"Yes, aren't they? I've always loved roses—maybe because they're so fragile and delicate, yet they're survivors. Here it is, the last of summer, and they're still struggling to bloom. We all admire survivors, don't we?"

Pam shifted her gaze from the rose to the woman's face, wondering if she was trying to make a further point.

But Anna looked up at the sky, then toward the turning leaves, some already falling from the large trees bordering the property. "Autumn is definitely in the air."

Pam leaned back, gently rocking, enormously relieved that her leg felt fine. "I think you're right." She looked back to the game in progress, automatically seeking and finding Patrick. He wore stone-washed jeans that clung to his strong legs and a bright blue sweatshirt that stretched over his wide chest. Stepping back, he feinted to the left, avoided Alan, who was closing in on him. Then he ran to the right and threw a high, arcing ball toward Kathleen, his expression intense. When she caught it and ran for the goal, he applauded vigorously.

"He loves football," Pam commented, almost to herself.

Anna followed her gaze. "He loves most sports and he loves competing."

"Has he always been that way?"

Anna rocked, smiling in remembrance as she nodded. "Even as a Cub Scout. He wasn't always the fastest or the best, but you always noticed Patrick because he played with everything in him. He gave the game all he had, in high school and later in college. As a man, I think he approaches his job with the same intensity he played ball as a boy."

"I've noticed that. Every facet concerns him, every player is important to him."

"He says the same about you."

Pam turned to study Patrick's mother. She looked to be in her late forties, though she had to be older. She was slender and attractive, with startling blue eyes, so like her son's, noticeable even through her fashionable gold-rimmed glasses. Pam had the feeling Patrick had inherited more from his mother than merely her eye coloring. "It's difficult not to get involved with the players in football and basketball. They're both such team sports."

"Patrick tells me you were a runner in the Olympics."

"Yes." She let out a ragged sigh. "That was a long time ago. I'm quite happy coaching from the sidelines now."

Was she? Anna Kelsey wondered. There was a sadness in the young woman's eyes, but more than that. Regret, maybe, and she couldn't help conjecturing why. Running was for the young, and perhaps, as her body matured, Pam had hated acknowledging her new limitations. Or perhaps the adjustment from gold medal winner to small-town high school coach was the source. Whatever it was, though she tried to hide it, there was something bothering Pam Casals.

Ordinarily Anna would have dismissed her curiosity regarding a new acquaintance. But the way Patrick spoke of Pam, and the way Pam's eyes followed her son, made her realize she would undoubtedly be seeing more of this young woman. Still, her policy of noninterference in the lives of her grown children brought her to her feet. "I've got to check on a couple of things on the stove."

"I'd like to help, if I may," Pam offered.

Anna placed a restraining hand on her shoulder. "Thanks, but why don't you just enjoy the afternoon. Or rejoin the game." Picking up her flowers, she went inside.

Pam resumed rocking as she saw Patrick gently shove his sister Laura out of the way of a flying tackle by Kathleen. His first thought, an inbred instinct, was to protect. Moments later, he caught her eye and waved. She waved back.

She felt good just looking at him. Absently, she rubbed her leg, finding it fine once more. She should tell Patrick, get it over with, because her MS wasn't something that was going to go away. But, recalling Bob's expression as he'd learned about her illness, his awkward visits to her in the hospital, she shivered. Could she bear seeing that look on Patrick's face? Could she handle another rejection?

Not yet, Pam decided. After all, perhaps nothing would come of their friendship anyway.

Rising, she felt strong enough to rejoin the game. Walking toward Patrick, she decided to concentrate on today and let tomorrow take care of itself.

THE HOMECOMING GAME in early October was always a big event at Tyler High, since nearly all the residents of the town had once attended the school. Pam had drilled the boys unmercifully, and again they'd come through. The final score, 34–10, had delighted the fans. As the team left the field, everyone had cheered until many a voice became hoarse.

Pam hadn't had to hustle the boys through their showers this time. They were all anxious to get home and change for the big homecoming dance that evening in the gym. Several faculty members and a few prominent people about town were chaperoning. Pam and Patrick were, also.

Gazing into her closet, Pam frowned, wishing she had something a bit special to wear. She'd heard the girls buzzing excitedly about the dance, about their formals. Some had ordered dresses from catalogs, others had shopped at Gates Department Store in Tyler, and a few had persuaded their parents to drive into Lake Geneva for something different. Rumor had it that a couple of the boys were even renting tuxedos.

In the teachers' lounge, Dora Knight, the red-headed home ec teacher who was also chaperoning, had described in great detail the taffeta dress she'd finished sewing for the occasion. Miss Mackie, when pressed, had somewhat primly stated she'd be wearing her black silk, the same one she'd worn to dances for ten years, since she believed a well-cut dress never went out of style. Pam didn't own a black dress, well-cut or otherwise.

Restlessly, she shoved several hangers aside. It was no big deal, she told herself. No one looked at the chaperons anyway. And she wouldn't care that much what she wore if it weren't for one fact: Patrick would be there.

Finally, she narrowed the choice down to one and removed the pale rose dress from the closet. She'd worn it to an awards ceremony in Seoul years ago and not since. She'd hesitated to bring it along when she came to Tyler, yet had stuck it and the matching shoes into one of her bags at the last minute. Long-sleeved and high-necked, it had a fitted bodice and drifted to a full, swirling skirt that ended at midcalf. And the entire back, from collar to waist, was bare.

"What do you think, Samson?" she asked the dog, who lay dozing in his usual spot across the doorway to her room. At the sound of his name, Samson raised his shaggy head, let out a loud snuffling sound, then went back to sleep. "Oh, who asked you, anyway?" Pam said with a laugh.

A bit nervously, she laid the dress on the bed and went to take a shower.

PATRICK MADE HIS WAY through the crowd, shaking hands with several alumni, congratulating the football players, admiring several ladies. The committee had worked hard and the gym looked great, with its blue and gold decorations. A mirrored ball hung from the ceiling and threw prisms of light on everyone as it spun. The disk jockey was set up off to one side, playing a collection of recent hits and some golden oldies that were always a big hit at the homecoming dance. Patrick scanned the crowd of young and not-so-young, but still he didn't spot the one face he'd been seeking.

Where was Pam?

Banking his impatience, he joined Miss Mackie at the punch bowl and told her how nice she looked.

"Why, thank you, Patrick. Are your folks going to be here?"

"No, they had some dinner they had to attend." He sipped the too-sweet punch she handed him. "Great game, wasn't it?"

"Yes, and there's the lady who made it happen." Miss Mackie nodded toward the door, where Pam was being greeted by several bystanders. "I take it you've gotten over your misgivings about our female coach, Patrick?"

Had he had misgivings? He supposed he had, but that seemed like a long time ago. "You could say that," Patrick said as he watched Pam. There was nowhere in town she could go without people wanting to congratulate her, to shake her hand, to have a word with her. Was it due to the way she'd turned the team around, or was she simply a charismatic personality? Probably a bit of both, he decided as he saw her toss back her head and laugh at something someone had said to her.

Setting down his glass, he gave Miss Mackie a distracted glance. "Excuse me," he muttered, then turned to walk toward Pam.

It was the first time he'd seen her really dressed up, and he thought her beautiful. The pale rose color flattered her lingering tan, turning her skin golden. Her hair was an auburn cloud just touching her shoulders and her dark eyes were shining. She was easily the loveliest woman in the room. With a frown, he watched Fred Palmer who taught math, whirl her off into a dance. He hadn't been fast enough, Patrick admitted ruefully. Jealousy was not a feeling he was used to, but he swallowed a dose of it now.

He was standing talking with George Phelps when the dance ended and Fred led Pam back to them, thanking her profusely. As she turned, Patrick reached out a hand to her. Taking it, she smiled up at him and stepped nearer.

He spoke in low tones, for her ears only, as he tugged her close to him for a private moment. "You're a knockout tonight, lady."

"You don't look so bad yourself, Coach."

His hand on the small of her back touched bare skin. Patrick felt a ripple of awareness skitter through her as his fingers caressed. Easing her around, he introduced her to Dr. Phelps, who shook hands with her, giving her one of his gentle smiles.

"Your name keeps coming up around this town, Pam," the older man said. "The miracle coach, isn't that what they call you?"

Pam felt her concentration slipping under Patrick's warming touch. "The Tyler fans are very generous. It's good to meet you, Doctor. I believe my roommate, Rosemary Dusold, works with you on occasion at the hospital."

He narrowed his eyes as if suddenly placing her. "Yes, she does. Rosemary's an excellent therapist. How did you two meet?"

"In Chicago." Pam felt a rush of panic, wondering if Rosemary had mentioned her illness to him. She hurried to change the subject. "And Patrick's mother works for you, too, I hear."

"Yes. I like to surround myself with lovely women." George fingered his graying mustache and glanced around the gymnasium as another record began. "I hope you'll excuse me. I see someone I need to speak with. Good to meet you, Pam. Patrick, see you later."

"He's very distinguished looking," Pam commented as the doctor strolled off, his back ramrod straight. "Is his wife here?"

Before anyone else could interrupt them, Patrick guided her onto the dance floor. "No, George and his wife are seldom seen out together."

"Really, why? Is she not well?"

Wrapping his fingers around hers, he drew her closer with his other hand, touching the silky softness of her back. "Mary's sort of reclusive, I think. I've heard they don't get along." He tipped his head to inhale the fragrance of her hair. "Mmm, you smell good. You were late getting here. Everything all right?"

"It is now. I had a flat tire that I didn't notice until I was dressed. So I had to change clothes, change the tire, then get cleaned up all over again."

Pulling back, Patrick frowned. "Why didn't you call me? Or road service? You shouldn't be changing tires."

"Why not? I've changed plenty. My father wouldn't let me get my driver's license until I knew how to change a tire, change my own oil and pump gas. It's just as important for a woman to know these things as a man. Maybe more."

He didn't want to debate with her tonight, so he swirled her into the crowd. "You dance well. Something else your father taught you?"

"No, my brother Don. I can even jitterbug. Can you?" Her laughing eyes challenged him.

"We'll soon find out. They'll probably throw one in for us old folks."

At the edge of the crowd, the father of one of the football players spotted Pam and beckoned them over. "I just wanted to thank you in person, Coach," he said to Pam. "Tommy's a different kid since you took over and the team started winning. Feels real good about himself. Sort of strutting proud, you know."

"He's a good ball player, Mr. Maxwell, and a fine young man."

Beaming, the father went back to his friends, while Patrick maneuvered Pam toward the middle of the crowded dance floor. She let him lead, following him easily. In heels, she was tall enough that her hand stretched to his shoulder, and she longed to encircle his neck, touch the soft hair there. But this was a public dance and she was supposed to be chaperoning.

Already his warm breath on her cheek was making her forget where she was and who she was. In an effort to distract her thoughts, she studied nearby dancers. Spotting a familiar couple, she drew Patrick's attention to them. "Look over there. Isn't that Marge Peterson from the diner dancing with Dr. Phelps?"

Patrick swung about and glanced over. "Sure is. Looks like Mary Phelps should have come to protect her interests. If she still cares, that is."

"They do look like they're fairly close friends. Maybe they're just lonely."

He squeezed her hand. "What about you, are you lonely?"

Close up against him, she felt his heart beat, strong and sure. "Not when I'm with you."

It was what he wanted to hear. Patrick tightened his arm around her slender waist, drawing her nearer, locking his gaze with hers. The recorded music swirled about them, a Johnny Mathis tune, one the singer had recorded with Jane Olivor.

"The last time I felt like this," Johnny sang out, "I was falling in love. Feeling and falling..."

Staring into Patrick's beautiful blue eyes, Pam felt herself falling, falling.

CHAPTER SIX

PAM HAD NEVER BEEN FOND of rainy days. When she'd been younger, the inclement weather meant she couldn't be outside running or doing any of the things she enjoyed, most of which depended on sunny skies. Since she'd learned of her MS, her dislike of wet, chilly days had increased. Huddled in her raincoat on the sidelines, she watched her players halfheartedly going through practice in the light drizzle of a fall afternoon.

The doctors in Chicago had warned her that extremes of temperature were hard on MS patients, and she'd studiously avoided undue exposure since then. She had to be out here today, but she was paying the price, she realized, rubbing her tingling hands together. A glance at the gloomy sky told her the weather wasn't likely to change anytime soon.

Needing to keep moving, she paced the boundary line, her eyes on the players and their maneuvers. Her mood wasn't helped one iota by the fact that Ricky Travis wasn't at practice again. The sturdy quarterback was good—good enough to have drawn the attention of a few college scouts. But his cocky attitude and a firm belief that the team was lost without him was getting on her nerves. She'd warned him, excused him; and yet his behavior was totally self-serving. It seemed she would have no choice but to teach him a lesson or lose all credibility with the other boys regarding discipline.

Pam sneezed, then blew her nose. That was all she needed—to catch a cold. She watched the lineup go into motion, noticed two eager boys offside, which would surely have justified a flag during a game. B.J. stepped back, searching for his receiver, and finally let go of the ball with a teetering throw that was immediately intercepted. Terrific. Pam blew her whistle.

Gratefully the boys came running over. Squinting, she saw that the rain was coming down harder. Better to quit practice early than have everyone come down with pneumonia. "Let's call it a day, guys," she told them. "I don't want anyone to get sick. Take a warm shower before changing." She peered up at the darkening sky. "Maybe tomorrow we'll have better luck."

Wet and weary, the fellows strolled toward the locker room. Following, Pam felt another sneeze shake her. She hated to give in, but there was no putting it off. She'd better pay George Phelps a visit and let him in on her little secret. She simply couldn't risk a relapse, not now, when her team needed her.

DR. PHELPS LEANED BACK in his leather chair and reached for the pipe lying in a large glass ashtray. The ashtray was spotless, Pam noticed, and though he bit on the stem, he didn't fill the pipe or light it. "So you've been in remission about six months then?" he asked, looking across his desk at Pam.

"Yes, about that."

"This tingling you felt yesterday out in the rain, has it occurred before? Recently, that is?"

"Only once, a little more than a week ago." Pam crossed her legs, remembering the sunny afternoon in the Kelsey backyard, the fear that had gripped her then. "Several of us had been tossing a football around. I caught the ball, turned to run, and my left leg suddenly went numb."

"You fell?"

"Yes. I pretended that I'd turned my ankle, but I hadn't."

"I see." Thoughtfully, George fingered his pipe. "Then no one in Tyler knows of your condition."

"No one except Rosemary, and now you." She leaned forward, anxious to clarify her position. "I'm not trying to deceive anyone, Doctor. I can carry out the terms of my contract with Tyler High. But I want to prove myself and not give anyone the opportunity to feel sorry for me. I can live with MS. I can't live with pity."

"I understand, and I respect your wishes. You're an intelligent woman, Pam, one who's learned as much as possible about MS, I'm certain. Therefore, you must know that stress can aggravate your condition, and also that it's not good for you to be out in cold, rainy weather."

"I feel I'm handling the stress, and really, one isolated rainy day..."

Dr. Phelps ignored her explanations. "As to the numbness, the tingling—well, you may not experience more for quite some time, if you're careful. Or they might be warning signals that the period of remission is ending.''

Pam swallowed, digesting that, although his words merely confirmed what she'd already been thinking.

"From my examination, I can tell you that I see no damage to the optic nerve, no slurring of your speech and only a little topical numbness." He glanced up from his notes. "And you walk very well in high heels, something many MS patients don't even attempt."

It had been a major challenge, walking in high heels, one she'd vowed to master after she'd been released from the hospital. She'd worn them today, not to show off but because she'd needed the confidence they gave her.

"I'm sure you've had all the neurological tests," Dr. Phelps went on.

"Every one."

Nodding, he closed the file,. "Then I think we can safely assume that this sort of thing is to be expected from time to time."

"That's what they told me in Chicago. I just wanted to inform you of my condition, perhaps have my records from the hospital transferred to you, in case I... if there's a need in the future."

"Fine. I'd like to go over them. And please, if you have any more episodes, or if you need to talk, feel free to call me."

Pam stood, feeling a bit hesitant and embarrassed. She'd discussed this before, but it was worth repeating. "Is there any reason why I shouldn't have sex, get married, even have children?"

Dr. Phelps stood, shaking his head. "None whatsoever. As a matter of fact, I've read of cases where patients experienced longer periods of remission when they were involved in loving relationships. As you're aware, a positive mental attitude is extremely important to any illness."

Feeling reassured, Pam reached to shake his hand. "It was good of you to see me on such short notice."

The doctor gave her his professional smile. "My pleasure. Give my best to Patrick."

Leaving his office, she pondered his last remark, then remembered that she had been with Patrick at the homecoming dance when she'd met Dr. Phelps. Was the town beginning to see them as a twosome? Was she?

Cutting across the parking lot from the medical building to the adjacent hospital emergency area where she'd left her car, Pam was lost in thought. But the arrival of an ambulance turning up the winding drive and stopping at the hospital entrance caught her attention. When she saw the double doors open and Patrick step out, she changed her route and hurried over.

The ambulance attendants rolled out the cart, releasing the retractable wheels as the emergency crew came out to assist. She reached Patrick's side as they wheeled the cart away and immediately recognized the boy as Tommy Maxwell. His face was white and he lay very still.

She grabbed Patrick's arm. "What happened to Tommy?" She'd left school right after lunch today, intent on her doctor's appointment.

Patrick's face was grim as he walked along behind the moving cart. "Gym class. We were doing rope climbing exercises, stuff we'd done a hundred times. Suddenly Tommy slid to the floor, really fast, as if he'd let go. He didn't yell, didn't try to grab the end, just whack! and he hit the gym floor." He ran restless fingers through his windblown hair. "I can't imagine what happened to him. I was standing right below watching."

A nurse stopped them as Tommy was wheeled into one of the partitioned cubicles. "The doctor'll speak with you in a moment," she told Patrick. "Are you the boy's father?"

"No, his teacher. His father works at Ingalls Farm and Machinery. He's been notified and is on his way. His mother wasn't at home when I phoned there."

"Fine. If you'll have a seat over there, please." She indicated the waiting room.

"I don't want him to be alone," Patrick protested.

"No one's allowed in during the exam, not even parents. We'll keep you informed."

Reluctantly, Patrick walked over to the bank of plastic chairs, but he was too agitated to sit down. He stood looking out the window, his face filled with concern.

"Is there anything in Tommy's health records that might tell us what happened?"

"Not that I've seen. He had the usual required physical at the beginning of the school year, and there was nothing new. Far as I know, he's strong and healthy. Have you run into any problems with him on the football field?"

"No, I haven't. As a matter of fact, I've seen only improvement. Just last week, Tommy told me he wanted to go on to play college ball, maybe even consider football as a career." She moved to stand alongside him. "How did he fall—on his back, or..."

Patrick let out a rush of air. "Kind of on his side, landing heavily on one knee." He turned anguished eyes to her. "On his knee, Pam. Do you know what that means?"

She touched his arm. "You're jumping to conclusions. Even if he hurt his knee, they've come a long way in surgery techniques." What worried her more was that the boy had been unconscious when they brought him in. If only his knee was injured, he should be awake by now.

Patrick made a disgusted sound. "Not far enough. I've had knee surgery several times. It can end a career like that." He snapped his fingers.

So that was where he was coming from. "It's difficult when physical problems make you change a career choice. But it's not impossible. People do survive disappointments."

He turned to stare out the window. "Some do. Others waste a lot of years regretting."

The double doors whirred open and Tommy's father, Henry Maxwell, came rushing in. Pam stood back as Patrick went up to him. Together, the two men walked toward the treatment cubicle. Pam sat down to wait.

It was a very long half hour before Tommy's father came into view, his shoulders sagging, his eyes red.

Walking beside him, Patrick patted the big man on the back.

"Don't blame yourself, Henry," Patrick said. "You thought you were doing the right thing."

"But it could have been worse. I should have seen that. Tommy could have...could have..." He seemed unable to complete the thought.

"But he didn't. Knee surgery isn't a piece of cake, but it's not life-threatening. Tommy's aware of what happened and in good spirits, considering everything."

"Yeah, you're right." Henry Maxwell ran a hand across his florid face. "I've got to go home and get his mother. We don't have a second car and she'll want to be with Tommy." He reached to shake Patrick's hand. "Thanks, Patrick. I'm sorry I wasn't honest with you from the beginning."

"It's all right, Henry."

Patrick watched Mr. Maxwell walk off, then turned when Pam came up to him. He'd all but forgotten she was here. He gave her a wan smile as he led her over to a secluded corner of the waiting room and sat down with her. "Tommy Maxwell has epilepsy."

"Oh, no," she groaned.

"His parents didn't tell us because they didn't want him to be treated differently. They wanted him to be like everyone else. They persuaded his doctor to keep it off his school medical records."

Pam almost groaned, but she could understand. "Their thinking is not uncommon. In high school, I ran with a girl who had a heart murmur. She had a doctor friend of the family fudge her medical records so she could compete. She never had a heart attack on the track."

"But she may have shortened her life."

Sitting back, Pam shrugged. "That's an old debate. Quality of life versus quantity of years. I believe each person has the right to decide that one for himself."

"Not when you're only a kid. Parents have an obligation to protect their children."

"Maybe they thought they were—from prejudice, from uninformed and unreasonable fears, from pity."

Patrick's eyes narrowed. "How would you know so much about it?"

Pam rose. "Let's just say I do. Keep me informed about Tommy's condition."

He walked her to the door. "I'll drive you home."

"Thanks, but my car's over there. Give Tommy my best." Pam belted her raincoat tighter and left him there, berating herself for being the coward she was. She'd had the perfect opportunity to confide in Patrick, and again she'd put it off.

Unlocking her car door, she recalled his tight expression when he'd condemned Tommy's parents for not informing him of the boy's epilepsy. Her case was different, but would Patrick think so?

Probably not. Soon, Pam promised herself as she got into her car. Soon she'd have to have that long talk with Patrick, for better or worse.

"GET OUT OF THERE, you big lug." Pam shoved Samson's inquisitive nose away from the hot water in the basin. Gingerly she tugged her jogging pants high up on each leg, then slowly lowered her feet into the steaming basin. Leaning back in her chair, she closed her eyes for a moment.

Not easily thwarted, Samson moved to her side and stuck his head onto her lap. "The heat feels good, Samson," she told the nosy animal. "But not for you." Brushing his shaggy hair from his eyes, she smiled at him. Maybe after this footbath, she'd warm up. Returning home from this afternoon's chilling practice, she'd wondered if she'd ever thaw out.

"Anyone home?" Rosemary called out, coming in the front door.

"We're in the kitchen," Pam answered.

Shrugging out of her raincoat, Rosemary walked to the back. As soon as she saw Pam soaking her feet, she frowned. "Are you having trouble? Numbness?"

"No, just cold. I was out on the field for three hours and I can't seem to warm up." It had rained for two days, and although the rain had finally stopped, the damp cold lingered in the fall air. "I think I'm getting old."

"Decrepit at thirty. What a shame." Rosemary ruffled Samson's shaggy mane, then put a kettle of water on to boil before she pulled up a chair. "Seriously, do you think it's your MS or are you catching a cold?"

Pam rubbed her feet together as the heat permeated. "Neither. It's just lousy weather to be standing around in." She disliked dwelling on her health so she tried to change the subject. "How are things at the hospital?"

"Fine. George told me you were in to his office a couple of days ago. He's nice, isn't he?" Rosemary removed her thick-soled white shoes and wiggled her toes.

"Yes, I liked him. Fortunately, he's familiar with MS, so I feel comfortable if I should need him one day."

Rosemary rose and fixed their tea, placing both cups on the table to steep. "This should help." Sitting, she eyed her friend. "You're not worried about anything, are you?"

"Not really." Absently Pam rubbed Samson's head as he sat snuggling his face into her lap. "Except maybe my quarterback. Ricky Travis is a good kid and a very fine ball player. But he's irresponsible, and I may have to do something about him if he keeps missing practice."

"I know his family. He's got an older brother, Tony, who's away at college. Both boys are good-looking, and talented athletes, but kind of arrogant."

"Mmm. Maybe it's time for Ricky to be taught a lesson."

Rosemary removed her tea bag and took a careful sip. "Good in theory, but you need him to win games."

"Football's a *team* sport. No one player should make the difference. Besides, I've got a backup quarterback who's coming along nicely."

"That's good. What does Patrick think?"

Pam frowned over the rim of her cup. "I haven't asked him. Why should I?"

Rosemary shrugged. "I just thought that, since you're both coaches, you'd naturally discuss the teams. And it's no secret you see quite a bit of each other."

There it was again, the assumption that she and Patrick were "together." Pam hated being the subject of gossip. Setting down her cup, she reached for the towel. "This really is a small town, isn't it?" she asked dryly.

"Oh, yes. I'd never lived in one, either, before moving here. Everyone seems to know everyone, and their business as well. It can be annoying."

"It certainly can." Pam dried her feet.

Rosemary studied her friend a long moment. "Is there any truth to the speculations? Are you and Patrick more than just friends?"

"You can report back to the multitudes that as of this moment we are friends and only friends." Feeling a rush of anger, she rose to dump the cooled water.

Rosemary turned slowly toward Pam as she stood at the kitchen sink. "I'm sorry if I got too personal. I thought we were friends and . . ." She let the thought drift.

Pam took in a deep, calming breath. "It's okay, and we *are* friends. It's just that I'm not sure what I feel for Patrick, and so it's hard to talk about it."

"Listen, I'm just glad you're over Bob."

"Over Bob, but having to face a similar situation."

It took Rosemary a moment to catch Pam's meaning. "You're worried about Patrick's reaction when he learns about your MS."

Pam stared out at the darkening evening sky. "I keep remembering Bob's reaction. And Patrick's so athletic, so strong and vigorous. Then there's his family. How would they feel about their only son's involvement with a woman who has a potentially crippling disease?"

"I don't know Johnny Kelsey well, though I've heard he's very well thought of. But Anna is one of the warmest people I've ever met. I can't believe she'd be against any woman who loved her son." Rosemary met her friend's troubled gaze. "Do you love Patrick?"

"I don't honestly know." She brushed a strand of hair from her face. "I think I do, but we haven't known each other for very long, and there are so many things that worry me. He's so protective that I'm afraid if he knew about my illness he'd have a tendency to hover, to not want me to do things. He's a take-charge man, like my father, and I don't want anyone to take charge of me."

Rosemary moved alongside Pam. "Have you talked to him about this? If he loves you enough . . ."

"I don't know if he loves me at all." Pam shook her head as she crossed her arms over her chest. "I know the doctors say there's no reason I shouldn't marry, even have children. But would that be fair to Patrick, considering I might not be around to help him raise those children?"

"Hey, listen." Rosemary put her hands on Pam's arms and forced her to look up. "None of us knows how long we've got. He could marry a perfectly healthy woman and she could develop cancer the next month or have an accident. Remember when we were working together in Chicago, getting you out of the wheelchair, I told you that your mental attitude is more than half the battle? You could live a very long and fruitful life and I could get hit by a bus tomorrow. Life's a gamble, Pam. Just like going for the gold, remember?"

Pam nodded, trying to find a smile for her friend. "I remember," she said softly.

"If you love him, go after him. But first, tell him, Pam. Trust him enough to tell him. I haven't known Patrick Kelsey long, but I feel strongly that he'll come through for you."

She knew Rosemary was right; she had to tell Patrick. "I hope so." On a sigh, Pam hugged her friend. "Thanks."

"You're welcome." Rosemary moved to the refrigerator as the phone rang. Absently, she answered it. Listening for a minute, she struggled to keep her expression bland. "Sure." Turning, she handed the phone to Pam. "For you."

It was the end of the grading period and they had a three-day weekend. Pam was intending to use the time to rest up. Reaching for the receiver, she hoped no one would interfere with her plans.

"Hi," Patrick said. "I missed seeing you today, so I thought I'd call. How are you?"

Rosemary busied herself making a salad, yet Pam felt the color rise in her face. It felt odd having Patrick call just when they'd been discussing her feelings for him. "I'm fine. What's up?"

"You are, I hope. Up to going out with me tomorrow."

To go out with him again, to be alone with him, would mean she'd have to find a way to tell him about her illness. She didn't think she was ready to do that just yet. "I thought I'd take it easy this weekend."

"You don't know what I had in mind."

She didn't, at that. She could at least hear him out. Feeling chagrined, she put warmth in her voice. "All right. What did you have in mind?"

"The circus. Baraboo's about an hour's drive from here, and that's the home of the Ringling Brothers circus. I understand they're in town, trying out fresh acts and signing on new people before they do their winter swing down South. I thought you might like to be a kid again and go with me."

He'd remembered that she'd never been to a circus. His thoughtfulness warmed her and had her reconsidering. "It does sound like fun."

"I could pick you up about noon so you could sleep in. How's that sound?"

A whole day with Patrick. Very tempting. Perhaps she'd find an opening to have that serious talk. "Noon sounds good."

"Great. See you then." She could hear the smile in his voice as he said goodbye. Pam turned to see Rosemary glance up from tearing lettuce into a bowl. "Go ahead and say it. I gave in awfully easily."

"And why shouldn't you? You like the man and like being with him. What's wrong with that?" She nodded toward the refrigerator. "It's my turn to make dinner. How do you feel about broiled shark?"

Feeling much better than she had a mere hour ago, Pam smiled. "I love it, but Samson doesn't."

"Tough. He'll have to settle for bologna tonight."

Pam glanced over at the big sheepdog, whose sad eyes gave the impression he'd understood what his dinner was to be, and he wasn't pleased. "All right, but you explain it to him. I haven't the heart."

Rosemary gave an exaggerated sigh as she stared at the suddenly forlorn dog. "Okay, pouty face. I'll make you a hamburger."

"Better make that two. He's a big dog."

Shaking her head, Rosemary returned to the refrigerator. "The things I do for friends."

BARABOO WAS BUSTLING. The sleepy little town doubled its population and came alive when the circus was in town. Patrick parked his truck in a lot some distance from the big top and held out his hand to Pam.

It was a beautiful day. Fall had come in triumphant splendor. Leaves of rust and gold and burnished copper drifted to the ground and crunched underfoot. An autumn breeze rustled those still tenaciously clinging to near-naked limbs. The cool air was spiced with the smell of burning leaves.

"Am I going to have to hold on to your hand to keep you from running off to sign up with the trapeze artists?" Pam teased as they walked.

"I think I've outgrown that stage." She wore a long plaid blazer over a soft turtleneck and wool slacks. A simple enough outfit, yet on her he thought the clothes looked wonderful. Every day he was more enamored of her, Patrick acknowledged. He was no longer in-

clined to fight the feeling. Looking down at her, he
smiled. "But I'd like you to keep your hand in mine
anyhow."

Instead of answering, she squeezed his fingers.

As they entered the tent, familiar smells and sounds
brought memories rushing back to Patrick. The unmistakable aroma of roasting peanuts and sweet car-
amel corn. The musky scent of animals and dusty
canvas. The blaring of a bugle drawing attention to the
center ring, and a man in a formal red cutaway coat
bellowing through a megaphone. The roar of a big cat
in the third ring, followed by the crowd's noisy appreciation and applause. Clutching her hand, he led
Pam up the wooden steps to their tenth-row seats.
"Best I could get," he explained as they sat down.
"It's opening week and nearly sold out."

She could see that as the eager crowd welcomed the
lumbering elephants entering from the side. As the
trainer guided them into their first number, she leaned
her shoulder into Patrick's. "I'm glad you asked me
along."

"So am I. Want me to get some popcorn?"

Pam shook her head, her eyes on the sleek tigers lazily pacing their cages. The cat trainer held up a hoop
and tapped the floor with the edge of his whip. The
largest cat leaped through, then turned to yawn ex-
pansively toward the audience, revealing the strength
of his powerful mouth. Pam sucked in a breath as the
lights glinted off his sharp teeth, wondering what kind
of man his trainer was, daring to enter that cage daily
to confront a wild beast.

"After a while, it's probably just a job to him," Patrick said when she voiced her thoughts to him.

"One he'd better not show up for if he's having a bad day. One careless mistake and that tiger would be enjoying lunch." The trainer set the hoop on fire next and held it out for the tiger, who executed a smooth leap through the flames. Pam felt herself shudder. "I wonder how long these animal trainers last on the job before burnout. No pun intended. I should think the turnover would be terrific."

Patrick slid his arm about her, subtly drawing her closer. "Actually, circus people are very committed and often stay for life. My dad used to bring me here, probably thinking that firsthand information would discourage me from wanting this life. He'd walk me behind the scenes, talking with the various performers. Some are third and fourth generation."

The tiger act finished and the high-wire performers stepped into center ring. "Oh!" Pam exclaimed as she realized the set-up. "They're going to do their act without nets."

Patrick shrugged, his hand comfortably on her shoulder. "Draws a bigger crowd, I suppose." He felt her wince as the first acrobat climbed up the rope and swung onto the trapeze. Expertly, the man executed several maneuvers with sudden fast drops that had the crowd gasping in fear for his safety. Pam was no exception, averting her eyes at one point. "Not for the fainthearted, is it?" he asked.

"Oh, my, no." She watched a woman in sleek pink tights swing off her platform. "Flying without a net is more of a risk than I'd be willing to take, even as a well-trained trapezist. So much can go wrong." Dangling from the swinging bar by her bent knees, the woman jumped as her male partner swung toward her and grabbed her hands. The audience let out a sound of pure relief. "Split-second timing. She could so easily have fallen."

"It's sort of like falling in love," Patrick said, his voice low, his face close to hers. When she turned to look at him, he went on. "Allowing yourself to love is like flying without a net, taking a huge risk—so much can go wrong. But if your partner is there for you when you need him, then nothing usually goes wrong."

Pam stared into the blue depths of his eyes. What she saw there had her heart picking up its tempo.

"Are you a risk taker, Pam?" he asked solemnly.

She swallowed hard. "I've been known to be. But I'd feel more comfortable with a safety net."

He shook his head slowly. "Not possible in affairs of the heart. You just have to jump, and trust your partner."

Trust your partner. Could she do that? Uncertain, Pam turned her attention back to the performance.

THEY WANDERED the city afterward, stopping at a building that housed circus memorabilia, a museum of sorts. The history of circuses past and of performers long-dead intrigued them as they strolled the halls, reading the plaques alongside the many pictures, and the available leaflets.

The sun was setting as they headed for the highway, but Patrick was hungry and reluctant to end the day too soon. Pam readily agreed to stop for dinner at a restaurant just outside town.

The Owl's Nest was up a winding road, its field-stone front and glowing carriage lamps inviting travelers to rest and to eat. Though the main dining room was somewhat crowded, a deft exchange of a folded bill from Patrick to the maître d' secured a quiet corner table for them in a more secluded section.

After ordering, Patrick picked up his wineglass and held it toward Pam. "Here's to the miracle coach."

Pam frowned. "Oh, let's drink to something else. This coach doesn't feel too miraculous right now."

"Troubles?"

"Just the usual stuff, but we've got seven weeks remaining before Thanksgiving play-offs. A long way to go and anything can happen." She lifted her glass. "How about here's to a lovely day? Thank you."

He touched his glass to hers, then tasted it. The wine was cool and tart on his tongue. He saw Pam take a sip, then gaze somewhat moodily into her glass. Since picking her up earlier in the day, he'd had the feeling she had something on her mind, something troublesome. Patrick wondered if he could get her to open up to him. "Having problems with the team?" he began.

She shook her head, but didn't meet his eyes.

"Good, because I think they're doing very well. I wouldn't be a bit surprised if you walk off with the championship. And that would cinch it. The school board would take you off probation and ask you to stay."

"You make it sound so easy."

"Not easy, perhaps, but a goal within reach. That is what you wanted, isn't it? To have a winning team, to stay on?"

That had been all she'd wanted when she arrived. But things had changed, and the one who'd changed them for her sat across the table, trying to get her to play true confessions again. Back in the tent, he'd compared falling in love with the risk of high-wire performing. Right now, Pam felt as if she were all alone on the swinging bar and someone had removed the net.

"I admire your confidence, Patrick," she told him sincerely. "You've undoubtedly come by it honestly. You played high school football here, the hometown hero. You went on to star as a quarterback in college. The pros were all after you, so I heard. You've always gotten what you wanted and, although I realize you had to work hard, most things come easily to you. With the possible exception of this football coaching job I now hold, you've had everything you've ever wanted. But for some of us, nothing came easily. So if we don't attack new challenges with the utmost of confidence, that perhaps is why."

He hadn't known that was what she'd been thinking. He needed to set the record straight, even if it meant baring his soul. "You're wrong. I once wanted something more than anything else in the world, and I never did get it." He saw he had her surprised attention now.

"Go on."

Patrick took a deep breath, his hand fiddling with his napkin. "I did have it pretty easy at first. Schoolwork came effortlessly to me and so did playing football, both at Tyler High and at college. I was at the top of the draft list for four pro teams, and I thought I was on my way to realizing a dream. Only I hadn't counted on my body giving out on me."

"You became ill?"

"No. My knees were badly damaged on two separate occasions. I had surgery four times, then a long, painful recovery. Worth it though, I thought, because then I'd be fit again." His eyes were filled with the bleak memories. "Finally, I had to face a fact: I couldn't hack it. I had two choices, take a chance and maybe wind up in a wheelchair, or give up my dream." He folded his hands on the tabletop and felt Pam's soft touch on his fingers.

"I knocked around for two years after that, hardly letting my family know where I was, what I was doing. I was wallowing in self-pity. One day I called my mom and heard that my sister Kathleen was very sick. I came back and finally was able to put the past to rest. I didn't want anything to do with sports ever again. It hurt too much. But, after a while, Josephine Mackie called to tell me they really needed a basketball coach. I decided to give it a try."

"Does she know about this?"

"No, only my family knows. I saw no reason to spread the news. I know Miss Mackie and half the town think I wanted your job. It isn't so. Basketball allows me to coach, yet it's easier on my body. Even so, I give a lot of instructions, but rarely scrimmage with the boys. You probably don't understand, but the fear of winding up in a wheelchair keeps me on the sidelines.''

She withdrew her hand, hoping he couldn't see the truth in her eyes, that she understood all too well. Another thought occurred to her. ''Did you tell this story to B.J. when you talked with him?''

He nodded. ''I thought he needed to know that sometime in life nearly everyone has to compromise. And that you can live through the experience.''

Pam smiled at him then, letting her admiration show. ''You're quite a man, Patrick Kelsey.''

He made a dismissive gesture. ''I just wanted you to know that, despite how things may seem, it hasn't been a bed of roses for me. You, with your Olympic successes and your wonderful job offers and your inspirational coaching—you've worked for and gotten what you've wanted more readily than I.''

Tell him, now, a voice in her head insisted. But just then, the waiter arrived with their dinner, and the moment was lost.

Soon, Pam vowed as she ate. Yes, in light of what he'd told her, she would find a way to tell him soon.

CHAPTER SEVEN

"JUST TRIM A LITTLE off the ends," Pam said as she settled back in the beauty shop chair.

Tisha Olsen draped the plastic cape over her client's shoulders, her professional gaze scrutinizing Pam's thick brown hair. "Even out the back a bit and perhaps thin the crown?" she asked, running her fingers through the strands.

"Yes, that'd be fine." While Tisha searched through her drawers for the right comb and scissors, Pam looked around the small shop. At seven in the morning, she was the only customer, but she imagined that later in the day and probably on weekends, all four chairs would be filled. The Hair Affair was the only beauty shop in Tyler, so unless a customer wanted to drive some distance, Tisha's place was it.

The floor was a black-and-white-checkered vinyl, the walls filled with pictures and memorabilia, the red chairs a bright splash of color. The sinks and counters were spotless. A row of hair dryers stood along the back wall, and in the corner a brass coatrack was draped with three colorful feather boas. A comfortable clutter gave the shop a homey feel.

In the mirror, Pam watched Tisha move behind her to anchor the cape about her neck. The beautician was certainly attractive, with her red hair piled high on her head today and her large eyes a smoky gray color. Pam guessed Tisha to be in her mid-forties. She had a well-maintained figure and wore a bright pink coverall over a black sweater and slacks. Her cigarette smoldered in a nearly overflowing glass ashtray.

"So, how do you like living in Tyler?" Tisha asked as she divided Pam's hair into sections.

"I like it fine. I've never lived in a small town before, though, and I'm amazed at the closeknit community friendliness."

Tisha's husky laugh rang out. "Nosiness, you mean. That's Tyler's favorite pastime, keeping track of everyone else's business."

"Have you lived here all your life?"

"No. I was born here and could hardly wait to leave, which I did as soon as I turned eighteen." Tisha pumped Pam's chair higher so her hair would be at eye level. Before beginning, she took a long pull on her cigarette.

"Where'd you go?"

"Chicago."

"My hometown."

"I know. It's a real swinging town, or was back then. I was a dancer with big dreams and a small bank account. I played every small club in Illinois, I think. But I never hit the big time." She sighed heavily. "That was a lot of years ago. Much water under the bridge since then."

"Bonjour!" squawked a parrot from his cage in the corner.

"Good morning to you, Nouci," Tisha answered him.

Pam's eyes found the brilliant green bird in the mirror. "Your parrot speaks French?"

Again, Tisha chuckled. "He speaks several languages. Nouci's a big show-off."

"Nouci's a big show-off," the bird echoed.

"Go back to sleep," Tisha instructed.

"Where'd you ever find him?"

"A good friend gave him to me a long time ago." Tisha winked at Pam in the mirror. "He was quite a guy, so I named my parrot after him. Do you have any pets?"

"An English sheepdog named Samson."

"Ah, yes. I've seen you running with him a couple of times. I also saw you playing football in the backyard with the Kelseys. I live in the boardinghouse." Tisha swiveled Pam's chair so she could work on her sides. She took a final puff and put out her cigarette, blowing smoke toward the ceiling.

"Then you must know the Kelseys well."

"Honey, I know everyone in this town well."

"Is that why you moved back to Tyler—because you missed your friends and the people you grew up with?" Pam was no stranger to homesickness.

Tisha smiled at that. "Not exactly. You can only live on the edge for so long. Let's just say I ran out of options and I wasn't getting any younger."

She was a character, Pam decided, and she worked at being perceived as one. "Are you glad you came back?"

Tisha shrugged. "When you hit the forty mark, you get this hankering for roots. Yeah, I'm glad I came back."

She worked in silence for a few minutes. When a sleek silver Mercedes rolled past the big picture window, Tisha glanced out. "There goes the baroness. Wonder why she's out and about so early."

"The baroness?"

Tisha's artfully applied eyebrows rose. "You haven't met the baroness? Alyssa Ingalls Baron. Ronnie's widow and Judson's daughter. She's not to be missed." She sent a disdainful glance toward the disappearing car. "We didn't see eye to eye when we were young, and we don't now."

"I've met Judson Ingalls—he comes to most of our games. I feel sorry for him right now with all the whispering about this buried body they found on his property. He must be upset."

Tisha's expression turned serious. "He is. Judson's granddaughter, Liza, is very protective of him. She's been in here questioning some of my customers, trying to get to the bottom of things."

"Do you think the body is that of her grandmother?"

Tisha shrugged. "Could be."

"Oh, poor Judson."

"Judson's a good man and a strong one. He'll survive the gossip."

"I'll bet you hear more than your share of gossip in this place."

Tossing aside the scissors and her sober mood, Tisha laughed. "Honey, you don't know the half of it." Brushing Pam's hair, she followed by fluffing the sides with her hands. Then she lowered the chair and angled it toward the mirror so that Pam could examine her haircut. "How's that?"

"Very nice. Thank you."

"My pleasure." She unfastened the cape. "Lots of luck to you and your boys in the next game. Judson usually takes me, and I have to tell you, I think you've done one hell of a job with those kids."

Rising, Pam hid her surprise at Tisha's revelation that she was dating Judson Ingalls. If she was the same age as Alyssa Baron, he was old enough to be her father. "Thanks. The boys have really worked hard."

"Did you see this stuff?" Tisha indicated a small table off to the side and walked over to it. "Liza Baron designed them. She's real talented."

An assortment of Titan promotional items were spread on the table—pins and balloons and T-shirts, sweatshirts, whistles and matchbooks. Pam picked up a blue-and-gold mug with the Titan logo on it and smiled. "These are great."

"The Booster Club is selling them as a fund-raiser for the team."

The bell above the door clanged and both women turned.

"You're out early, Pam," Kathleen Kelsey said as she entered. "Hi, Tisha."

Pam smiled a greeting. She'd spent some time at the dinner table talking with Kathleen when Patrick had taken her to the Kelsey Boardinghouse. She'd found the youngest Kelsey to be interesting and genuine, with a delightful sense of humor. "I needed a trim and I heard this was *the* place."

"Don't tell me you want to cut that gorgeous hair of yours, Kathleen," Tisha said.

Kathleen acknowledged the compliment with a smile. "No, but I stopped in to look through some of your fashion books. I've got this hot date and I want to try something new with my hair."

"A hot date in this town?" Tisha looked shocked. "Be serious."

Kathleen's blue eyes sparkled as she turned to Pam. "Listen to her. No, not in Tyler. In Milwaukee. A friend of Patrick's."

"Ah, Patrick," Tisha said in appreciation. "Now there's a man for you." She shifted her gaze to Pam. "I hear you two are close."

Her throaty emphasis of the last word had Pam feeling suddenly flustered and she hoped it didn't show. "We work together and we *are* friends."

Tisha laughed aloud. "No secrets in this town, honey. The miracle coach and the hometown hero. It's a natural." The phone rang and, still smiling, Tisha went to answer it.

Disconcerted, Pam grabbed her purse and searched around for her wallet.

"Don't let Tisha get to you," Kathleen said, laying a hand on Pam's arm. "She means no harm."

Pam let out a rush of air. "I know. It's just that I feel everyone's eyes are on me when I'm on the field. And now with Patrick."

Kathleen nodded understandingly. "That's the trouble with small towns. I was engaged once several years ago to a man from Tyler—Ralph Anderson. Everywhere I went I had people asking me when we would marry, where we planned to live, did we want children.'' She shook her head tolerantly. ''It's their way of saying they care, but it can get to be a royal pain.''

Pam laid a bill on the counter and turned back to Kathleen. She was such a lovely woman, tall and slender, with those incredible blue Kelsey eyes. ''Did all that friendly interest get to you and you broke it off?''

''No. I broke it off because there wasn't that feeling of rightness, the one that says, *this is it.*'' Seeing Pam's puzzled look, she stepped closer. ''My mother always told me that when I found *the* man, there'd be this feeling of rightness, as if I'd been waiting all my life for this one person. I tried to convince myself that Ralph was the one, but it's not something you can fake.'' She shrugged, looking a bit embarrassed. ''You probably think I'm crazy.''

''Not at all. I tried it once, too. Afterward, I realized I'd been kidding myself that he was the right one, giving him traits he didn't have so it would feel right.''

Kathleen smiled. ''That's it exactly. Well, hopefully we've learned our lesson, right?''

''I think so.''

Tisha hung up the phone and walked over to join them. ''Did you ladies solve the problems of the world?''

''Just a few local ones.'' Pam slid the money across the counter toward her. As Tisha made change, the parrot shouted out a phrase in another foreign language. ''What'd he say?''

"The same thing he always says," Kathleen said with a laugh. "And he can say it half a dozen different ways."

Pam put away her wallet. "And what is that?"

"Let's go to bed," Tisha and Kathleen chimed in together. All three of them laughed.

"Was he raised in a bordello?" Pam asked.

"I'll never tell," Tisha answered.

With a wave, Pam left the shop, Tisha's deep laugh following her out the door.

PATRICK SAT on the porch steps of Pam's apartment house on Morgan Avenue, gazing up at a cloudless twilight sky. A cool October breeeze sent a handful of dry leaves scurrying, but at least the rain had stopped, several days before. He'd walked over to ask Pam to go somewhere with him and found both her car and her dog gone. Knowing her habits, he assumed she'd driven to a country road, then gone running. He leaned back on his elbows, prepared to wait.

There would be a moon tonight—a sliver of one, but nonetheless a moon, Patrick thought. He wanted to go walking in the moonlight with Pam. He wanted to see that slow smile spread across her face, to hear her low laugh. He wanted to hold her hand and stroll around the town square. Like a smitten teenager, he wanted people wandering about to know that she was his. Ah, but was she?

Not yet, certainly. He knew she cared about him, that physically she was attracted to him, that they had more things in common than either had originally thought. Yet she was fiercely independent, even changing her own tires. She was a private person who didn't share her concerns easily, a modest champion who wouldn't show off her medals, a woman who was still a mystery to him in many ways.

She'd seemed drawn to family life—his own family, for instance—and had spoken almost reverently about having a child. Yet she loved her work and would not love a man who would oppose her need to have it. She wanted to make it on her own, with no help from anyone, including Patrick Kelsey himself.

And she'd changed him. In the silence of several sleepless nights, he'd had to admit that perhaps ne had been a bit of a chauvinist. He and his father before him had always looked after the Kelsey women, trying to ease their burdens and lighten their load. But Pam would have none of it, so he'd changed. If John Kelsey only knew, he would chuckle to think that this tiny woman had been able to change his stubborn son.

Lately Patrick's thoughts had wandered down new avenues. He was ready, he decided as he watched the first evening star come out. Ready to settle down, marry, make a home, have a family. He was a traditional man with roots buried deep in the fertile Wisconsin soil. But could Pam be happy here, living the small-town life? Had she had enough traveling, enough big-city excitement?

Then there was the sixty-four-thousand-dollar question. Did she love him as he'd come to love her. Yes, that was the biggie.

Hearing a car turn onto Morgan Avenue, Patrick sat up. It wasn't Pam's sporty white convertible, but a sedate four-door Lincoln. As he watched, the car stopped across the street, two doors down. Empty pipe in his mouth, Dr. George Phelps stepped out, walked up onto Marge Peterson's porch and rang the bell.

Patrick sighed. So that was how it was, he thought as Marge came out, chattering happily. They were so engrossed in each other that they didn't spot him on Pam's steps. Taking her arm, George guided Marge to his car.

Patrick had suspected that the Phelps's marriage hadn't been happy in years. No wonder, with Mary so reclusive. Now it would seem George had found a sympathetic ear. He'd always liked Marge and he hoped she knew what she was doing. None of his business, Patrick decided as he watched the Lincoln move on down the street.

He glanced at his watch and saw it was nearly seven. Perhaps Pam had gone to visit someone. Feeling a wave of disappointment, he stood just as another car turned onto the street. He stepped off the porch as Pam's convertible swung into her drive. Samson's deep baritone bark greeted him through the open window of the car as Pam climbed out.

Her smile was soft and warm and just for him. "What a nice surprise," she whispered.

"Were you out running?"

"No, I just took Samson for a ride." She'd needed to think, to be alone on the open road with her thoughts.

Patrick couldn't wait to touch her, couldn't wait to hold her. Wordlessly he pulled her to him and buried his face in her hair. He felt her arms tighten around him and gave in to his impulse to kiss her.

Her lips were cool, her mouth warm as she went up on tiptoe and returned his kiss. He crushed her closer, quickly losing himself in her special taste. He'd passed her in the halls at school several times today, and each time he'd wanted to kiss her like this, to slide his hands down to the small of her back, to feel that quick jolt of awareness that she always brought to him.

They heard two boys on bikes passing by, giggling and whistling. Samson let out another bark. Embarrassed, Pam eased back. "Do you believe in public displays, Coach Kelsey?" she asked, her eyes teasing.

"No, I'm all for dark, quiet corners."

"Then maybe we'd better go in." She led the way, shooed Samson into the backyard and returned to Patrick in the living room. "To what do I owe this pleasure?" she asked as she snapped on a table lamp.

"I'm on my way to Worthington House to visit my grandmother, and I thought you might like to come along." He placed his hands on her arms, keeping her near.

She'd wanted to see the refurbished retirement home and to meet the lady she'd heard so much about. "You mean the grandmother who calls you Paddy?"

"One and the same. Martha Bauer, my mother's mother. Her maiden name was O'Malley, and she's as Irish as they come, but my grandpa was German. She's seventy-nine going on seventeen, I think. And she's only about five-three. I thought you'd enjoy meeting someone smaller than you."

She punched him lightly. "You trying to say I'm short?"

He pulled her closer within the circle of his arms. "I'm trying to say you're perfect in every way." Dipping his head, he captured her mouth once more.

There were kisses, Pam thought, and then there were kisses. Some made you feel more than others. But she hadn't known there was the kind that could bring her to her knees. Not until Patrick had kissed her.

Feeling drugged, she let him draw her nearer, shivering when his hands inched under her sweatshirt and crept up her back. Almost lazily, his mouth moved over hers, seducing her slowly, captivating her completely.

His strong, restless hands slid down her sides, straying toward the front. When they closed over her breasts, Pam gasped. His mouth moved to her ear.

"No bra, Coach Casals. I'm shocked."

His voice was low, his warm breath sending shock waves through her. "I usually wear one, but..." She couldn't talk, could scarcely think. His fingers on her flesh felt so good and it had been so long.

"I like you better this way." And his mouth returned to hers.

She was losing ground rapidly, the sensations caused by his clever hands and his seeking tongue nearly causing her knees to buckle. Grasping at a thin thread of control, Pam pulled back. "Patrick, I have to change. Your grandmother's waiting."

"There's always tomorrow."

It was clearly going to be up to her. Pam gently shoved at his chest, easing herself free. Please. Not like this. Let's wait."

With a ragged sigh, Patrick stepped back. "What *are* we waiting for, Pam?"

She swallowed hard, trying to calm her erratic breathing as she straightened her shirt. "For the right moment. Rosemary's due home any minute. I have this thing about privacy."

He ran his hand through his hair. "You make me lose all sense of time and place."

She smiled at that and touched his face. "You make me a little crazy, too. I'll just freshen up and be right back."

"Sure you don't want me to help?" he called after her.

"*Real* sure. Have a seat." Pam hurried down the hallway with a racing heart, knowing she couldn't put him off much longer.

The truth was, she was as eager as he. But first, they needed to get some things said. She would not take Patrick into her bed unless he knew the truth about her. If after the telling, he still wanted her, then she would reach for him willingly, happily.

She closed the bathroom door and turned on the shower.

In the living room, Patrick sat down and stared out the window, trying not to picture her behind that closed door.

"MMM, CHOCOLATE CHIP. My favorite." Martha Bauer looked up from the cookie tin she held, her blue eyes dancing. "Paddy, you never forget. Thank you."

"How could I forget?" Patrick asked, giving his grandmother's hand a gentle squeeze. "You're the one who taught me to make them, remember?"

"Certainly I remember." She touched his cheek affectionately. "One for the jar and one for the tummy, wasn't that what we used to say as we slid the cookies off the baking sheets? Your mother used to scold me for ruining your dinner."

"I'd still rather have cookies than dinner." Seating himself alongside Pam on the couch across from where Martha sat in her bentwood rocker, Patrick stretched his legs. They'd found his grandmother working on her sewing, but she'd quickly set it aside and welcomed them warmly, hugging Pam when they were introduced as was her way.

Then, because Pam had voiced an interest, Martha had taken them on a tour of Worthington House—the small, second-floor apartments like her own, the lower level with its nurses' station, the spotless kitchen, the spacious dining room where the residents all shared meals and the addition at the back for extended-care patients.

Martha had introduced Pam to half a dozen of her resident friends, who much to Pam's surprise had all heard of the miracle coach and her success with the Titans. Afterward they'd taken the elevator back up to Martha's old-fashioned living room, where Patrick had presented her with the cookies.

Martha held the tin toward Pam. "Would you like some cookies? I could get us some milk." She gestured toward the small pullman kitchen. "I take most of my meals in the dining room, but I have a small refrigerator.''

Pam shook her head. "No, thanks, really." She turned to Patrick. "I had no idea you were a cookie baker."

Patrick just grinned as Martha chuckled. "Paddy and I spent many a Saturday afternoon baking. Later, when the girls were born, we'd all bake and decorate Christmas cookies. We had colored icing on our faces and those little silver balls all over the kitchen floor. Of course, that was back when I had my own home."

Pam glanced around the cozy room, with framed pictures of Martha's family everywhere. "This place is very nice. I love these old houses."

Martha set the tin of cookies aside and resumed her rocking. "So do I. They get my vote over those modern cement structures that seem to go up overnight. Tillie lived in an apartment building like that over near the freeway for a couple months after she sold her house. She hated it, so I coaxed her over here for a visit. She moved in the next week."

"Tillie Phelps is George's aunt," Patrick jumped in to explain to Pam. "She and Grandma go back a long way."

Martha adjusted her rimless glasses higher on her nose and nodded. "We sure do. Tillie and I grew up in Tyler when there was hardly anything here but a couple of spread-out farms. 'Course, Tillie's older than me. She turned eighty last week and I won't reach that milestone until Christmas Day."

"You were a Christmas baby? What fun!" Pam was enjoying Patrick's grandmother immensely. She was also keenly aware of the man beside her, who kept her hand firmly clasped in his own. The love and affection between Patrick and Martha Bauer was evident in every word they exchanged.

"My father used to call me his Christmas angel," Martha confided.

"Eighty. That's really something." Pam turned to Patrick and found his eyes on her. "You seem to come from hardy stock."

"That he does," Martha answered for him. "I promised myself I wouldn't give up the ghost until I hit the century mark." She reached a freckled hand to rub her right knee. "Some days I'm not sure I'll make it."

"You will, Grandma," Patrick interjected. "The ladies would be lost without you. Grandma belongs to a group of ladies who do quilting, kind of a lost art," he went on to explain to Pam. "They meet here twice a week."

"Really? I'd love to see some of your work."

Martha's blue eyes lighted with pleasure. "Then you shall. I've got a couple in my bedroom." Rising, she led the way through the arch and down the hall.

Following Pam, Patrick flipped the hall light switch. Nothing happened. Frowning, he gazed up at the light fixture. "Grandma, I think you've got a burned-out bulb here."

Already in her bedroom, Martha turned on her bedroom lamp. "Yes, I know. I keep forgetting to replace it."

Reaching up, Patrick unscrewed the bulb from the oval fixture. "I'll go to the storage room and get you one."

Pam stood at the bedside admiring the quilt on Martha's bed. Triangular pieces of cloth were sewn together in an exquisite blend of light and dark, moving from the palest yellow to deepening shades and ending with a burnished gold. "This is lovely. I've seen the pattern before."

"It's called sunshine and shadow," Martha explained, holding up the end for Pam to examine more closely. "It's from the Amish, who are really experts at quilting."

Pam traced the pattern with her finger. "Everything is hand-stitched."

"We use heavy silk thread to cross-stitch the pattern on each seam."

"I'm amazed at the amount of work that goes into these."

"And a lot of love. Five or six of us get together afternoons and sew and talk. Mornings, too, if we're meeting a deadline. Some quilts we sell at specialty shops, others we donate to churches for raffles and a few special ones, we keep. We've tried a great many patterns over the years."

"I've heard that each pattern has a meaning."

"That's right. This one symbolizes the tragedies of life in the darker colors—the shadows—then moves to the hope and joy we can look forward to when the dark moments pass and we move into the sunshine."

"You must get a lot of pleasure from working on something so meaningful."

"I do. Let me show you another." Martha removed a box from the closet shelf and pulled from it another rich quilt. "This is called the wedding-ring pattern."

The quilt was very large and consisted of a variety of colors sewn together in overlapping circles. "Beautiful," Pam told her with honest admiration.

"I've made one of these for each of my grandchildren. There are still two in the closet, for Kathleen and Paddy. One day I'd like to give them theirs, and dance at their weddings."

"I'm sure you will." Pam stood aside as Martha rewrapped the second quilt and put it away.

"You must be a special person in Paddy's life," Martha said, studying Pam closely. "He's never brought a woman here before."

"I'm surprised. Not even when he was younger and a big football hero?" She was trying to keep it light, but her heart had lurched at the news.

"No, not even then. Paddy takes his time making up his mind about things. But when he does, he seldom changes it."

In the light of that blue-eyed scrutiny, she could not back away. "I like your grandson very much."

After a long moment, Martha nodded. "I'm glad, because he needs someone, I think. It's not good for a man his age to live alone."

Martha was moving a little fast for Pam. "Well, actually, we're just friends at this point...."

Slipping her arm around Pam's waist, Martha guided her toward the living room. "I understand." She glanced up as Patrick finished replacing her hall light bulb. "Thank you, Paddy."

Patrick took Pam's hand. "You're welcome. Anything else need doing around here before we go?"

"Not that I can think of." Martha walked with them to the door, where she turned to Pam. "I enjoyed your visit. Thank you for coming. I'll probably see you at one of the football games, if the weather doesn't turn too cold. I often go with my quilting group." Giving her a hug, she then reached up to kiss her grandson. "And you, I always enjoy."

"Me, too, Grandma. Take care and I'll see you soon."

"It was a pleasure meeting you, Mrs. Bauer," Pam said.

On the sidewalk, Pam looked at Patrick. "I like her."

"I thought you might. In a changing world, Grandma's a constant." He swung their clasped hands. "How about a walk in the moonlight, lady? Maybe we can find a deserted park bench where we can neck awhile."

"Didn't you outgrow that sort of thing in high school?"

Patrick grinned. "Men never outgrow necking, sweetheart."

"THAT'S IT then," Pam said, her voice firm with determination. "Ricky's benched."

The boys who'd gathered around her after practice did not take the news well.

"Coach, you can't bench Ricky Travis," Moose said, clearly agitated. "We need him to win Friday's game."

She'd known she'd receive opposition to her decision, and she hadn't made it lightly. But her credibility and the discipline of her team were at stake here. "I understand how you feel, how you *all* feel. But I told you from the first day that if you miss practice, you won't play. I've been more than lenient with Ricky's constant excuses. When he didn't show up today, that was the final straw. He won't listen, so he can't play." She bent to gather up her things.

"We can't win without him, Coach," Jamie added above the mumblings of the others.

"We *can* win without him. Football is a team sport and not dependent on any one person." She looked into their doubting faces. "We can't defeat ourselves with negative thinking. We can and will win Friday without Ricky Travis. Now, let's hit the showers."

They didn't run off the field as usual, she noticed, but walked dejectedly. All except B.J., who hung back, wanting a private word with her.

"Coach, I don't know if I can do it," B.J. began. "I'm too small. I do all right in practice, but they'll kill me out there in a real game."

Her backup quarterback with a case of nerves. Wonderful. She had to convince him he was capable, for she knew he was. Slipping her arm around his shoulders, Pam led him to the bench. "B.J., when I was competing for the Olympics, I was the smallest runner in the lineup. Some of the taller, stronger women were able to take such huge strides with their long legs that I almost psyched myself out thinking I'd never keep up, much less beat them."

She stared into his worried eyes, anxious to make her point. "Ninety percent of your adversaries will be bigger than you, maybe stronger. Your biggest asset is your mind. A quarterback has to think, to plan, to be quick and clever. You can outthink your opponents if you put your mind to it. I had to work hard to beat those long-legged women, twice as hard sometimes. But I made up my mind I could do it. Can you do that? Can you make your mind rule your body?"

B.J. sat a bit taller, though he didn't look utterly convinced. "I can try."

Pam gave him an encouraging smile. "That's all I can ask. Do a little private practicing in your mirror at home. Tell yourself you can do it. Believing is half the battle."

"Okay." B.J. got up and ran toward the locker room.

Letting out a ragged sigh, Pam grabbed her clipboard and trailed after him. She was nearly to her office when she glanced up and saw Ned Connor, the father of one of her wide receivers, waiting for her. She greeted him with a curious smile.

"I just talked to my boy, Coach." The big man removed his unlit cigar from the corner of his mouth. "He tells me you've sidelined Ricky Travis. Forgive me for saying so, but that's not a good move. The Titans can't win without Ricky."

It was beginning to sound like a broken record. "Ricky is a valuable player, but he's flouting the rules. I can't have that. These boys learn more than merely how to play football from participating in high school athletics. We can't have certain players exempt from the rules. Winning isn't all there is to sports, Mr. Connor."

He rubbed a beefy hand across his unshaved face as he shook his head. "You ever hear of a fella named Vince Lombardi? Coached the Green Bay Packers for years. He said winning isn't everything—it's the *only* thing. Or something like that. Anyhow, you get his meaning?"

"Yes, I get his meaning. But these boys aren't the Green Bay Packers, Mr. Connor. They're not being paid to play, they're playing a team sport and hopefully learning some important lessons about life. And one of those lessons is that if you don't follow the rules, you pay the price. Isn't that something you want your son to learn?"

Mr. Connor shuffled his feet, his expression stormy. "I want my son to play on a winning team. That's what I want."

Pam struggled not to let her annoyance show. "Well, we'll try really hard to win for you. Now, if you'll excuse me." Stepping around him, she unlocked her office door and escaped inside.

Lord, she thought, sitting down heavily in her desk chair. She couldn't help but wonder how many other parents were going to feel as Mr. Connor obviously did. She knew from Josephine Mackie that the Titans had for many years finished near the bottom of the ratings. But could these parents honestly want victory at any price? Weren't the lessons of life as important as winning the game?

Wearily, Pam tossed her clipboard onto the desk. Well, at least Miss Mackie would back her. She'd promised her complete control, and Pam would hold the principal to her word, if necessary.

Standing, she stretched, trying to relieve the tense muscles of her shoulders. She hadn't had any recurrence of the numbness or the tingling, and she fervently hoped she wouldn't, at least until after football season.

Quickly, she gathered up the notes she'd made during today's practice. With Ricky out for now, she'd have to work more with B.J. and get the receivers ready for the subtle difference in his approach. She'd run over the various plays tonight so tomorrow's practice would go well. She wanted to bolster the boys' confidence, to make them believe they could win. She wanted them to trust her decision.

At the door, Pam paused a long moment, her eyes closed. She had made the right decision, hadn't she?

CHAPTER EIGHT

"IT'S AMAZING how quickly a person can go from hero to villain in this town," Pam commented, her voice heavy with disappointment. Needing to keep her hands busy, she arranged and rearranged the items on her desktop.

Seated at his own desk opposite hers, Patrick leaned back in his swivel chair and quietly watched her. He'd come in after school to find her brooding in their office. He knew the reason why, had heard the disgruntled comments all around town. Pam's fall from grace had her fuming.

"I mean, you would think I had committed a heinous crime here." Pam crammed two files into a drawer and shoved it shut. "What kind of morals do these people have that they think winning a silly championship is more important than molding character and fostering integrity and ... and ..."

"Honoring commitments?"

"Honoring commitments. Yes, thank you." Slamming a pile of charts onto the far corner of the desk, she eyed him suspiciously. "Are you humoring me?"

"I thought I was agreeing with you."

"If you do, you're the only one in Tyler who does."

Patrick placed his hands on the back of his neck and stretched back as far as his ancient chair would lean. "Have you considered the possibility that you're overreacting a tad here?"

She glared at him, her dark eyes blazing. "*Me* overreacting? At lunch in Marge's Diner I was besieged by no less than eight people, and in the grocery store later I was harassed by a persistent old guy whose grandson has never even left the bench. Even this morning, while Samson and I were out running, this farmer pulled over in his truck and gave me his not so subtle opinion of my coaching decisions." She reached for a handful of pink slips and held them up to him. "Look at these. Probably a dozen phone calls from upset parents." Pam shook her head. "I can't believe this town."

If the situation hadn't been so serious for her, Patrick might have smiled. She'd been queen for a day and she missed being well thought of. But he had to give her a lot of credit. So far, she was sticking to her guns. "Don't be so hard on them. It's just that they thought the Titans had the championship wrapped up, and now they're unsure again."

"Don't defend them. They're in the wrong. Besides, we haven't even played the first game without Ricky. Did it ever occur to anyone that B.J. might come through? And how must he be feeling with all this lack of confidence in his ability?"

"I admit that must be hard on him. He's never been overflowing with self-confidence."

"That's right. I spend three hours at practice telling him he can do anything he sets his mind to. Afterward, he walks into Marge's Diner, and in two minutes he begins to doubt himself.'' She felt like hitting something, but instead folded her hands together tightly and stared at her white-knuckled fingers.

Patrick decided to play devil's advocate. ''Maybe there's a compromise to be found here somewhere.''

Always the peacemaker. ''If you can find one, please let me know.''

''I just wonder if your hard-line approach is really best for everyone.''

She raised angry eyes to his. ''What do you mean?''

''I mean that when you first announced the rule about if you miss practice you can't play, perhaps you could have set a limit. Like, if you miss practice, you can't play in the next game. But to remove a kid for the whole season . . .''

She must calm down, Pam reminded herself. Stress was very bad for her. She searched for the right words. ''Look, Patrick, I realize you've lived here a long time and you know these people far better than I do. But I believe we're teaching more than football here. We teach cooperation, pulling together for the whole, commitment, unselfishness.''

''I agree.''

''Ricky Travis knows how to throw a football, but he knows very little about group effort. He's letting his teammates down for his own selfish purposes. He didn't miss practice because he was ill, or for any other good reason. His father told him he couldn't go out if he didn't complete his farm chores. Ricky chose to do them when he should have been at practice so he could go out evenings.''

"That's what I'd heard, too."

"And, as far as I'm concerned, his father isn't much better. He knows what Ricky's been doing and he allows it to continue, which is tantamount to condoning his behavior."

"Oh, Albert Travis isn't such a bad sort," Miss Mackie said from the open doorway. Entering the office, she walked to the filing cabinet and leaned against it. "I've just finished meeting with him and his wife."

Here it comes, Pam thought. "And he wants me to reinstate Ricky, right?"

"Yes, he does."

Disgusted, Pam shook her head. "How is that boy going to learn responsibility for his actions if his father pleads his case and we fold?"

Josephine Mackie sighed. "I rather thought you'd feel that way. In theory, I do, too. However, I truly hate to see the Titans lose this opportunity. You've brought them along beautifully and they're so close. So very close."

Pam drew in a calming breath. "I hate to disappoint the team and the town as much as you do. Maybe more. Yet I'm highly annoyed that everyone places such importance on Ricky's performance and so little on his integrity."

"You're right," the principal said. "I came because Mr. and Mrs. Travis asked me to tell you that they'll watch Ricky, make sure he gets to practice daily, should you change your mind."

Patrick could see that Pam was close to exploding. Though this wasn't his battle, and she'd likely be furious at his interference, he could no longer be silent. "Miss Mackie, what lesson would Ricky learn if that were to happen? That he'd better behave when someone is policing his actions, but when their backs are turned he can do as he pleases? I'm afraid I have to agree with Pam."

Josephine nodded as she walked to the door. Her job was never easy, but keeping the school board happy, the Booster Club members pleased, the parents cooperative, the students from rebelling and the teachers contented was a juggling act that easily fell out of balance. This was one of those occasions. Hand on the knob, she turned back to Pam. "Maybe B.J. can pull it off. What do you think?"

"I believe he could, if people would stop worrying about Ricky and start showing some confidence in B.J."

"I did tell you you could run the team your way, and I'm not sorry. I want you to know that. I am sorry so many people are upset." She left the room, closing the door.

Patrick looked at Pam, noticing how tensely she held herself. Rising, he went to her and placed his hands on her shoulders. He began to massage the bunched muscles, his hands strong yet gentle. Finally he felt her let out a breath and start to relax.

His hands on her felt so good. Pam let her head drop slowly forward. "Thanks," she whispered, "for agreeing with me, at least in part."

He worked on her in silence for a bit, then said, "Tell me, if Ricky came to you with a change of heart, what would you do?"

Pam took her time answering. "If he honestly had a change of attitude, if he admitted he'd been wrong and dropped his arrogant manner, and promised to faithfully attend all future practices, I would limit his suspension to a couple of games. But I doubt if that'll happen. He was in the diner the other evening, surrounded by his friends—you know the scene. He seemed so confident that I'd give in to the pressure and he wouldn't have to change a thing."

Swiveling her chair around, Patrick drew her up and into the circle of his arms. "He doesn't know he's up against the toughest football coach around, does he?"

But Pam pulled back. "I can't laugh about this, Patrick. I worry about the effects of my decision, but I honestly feel I'm doing the right thing."

He moved his hands up to frame her face. "That's what I love about you, Coach Casals. You've got principles." He lowered his head to kiss her.

As her mouth softened under his, Pam's heart jumped about erratically. Love? Had she heard him right?

THE STADIUM WAS FILLED to overflowing for the Titan's Friday night game, Patrick noticed as he climbed up into the bleachers looking for a seat. When he spotted his grandmother, he smiled and squeezed past several people to reach her.

Sliding over, Martha Bauer made room for her grandson on the wooden bench. "We're crammed in here like sardines in a tin can tonight, Paddy," she said, accepting his hug.

"It's a big game. Everyone's here to see if the Titans can win without Ricky Travis." He gazed down over the rows of spectators. Under the lights, the referees stood around talking, but the teams hadn't come out yet. The cheerleaders were already in action on the sidelines, charging up the fans. He glanced back to his grandmother. "Did you come alone?"

"Oh, my, no," Martha said, tightening her head scarf against a cool evening breeze. She pointed down several rows. "I came with Rose Atkins over there. I persuaded her to leave that silly tricycle contraption that she rides everywhere at home and we strolled over. It's a lovely night."

"Yes," Patrick agreed. "Why isn't Rose sitting with you?"

"She just went down there to talk to that Santori fellow. Joe's his first name, I think. He's the building contractor who's working on the renovations at the lodge." She leaned close to Patrick. "Rose is awfully curious about that body they found, you know."

"I guess everyone is. Is that what she's asking him about?"

"I expect so. Little old ladies can get away with asking all kinds of questions, Paddy. People humor us by answering when they'd likely not tell a younger person."

He smiled down at her. "Grandma, you're incorrigible."

Martha chuckled. "Rose is all excited because her granddaughter Susannah's coming to visit her soon."

Across the field, the teams were lining up in preparation for their introductions, Patrick saw. Watching for Pam, he tried to keep his mind on the conversation. "I don't think I've met Susannah."

"Probably not, but you will. She has her own local television show. Household hints, that sort of thing."

"Uh-huh." The announcer had begun, and players were running onto the field as their names were called. Patrick wondered how Pam was doing, but had decided not to stop in the locker room for a pregame visit. Now he wished he had.

"My, my, will you look at those two," Martha commented.

Patrick drew his attention back to her. "What two?"

"Over there. Judson Ingalls is sitting with that redheaded Tisha from the beauty shop." She shook her head. "Some old men seem to prefer these young chickadees. Wonder if she's after his money?"

"Come on, Grandma. Maybe they just enjoy each other's company."

"That's possible, I suppose." At the sound of her name being called, Martha craned her neck, then smiled and waved to a young woman by the railing. "There's Liza Baron," she pointed out to Patrick. "She was over at the house the other evening, asking some of us what we remember about Margaret Ingalls. She's determined to find out what happened to her grandmother and clear up the suspicions about Judson."

Patrick shook his head. "I can't believe anyone in this town would think Judson killed his wife, then buried her on the grounds of his lodge. That's ridiculous."

"Stranger things have happened, Paddy. She was a wild one, Margaret was. I remember. Judson simply couldn't control her. Still, I believe he loved her."

"Then it stands to reason he wouldn't have killed her. I'm more inclined to believe they'll find it's an Indian, and I don't understand why it's taking them so long to identify the body."

But Martha was still convinced of her own theory. "I believe Judson's involved somehow. When infidelity enters a marriage, lots of things can happen. Which might be a warning for George Phelps. I heard he's been seen taking Marge Peterson here and there. What do you make of that friendship?"

Patrick had long been aware that the quilting ladies loved gossip almost as much as sewing, but occasionally it annoyed him. This was one of those times. "I think they're both adults and have to make their own choices."

"Well, of course. But I do think a man ought to get divorced before he starts up with another woman." She touched Patrick's arm. "I like George, Paddy. And Judson, too. I'd hate to see them get hurt."

"Grandma, aren't you the one who told me that sometimes we have to get hurt in order to learn important lessons?" At her nod, he kissed her powdery cheek, then stood. "I see Rose is coming back. I'm going to go down toward the Titans' bench. I'll see you later."

"Say hello to Pam for me. And be careful, Paddy."

Making his way down the stairs, Patrick thought about his grandmother's words. *Be careful.* He didn't think she was warning him about taking care of himself physically. More likely emotionally. She had voiced concern about George and Judson, as well. Martha always seemed to worry more about the male in any given situation. Yet she'd seemed to take to Pam. What, he wondered, need he be careful of?

Reaching the lower level, he stopped at the railing and watched Pam in a huddle with her boys. She looked calm and in control. He hoped she was both. He badly wanted this game to go well, for the Titans to win, for Pam's decision to be justified.

Perhaps that was what his grandmother, with her finely tuned female intuition, had been warning him about—his tendency to worry about the women in his life. But how could he stop?

Leaning on the railing, he watched the opening kickoff, knowing it would be a very long ball game.

THE BUZZER SOUNDED, warning the players that only two minutes remained before the end of the game. Pam watched her quarterback come off the field for final instructions. With a sinking heart, she wondered what to tell him.

The Eagles were a tough team, but not spectacular. Though the Titans had tried hard, at this crucial moment they were behind 19 to 14. It was fourth down with eight yards to goal. A field goal would be hard to miss at that distance, but that would mean only three points. Not enough to win.

Across the field at the Eagles' bench, she saw team members playfully patting one another, seemingly confident of victory. Everyone expected that the

Titans would kick it away, turning the ball over to the Eagles. Pam waited until B.J. came up to her.

Despite the cool night, B.J. was sweating. He pulled off his helmet and wiped his face. Pam quietly watched him as he drew on the straw in the cold drink one of the assistants held out to him. Finally, he made up his mind. "I want to try it," he told Pam.

It was what she'd been hoping he'd say, but she'd wanted B.J. to make the decision. "It's a long shot, you know that."

Hands on his slim hips, he nodded. "We're trapped, Coach. A field goal would shorten the point spread, but we'd still lose. I want to run the ball in myself."

Pam felt pride in this young man rise within her. She touched his arm. "I believe you can do it."

B.J. let out a huff of air. "I believe it's our only chance."

She patted his shoulder. "Go to it, then."

The whistle sounded and the players returned to the field, taking up their positions. She'd wanted her boys to win so she'd feel vindicated in making her decision. But things had shifted for her with B.J.'s willingness to gamble. Now she wanted them to win for his sake.

There was an almost palpable buzz of excitement in the air when the fans realized the Titans were going to run the play. Pam tried to shut out the sounds, to concentrate. She held herself rigid, clutching her clipboard to her chest, her eyes on B.J.

She saw the handoff to the quarterback, then B.J. moved back, feinting, changing directions, searching for a break in the formation. Finally, he found one and scrambled forward. Pam's heart leaped to her throat as she saw him running, his strides sure and filled with purpose. Close at his heels, a stunned linebacker pivoted and ran for him. But he was too late.

B.J. crossed the goal line a split second before the linebacker tackled him. The referee raised his hands, signaling a touchdown. The scoreboard changed, the new reading 20–19. The stadium erupted in surprised celebration, and the cheers were deafening.

Pam blinked back a sudden rush of tears as B.J. got to his feet, accepting the pats and punches of congratulations from his teammates as they ran to his side. The rest of the Titans gathered at the sidelines, hugging and hand-slapping one another. Pam saw Ricky Travis rise from the far end of the bench and quietly walk off the field. It was a shame Ricky wasn't a big enough person to enjoy his teammates' triumphs, she thought fleetingly. She swung her eyes back to B.J. He'd badly needed this win. And so had she.

Jamie made the extra point, bringing the final score to 21–19, but that was anticlimactic. The real hero was B.J., and everyone knew it as they cheered and clamored. Letting him revel in his victory, Pam stood back, watching him accept his accolades with an awkward shyness that touched her. It wasn't until she felt a hand on her shoulder that she tugged her eyes from the field.

"Hey, lady," Patrick said, "that was *some* ball game."

Because she felt so good, she hugged him and let him swing her around, enjoying the pleased grin on his handsome face. "Wasn't B.J. something? Lord, what a gamble. If he'd missed, everyone would have left here certain that Ricky was vital to the Titans' ever winning again. But B.J. changed all that."

Patrick walked with her as she followed the team off the field toward the locker rooms. "He's a good kid, one who's had to work hard for everything he's ever had. His father died when he was quite young and his mother raised B.J. and his older brother single-handedly. I think she works in the dairy, and I know money's always in short supply. If he keeps improving, maybe B.J. will win a scholarship."

"Well, for sheer guts he deserves one tonight." Pam paused at the far end of the hall, noticing a girl, one of the cheerleaders, who'd stopped B.J. at the locker room door. They stood talking, the girl obviously praising B.J.'s performance.

Patrick followed her gaze. "It seems our young quarterback is about to win back the girl who wouldn't give him a tumble a while ago. That's Cindy Crane, isn't it?"

Pam nodded. "It looks like Cindy prefers dating winners. I wonder if she'd have come up to console B.J. if he'd lost."

Patrick squeezed her arm. "The road young lovers travel is sometimes rocky, haven't you heard?"

She shifted her gaze to his face. "We older folks have a few rough moments now and then, too."

He leaned close to her ear. "I have plans for a quiet little victory celebration that I'd like to run by you. I thought we'd skip Marge's Diner and your public congratulations, deserved though they are. How about coming to my house? I'll build a fire and we can roast marshmallows and relax. What do you say?''

His plan sounded wonderful, but she couldn't give in too easily. Pam pretended to consider his proposal. "I don't know. Are there any homemade cookies left?" She saw him nod knowingly, then she smiled up at him. "It's a date, Coach Kelsey."

"Great. I'll wait here while you change."

Pam walked toward the lockers, her smile slipping a little. Tonight. She could put this off no longer. Tonight she would tell Patrick everything.

"CAN YOU GET TIPSY on cider?" Pam asked, accepting a second glass.

Seated facing her on the couch, Patrick shook his head. "Nah. It's only apple juice."

"*Fermented* apple juice. You wouldn't ask a woman to your home, then ply her with alcohol, would you, Coach?"

Scooting closer, Patrick smiled seductively. "What a good idea." He ran his hand along the couch back, resting it on Pam's shoulder. "Are you glad you came?"

"Mmm. This beats public celebrations." She turned to gaze into the fire crackling in the grate. Patrick had walked her through his small, two-story house, which hadn't taken long. Then he'd seated her near the fireplace while he built the fire. They'd sampled the cookies and cider, and now Pam felt relaxed and at ease.

"How long have you been renting this place?"

"I moved here shortly after I started coaching at Tyler High. My folks gave me a lot of breathing room at the boardinghouse, but I felt I needed to be on my own."

Pam angled toward him, lacing her fingers with his. "I know what you mean. After I left my college coaching position, I moved back home. My father's a great guy, but he can't resist trying to run my life."

"I guess lots of parents are like that. In an effort to keep us from getting hurt, even when we're grown up, they get overly protective."

"Do you think you'll be like that with your children?"

Patrick gave a short laugh. "I'd like to think not, but I probably will. I seem to lean in that direction."

"I've noticed."

"Does it bother you?"

"A little. That's why you worried when I suspended Ricky. You thought I'd lose my job if we didn't have a winning season."

He'd wondered if she'd seen his concern. "Yes."

The moment of truth. Pam raised her eyes to his. "Why? Why would you care if I lost this job?"

She wanted to hear the words. Well, he would give them to her. "Because I care for you far more than I'd planned to. And I don't want you to leave."

"I care about you, too." She leaned closer, reaching for his kiss, needing the contact, needing to borrow his strength.

His lips were gentle, coaxing, caressing. His hand touched her cheek lightly, with no sense of hurry. He seemed to be saying that there was lots of time and much to learn about each other. He seemed to savor, to enjoy, to cherish. Nothing could have won her over more completely.

Pam pulled back from him reluctantly, averting her gaze, gathering her thoughts. "Patrick, I need to tell you something."

He'd caught a flash of pain in her eyes for a moment there, and wondered at its source. He tried to lighten things. "Let me guess. You're the divorced mother of ten and you forgot to mention your brood." When she didn't react, he cupped her chin and tipped her face up to his. The look in her eyes was determined and a little frightened. "What is it?"

Pam swallowed hard and plunged in before she could change her mind. "When I came back from the Seoul Olympics, I had a cold. I felt tired and run-down, but I'd been working hard, so I chalked it up to that. I thought rest would take care of my fatigue. It didn't. I became listless and jumpy, as if I'd stayed in a sauna too long. I'd get this tingling feeling, and sometimes my hands and feet would go numb."

Clearing her throat, Pam forced herself to continue, knowing she was coming to the hard part. "Finally, my left leg gave out on me one day and I fell. That's when I decided to see a doctor. They weren't sure what I had at first, so they put me through endless tests. Finally, they pinpointed my illness."

She held his gaze now, and his attention. "I have multiple sclerosis." She waited silently for his reaction.

Patrick drew in a deep breath. "What exactly does that mean?"

She needed a little space. Edging back from him, she took a tissue from her pocket and worried it with shaking fingers. "MS affects the central nervous system," she began. She'd memorized whole sections of the many books she'd read. "Sometimes brain tissue hardens inexplicably and the spinal cord is affected. Something like a short circuit occurs. Often there's paralysis and muscle spasms and—"

He touched her arm. "No, I don't mean the clinical explanation. I mean how does this affect *you?*"

"Right now I'm in remission. No one can predict how long such a period will last. For the most part, I'm fine. MS patients can live normal lives much of the time. But not always. For instance, when I get a chill, or when I'm under a lot of stress, some topical numbness sets in."

"Is that what happened when you fell while we were playing football that day?"

So he had wondered about that. "Yes. My leg suddenly went numb from the knee down. But it didn't last long." He wasn't reacting. Of course, she hadn't known what reaction to expect or even what reaction she wanted him to have. She looked down, shredding the tissue methodically. "This isn't easy to talk about, which is one reason I haven't told many people. Everyone suddenly gets nervous around someone with a serious illness."

Pam found the courage to look up at him. His eyes were thoughtful, his expression unreadable. "Do you remember when we were in the hospital and learned about Tommy Maxwell's epilepsy? You wondered how I understood his parents—how they were trying to protect their son from prejudice and pity. Now you know why."

"And that's why you didn't tell anyone in Tyler?"

"Yes."

"Why didn't you tell me? For the same reason?"

"No. I . . . maybe. There was a man I was seeing at the time I found out about my MS. He couldn't handle it, couldn't cope. He walked away and I . . ."

"You thought I'd react the same?"

"I wouldn't blame you if you did." Her eyes as she raised them to his were overly bright. "I didn't set out to care for you, Patrick, or for anyone else. I needed to work and I felt I could do this job, so I jumped at the chance. When I met you, when we started to get close, I wanted to tell you. But I—I didn't know where to begin."

Patrick could see how difficult this was for her. He had to admit that what he'd just learned had shocked him. But it hadn't changed how he felt about Pam. He had to let her know that. Gently he took the tissue bits from her, then took her hands into his. "I'm not going to lie to you. This news has come out of left field. I don't know much about MS, but I mean to learn. One thing I do know. I'm not going anywhere. I want to be with you."

"Oh, God, Patrick . . ." She leaned into him, into the solid wall of his chest. He crushed her to him as she closed her eyes, the tears she could no longer hold back falling onto his shirt.

She hadn't cried in a very long time, not since those early days of learning to accept what she could not change. She didn't want to cry now, but she couldn't seem to stop. And Patrick held her, just held her, his hand touching her hair, his breath warm on her forehead.

He wasn't going anywhere, he'd said. But was he staying for the right reasons, or out of pity?

Pam pulled back after a while and wiped her face. "I don't want you to feel sorry for me," she said quietly.

Patrick paused a moment, then tugged her forward again roughly, his mouth capturing hers. Surprised, Pam opened to him as his lips devoured, his tongue took possession and his arms wound around her. Her pulse hammered in her throat as he deepened the kiss with an almost frantic urgency, the gentleness gone. She could do little more than follow his lead as he ground his mouth into hers, his breathing labored. Finally, he eased back.

His eyes when she looked at them were stormy. "Did that taste like pity to you?"

She took a deep breath. "No."

"Then don't ever say that to me again. I may need a little time to adjust to this, but I'm not that other man, and I'm not walking. Understand?"

Wanting desperately to believe, to hope, Pam nodded.

"I told you I care about you. Your having MS doesn't change that. Did you think it would?"

"Don't be angry. I couldn't know. For many it *would* change things."

She looked so damn vulnerable. Patrick felt his heart twist. She'd laid a big one on him today, and he could see she was still frightened, still wary. She'd been hurt by a man who'd turned from her. She couldn't have known he wouldn't also.

Of course, he had questions—lots of them. They could wait. Right now, she needed him. And maybe he needed her even more.

Gently he framed her face—her lovely face—brushing aside the last of her tears with his thumbs. "This man is exactly where he wants to be." With the utmost tenderness, he touched his mouth to hers.

Where before his kiss had been born of frustration and anger, this one offered comfort, offered love. He moved his lips over hers slowly, drawing out the pleasure for both of them. He felt the tension ease from her, felt her return the pressure slightly. He kissed the corners of her mouth, then slipped his tongue inside. She shuddered once, and he swallowed her sigh as he drew her closer.

He kissed her for a long time—every inch of her face, her closed eyelids and, again, her waiting mouth. Kissed her until she was relaxed and pliant and giving. Then he let his words flow over her, because he thought she needed them almost as much as his touch.

"You smell so good. How is it you always smell so wonderful? You're so lovely, Pam, so soft and lovely." His hands moved into her hair, his fingers sliding along her scalp until she shivered in his arms. "Your hair is beautiful, rich and silky." And always he returned to her lips. "I love the way you taste, like a fresh spring morning. Your mouth ... I think it was made for mine."

He knew the words themselves didn't mean as much as the feelings he was sharing with her. That she mattered to him, that she pleased him, that she excited him. Her pulse was throbbing in her throat now, and he was having a little trouble with his own heartbeat. He wanted her, yet he hesitated. He had a lot to learn about her condition, but some questions she'd have to answer.

"I have to ask you," he whispered in her ear. "Is it all right if we make love? I don't want to hurt you."

She sighed and held him tighter. "Oh, yes, it's very much all right." She smiled against his cheek. "Beneficial, actually. A deterrent to stress, you know." But then a new thought struck and she drew back. "That is, if you want to."

Patrick's smile was slow and very sensual. "I want to, all right. I've wanted to make love with you for a very long time. How about you?"

"I wanted to wait until you knew, until we both felt right."

"And now?"

She placed his hand over her heart so he could feel it pounding, pounding for him. "What do you think?"

"I think we need only to pick the place. I hate to leave the fire, and there is a soft rug in front of the hearth. But I have this great big old-fashioned four-poster upstairs that belonged to my grandmother and grandfather. Since them, no one has slept in it but me. Your choice."

She loved the way he'd told her that he'd not brought other women here, that she was special. "No contest. I choose Martha's bed."

Patrick smiled his approval as he stood, pulled her to her feet, then bent to pick her up into his arms. "I've been wanting to do this for a long time, too."

No man had ever carried her, certainly not off to his bedroom. Pam nuzzled his neck as he climbed the stairs with her. In his room, he set her down and went to light the hurricane lamp on the rolltop desk in the corner. One of his grandmother's quilts covered the huge bed, a design in browns and gold that she didn't recognize. Though she was trembling, it wasn't with fear. Anticipation had her blood heating.

Pam stood by the bed watching as Patrick walked slowly back to her. She pressed a hand to her stomach, where nerves fluttered and butterflies danced. Memories leaped to her mind—the way Bob had looked at her in the hospital, the near-revulsion and fear she'd seen in his eyes—and she fought them back. She must not dwell on the past nor measure this man by the legacy of another. She would not think of what had been, but instead would focus on what was to be.

He stood looking down at her with those incredible blue eyes. She loved him, Pam realized, loved him more deeply than she'd ever thought she could love. And she had such untapped reservoirs of love to give, to share. But she must not say the words, not until he did. She was a woman with a problem, and Patrick would have to come to grips with that his own way, in his own time. But for tonight, she would pretend no problems existed. They would just be a man and a woman reaching out to each other.

Patrick placed his hand on the top button of her blouse and felt her quick shiver. He dropped his hands. "Are you afraid?"

"Afraid? No. A little nervous." Nervous that she wouldn't please him. Nervous that he would find her lacking. She hadn't felt like this before, when she'd been more confident of herself, of her body and its reactions.

In the dim light, he stroked her satiny skin. "It's all right. I'm a little nervous myself."

That surprised her. "You, nervous? You're always so self-assured, so positive."

"Is that how I seem? It's not how I always feel. Men take risks in the bedroom, too." He smiled then. "We'll go slowly." He hoped he could keep that promise.

He bent to kiss her, his encircling arms drawing her close. Her hands, trapped between them, flattened against his chest as his mouth moved over hers. His tongue found hers and took it on a fanciful chase. Her fingers tightened and bunched his shirt. Unaware, she rose on tiptoe, rose to move closer to his hardening body.

It had been so long since she'd felt like a woman. The intimacy between them mounted as Patrick's hand at her back pressed her closer. Pam felt her body soften, needing him, wanting him. As the desire for him took over, she no longer felt hesitant or shy, or even terribly nervous.

Were those her fingers unbuttoning his shirt and pulling it from him? Had she given her hands permission to caress the thick patch of soft hair on his chest, then to wander and explore the firm muscles of his back? Was that her voice she heard moaning softly as the kiss went on and on, as her blood raced and her heart thudded against his?

She'd come alive under his touch, Patrick realized—slowly come alive. Her mouth scarcely leaving his, she helped him remove her clothes, then her eager fingers moved to assist him with his. His hands journeyed over her then, reveling in her fragile perfection, feeling her tremble as he lowered her to the mattress and followed her down.

The room was warm and nearly dark, the only sounds the ticking of the bedside clock mingling with their labored breathing. He found her skin smooth and slick, her body restless. Braced on an elbow, he rained kisses on her face as his hand moved lower. She jolted when he touched her, then relaxed and opened to him, offering the ultimate gift of trust. Her eyes on his were wide and aware, and Patrick felt a surge of emotion stronger than he'd ever known.

It was different for him this time, different because Pam was different. Special. And because his feelings for her were special. He felt her move against his hand, then saw a tear trail down her flushed cheek. He kissed it away, then, filled with an aching tenderness, he kissed her mouth.

Wonder filled Pam, wonder that she'd found something she hadn't known she'd been seeking. Here was power tempered by gentleness, strength seasoned by tenderness. His lips on hers tasted, teased and would not be rushed. She felt the passion build, build, until she could no longer lie still.

Suddenly eager, she felt a deep hunger leap alive inside her. Her mouth sought his now, losing patience, anxious and seeking. Her hands stroked, searching out his vulnerable spots, her body taut and straining as she reached for him.

She was so responsive. With openmouthed kisses, Patrick moved along her skin, trailing downward, then returning to her eager mouth. In the dim light, he saw that her eyes were full of unspoken need and lingering uncertainty. He would answer the one and chase away the other.

He encouraged her to learn him, to let her hands roam him, to send her lips on a voyage of discovery. Pam seemed to delight in the freedom to touch, to know, to experience. Then he rolled her to her back and shifted over her.

He touched his palms to hers, but she didn't feel entrapped. His eyes were steady on hers, as he lowered himself to her.

"I want to watch you," he murmured.

Pam couldn't speak, could scarcely breathe. She arched her back and sighed as he slipped inside her. He smiled then as he began to move, his chest rubbing against her sensitive breasts. Quickly, more quickly than she'd thought possible, he had her soaring, climbing, tossed into the eye of the storm. His mouth settled over hers, her moan merging with his.

Moving within her, Patrick watched her lovely face as she rose with him. She was everything he'd ever wanted, the dream lover he'd never believed he'd find. And now, at last, she was his.

Her eyes opened wide and she gasped at the unbelievable sensations that whirled her away. She whispered his name, then clutched him to her as she felt him join her in this world of their own making.

Breathing hard, limp and dazed, Pam waited for her heart to slow down. She wasn't certain how long they lay like that, entangled, euphoric. She only knew she felt safe and thoroughly loved.

Finally, Patrick shifted to look at her and smiled into her eyes, still hazy with passion. "How do you feel?"

"Wonderful."

"Why is that, do you suppose?"

Because I'm in love—really in love—for the first time. No, not the first. The last time. Pam raised a feeble hand and waved toward the window. "Because the sun is shining."

"Silly. It's dark out."

She tightened her hold on him. "Not in here, not for us. I feel absolutely bathed in sunshine."

He laughed, delighted. "I'm glad you feel that way, because we're far from finished here."

"Oh, I think we are. I'm so relaxed I couldn't possibly move for hours."

"Is that right?" Patrick had always loved challenges. Slowly, he began to move, to take her again along that seductive climb they'd only just sampled.

It wasn't possible, Pam thought, not so soon.

And then he showed her the impossible.

CHAPTER NINE

"I SHOULD LEAVE," Pam said softly, though it was the last thing she wanted to do. Her cheek rested comfortably on Patrick's chest and his arms cradled her against his large body under the warmth of his grandmother's quilt. In the dim glow of the hurricane lamp, she saw that the bedside clock read 1:00 a.m. and she frowned. "Positively scandalous, my being here in your bed at this hour."

"Mmm," Patrick agreed. "Positively."

"What would the members of the Booster Club say?"

"The smart ones would ask, 'What took you so long, Patrick Kelsey, getting that lovely woman into your bed?' The jealous ones would say, 'You don't deserve her.'"

His last words made Pam uncomfortable. It was *she* who didn't deserve him, she with her huge problem. He'd said he wasn't going anywhere, and she knew he'd meant every word. Under cover of darkness and in the heat of passion. How would he feel in the morning, in the brightness of day, when realities intruded and midnight promises brought regret?

Pam eased back and away from him, wondering how best to take her leave. She'd never been in this position before—in a man's bed in the middle of the night, only blocks from home. Running an unsteady hand through her hair, she sat up and started looking about for her hastily discarded clothes. "I have to go."

Patrick's fingers trailed down her back, sending shivers in their wake. "It's early yet and tomorrow's Saturday. Stay with me. In the morning, who will know if you spent the night or jogged over early to have breakfast with me?"

The thought frightened her, and she wasn't even sure why. "I can't." She reached for the silken panties on the floor.

Patrick recognized "after regrets." He'd experienced them himself a few times. His hand on her arm pulled her back down onto the bed. Quickly he leaned over her, ignoring the stubborn set of her chin. "Are you sorry we made love?"

The fight went out of Pam as she stared into his deep blue eyes, so unexpectedly anxious. "No, not in the least," she answered honestly. "But we're teachers and we can't—"

"We can't live our lives to please others. We aren't doing anything wrong and we aren't hurting anyone. We're both free, both consenting adults."

Pam sighed. "We have obligations to the parents, to the teaching staff, to Miss Mackie."

"We have an obligation to each other. Forget the rest."

"I can't. I'm on probation."

Patrick frowned, searching her eyes. "That's not it. What's the *real* reason you're so anxious to leave?"

She wished she had more of a poker face. "You're the reason. As you said earlier, learning about my MS is a real shock. I think it's best if I back away and give you some time to think things over. The fact that we made love doesn't obligate you in any way. I want you to know that. Some distance might—"

"I love you."

"—make you change your mind." She stopped, startled. "What did you say?"

"I love you, Pam."

"You can't mean it. You're just saying what you think I want to hear."

"Hardly that." He touched her face, realizing how much he meant what he said, acknowledging how the feelings had crept up on him. Yet they were strong, they were real. "I've never said those words to another woman. I told you before, I've never been in love, but I'm not a teenager. I know what I feel."

"Patrick, your family cares for you deeply. They'll want you to marry someone healthy and whole."

"My family will want what's best for me, and that's being with the woman I love. I promise you, they'll be all for us."

She wanted desperately to believe him. "But you haven't known me for long."

He smiled down into her eyes, eyes that were filled with hope, yet tinged with apprehension. "Oh, yes, I have. I've known you forever. I've known your intelligence, your sense of humor, your wit and charm. I've known your softness, your strength, your caring heart. Oh, yes, Pam, I know you. And I love you."

Pam felt something inside her burst open, letting the fear drain away, leaving only the love. "Oh, Patrick." With a soft cry, she buried her face in his neck, her arms tightening around him.

The tears ran freely, but she didn't care, didn't notice. Blindly she searched for his mouth, needing his kiss.

He made love to her then, slowly and tenderly, as if she were fragile and delicate, needing great care. Afterward, Pam fell asleep in his arms, feeling more cherished than she'd ever dreamed possible.

THREE O'CLOCK in the morning. Pam stared at the clock, then eased Patrick's arm from where it curved around her waist. Lying back, she let out a shaky breath.

The bewitching hour had passed, and again she lay watching the lamplight flicker across the ceiling, casting dancing shadows. The ambivalence was back full force, Pam admitted to herself unhappily. It wasn't a feeling she was used to or comfortable with.

Even in her youth, she'd always known the things she'd wanted and had forged forward to get them. She'd set her sights high—an Olympic gold medal, a career in sports, a loving husband, children. She'd managed the first two and had been closing in on the last two when fate intervened. Her illness wasn't keeping her from achieving them. Her love for Patrick might.

She turned to study his face, where sleep was softening the sharp masculine features. The gentleness that was so much a part of Patrick was there, as was the strength. His dark hair curled onto his forehead and she longed to reach up and brush it back. Touching him was a pleasure she'd recently become addicted to. But loving him carried an obligation she couldn't ignore.

With a ragged sigh, Pam eased from the bed, taking great care not to waken him. Loving someone, truly loving that person, meant caring more for him than for herself, she thought as she gathered her clothes and quickly dressed. Which brought her to the fact that perhaps she wasn't the best person for Patrick.

She couldn't help wondering what his family would say about their relationship when they learned of her problem. Despite what he'd forecast, they would warn him, would do their best to persuade him to let her go, as well they should. Loving Patrick, how could they encourage him to commit to a woman who could not offer him endless bright tomorrows?

Oh, but she loved him, too. And, oh, how she wanted him, especially after last night, after experiencing the passion he'd brought into her life. But she had limitations—severe limitations—and a questionable future. He deserved more.

Fully clothed, she stood looking down at him. He would be angry that she left like this, but she knew she had to go now, before he awoke. Before he touched her again and pulled her back into the magic of his arms. It was hard enough leaving like this. With his eyes on her, she'd never manage it.

Creeping downstairs, she found her shoes and jacket and quickly put them on. The moon as she stepped onto the front porch was full and bright, the neighborhood asleep and quiet. Pam hunched her shoulders against the chill and stuck her hands into her pockets as she set out for home.

How ironic, she thought, that when she'd at last found love, she felt compelled to run from it.

SHE'D KNOWN he would call and he did, at six in the morning. From her solitary bed, where she'd been tossing and turning since arriving home, she stared at the ringing phone and felt like sobbing. Fortunately, Rosemary was away for the weekend, and Pam didn't need to explain why she wasn't answering the early-morning call.

Finally the ringing stopped and she jumped out of bed. Patrick would guess what she'd done and come looking for her, she was certain. Quickly, she pulled on a pair of sweatpants and a shirt. From his corner, Samson eyed her curiously. Even he knew they didn't usually go running while it was still dark out.

But they would this morning. Grabbing her jacket and keys, she paused outside only long enough for Samson to visit a few bushes before she hurried him to her car. She backed out of the drive and took the long way around, fearful of running into Patrick on her usual route. On the open road, she stepped down on the gas pedal, shoving aside her cowardly feelings.

She drove around until a pale sun crept up on the dewy horizon of a country road. Parking, she pulled on her jacket and set out with Samson, hoping the clean air would clear her foggy brain.

Two hours later she returned to her car, exhausted mentally and physically. She knew better than to push herself so, but she'd needed the thinking time. Maybe now she was fortified enough to talk with Patrick.

The house was quiet when Pam entered. She gave Samson a fresh bowl of water and hurried into the shower. The phone was ringing when she turned off the spray. Wrapping a towel about herself, she took a deep breath and went to answer.

"Where the hell have you been?" Patrick rammed a fist into his jeans pocket. He hadn't meant to bark at her, but extended worry made him act stupid. He'd phoned, then gone to her house. Finding her gone, he'd cooled his heels on her porch swing until he thought her nosy neighbor was ready to call the cops on him. Fuming, he'd walked back home and put on a pot of coffee. He'd just finished the last cup when she finally answered.

"I'm sorry if I worried you," Pam said with sincerity. "I had some thinking to do." He was angry and she didn't blame him. Besides, she could deal with anger more easily than hurt.

Patrick's good sense kicked in and he took a calming breath. Personally, he'd had more time to think during the past few hours than he was comfortable with. "And what conclusions did you come to?" He might as well find out up front.

Pam shoved a hand through her wet hair, searching for the right words. "That last night was beautiful and that I care about you a great deal."

Patrick gave a somewhat relieved sigh. "Then why did you leave?"

"I want us to back away for a little while." When he tried to interrupt, she stopped him. "Hear me out, Patrick, please. I've got only a few weeks remaining in football season and our next two games are away, with our fiercest competitors. I need to concentrate on the team. And basketball practice is just beginning, so I know you're going to be busy."

"During working hours, yes."

"I want you to take some time, for both our sakes." She could not, would not, belittle his love for her, but she needed him to be very, very certain of his feelings. "I've got some books I'd like you to read on MS. One especially on what friends and family of MS patients can expect, the outlook for the future, that sort of thing. Blind love is for the young and the innocent. I need realistic love."

"And you don't think that's what I'm offering you?"

Pam shook her head, then tempered her thoughts. "I'd feel a lot better if you were completely aware of all the consequences, all the possibilities. As I told you, a man who claimed to care for me walked away, unable to cope when he learned what kind of a future he'd face with me. I care so much more for you than I did for him. If you left when things got rough—which they will—I'm not sure I could handle it. So I want us *both* to be very certain we know what we're getting into here."

She made sense. So damn much sense. Yet somehow it made him angrier. Patrick rubbed the back of his neck, feeling the tension building. "Loving should make a relationship easier, not more difficult, more complicated.''

Pam swallowed around a lump in her throat. He sounded angry, confused and frustrated. She'd gone through each emotion months ago and knew just what he was feeling. ''There are things that are never easy for an MS patient, or for the people who care for them. That's a fact they have to accept, to learn to live with.''

Patrick paced the length of his kitchen as far as the phone cord would allow him, then back. ''All right. We'll do this your way. But you're not getting rid of me this easily, lady.''

She smiled then, and blinked back the tears that once again threatened. ''I don't want to get rid of you, Patrick. I just want you to know what you'd be getting into, with no surprises.''

''You're the one who's going to be surprised. I'm in for the long haul.''

Hanging up, Pam walked slowly to the window and looked out. The clouds had moved off and the sun shone down on the fallen leaves shifting in a light breeze. It was a beautiful fall day, offering sunshine and hope.

Dare she allow herself to hope again?

''HEY, LOTTIE, Lottie, Lottie. Hey, Lottie, Lottie, Low,'' the football players and cheerleaders sang as the school bus lumbered back toward Tyler after the Titans beat the Bulls, one of their biggest rivals. The mood was jubilant, the victory atmosphere causing

them to sing even louder. Huddled in a window seat
near the back, Pam wished she felt like joining in.

Naturally she was pleased her boys had won, especially since they'd lost last week. Ricky had suited up
and sat out the game on the bench last Friday, swag-
gering over to her after that loss. He'd stood there expectantly, unwilling to ask, yet wanting her to tell him
he was reinstated. For a brief moment she'd almost
given in, more because B.J. was suffering with a sore
arm muscle than for any other reason. But she
couldn't undermine B.J.'s budding confidence. B.J.
had healed, worked hard and come through for them
again tonight.

So she should be happy, Pam told herself. But there
were several reasons why she wasn't.

Probably foremost was that she missed Patrick. He
was busy coaching the junior basketball team, since
many of the seniors were still playing football. They'd
had a preseason game scheduled for tonight or he
might have come along on the bus with them. It had
been a close game and she could have used his quiet
support.

Yet distance was what she'd asked for, so she could
scarcely fault him for doing as she'd requested. He'd
picked up the books she'd mentioned and presumably had read them by now. They'd talked in their
shared office, mostly about their respective teams, and
once had even gone for coffee together in the school
cafeteria.

Their eyes had said more than their lips, though,
and she couldn't help wondering what he was thinking. She hadn't realized how much she'd come to rely

on sharing her thoughts with him. But she desperately wanted to give him time.

Yet she missed his touch. She berated herself for having given in to his lovemaking, for now she knew what she was missing, and the loss left her feeling empty. He would phone her occasionally, and she'd try to keep the conversation general, yet she longed for him to say something personal, something to end what she'd begun. She wanted to ask about his reaction to the information in the books, but she was afraid of his answer. And she strongly felt the next move had to be Patrick's.

The team started in on another old favorite, counting bottles of beer on the wall, from ninety-nine on down. The monotonous tune left Pam isolated with her thoughts. Absently, she rubbed her left knee. It wasn't really numb, just tingling slightly. Probably from the cold. More than three hours outside in the chilly night air had made her feel stiff and cranky.

And a little frightened. She must ease up, not tire herself so, or she'd be in trouble. A warm bath tonight and lots of sleep would have her feeling in top form tomorrow.

Only she wasn't sleeping all that well. Her restive mind searched for new plays to finish the season with a bang. And her restless body yearned to have Patrick beside her, Patrick warming her, Patrick loving her.

A burst of laughter drew her attention and she looked up. Moose was clowning around, as usual. Across the aisle, B.J. sat with his arm around Cindy Crane. As one of the cheerleaders, she attended all the games, of course. And she'd been at his side whenever the team won. Pam had serious reservations about Cindy's feelings for B.J., and wondered if her quarterback would be able to see through his girlfriend's superficial ways. Pam watched as he smiled down at Cindy, so obviously in love.

Love. Such a confusing emotion, such an exciting place to be, such a frightening four-letter word. She was years older than B.J., yet she faced the prospect of love with the same vulnerability. Pam wondered if that would ever change.

When the school bus turned into the winding drive of Tyler High, she gathered her things and, holding on to the seat backs, made her way to the front.

"Okay, guys, let's have your attention." She turned to face them and waited until they quieted somewhat. "We won tonight, but don't let that go to your heads. Next Friday we play Tower City again. We need to beat them to make second place. Practice tomorrow, two o'clock." She listened patiently to the groans of protest. "Now is no time to let up," she said above the noise. "Be there."

The bus ground to a halt by the gymnasium and the driver hit the lever to open the door. "See you then," Pam called as she swung off the bus.

Hurrying to the parking lot and her waiting car, she envisioned a fragrant bath and eight hours of uninterrupted sleep.

THE THURSDAY AFTERNOON practice was not going well. Todd pulled a hamstring and was definitely out, probably for the balance of the season. Aaron was home with a bad case of the flu and would miss tomorrow night's game. And B.J. was off form, throwing wild.

Pam had all but lost her temper with her quarterback twice. The last time, when she'd noticed his eyes straying to his girlfriend, watching on the sidelines and interfering with his concentration, she'd ordered the field cleared of onlookers. The boys weren't happy with her. She wasn't any too happy with herself.

Winter was making an early visit to Tyler and it was suddenly bitterly cold. Frost covered the ground in the mornings, and even at four in the afternoon she could see her breath in the chilly air. Walking along the sidelines, Pam stomped her feet, trying to keep the circulation going. Glancing up at the grayish sky, she frowned. Were those snowflakes falling? She coughed into her fist, wishing she had more energy.

Checking her watch, she decided she'd cut the last hour by half and hope that they'd had enough practice before Friday night's game. She got the boys started in scrimmages, then came to a decision. Perhaps if she got out there and tossed a ball herself she'd warm up.

Walking briskly toward B.J., she felt a twinge in her right leg. Usually it was her left leg that gave her trouble. Pam decided to ignore the slight tremor.

"B.J., over here," she called out. He started walking to meet her, and she held up her hand when he was twenty feet away. "Okay, start throwing to me from there for a while. Then I'll back up and we'll go for distance. And please, B.J., keep your mind on what you're doing."

Catching for him, checking his form, Pam felt a shiver take her. Lord, but she wished the time would hurry by. She badly wanted to curl up in front of a warm fire.

The minutes seemed to crawl, but at last Pam dismissed the boys and rushed to her car, not even stopping by the locker room. She felt bone-tired and weak. Praying she was only catching a minor cold, she drove the dozen blocks carefully and slowly, grateful when she finally turned into her drive. She was on the porch when she felt the tingling begin, followed by the numbness that would have caused her to fall had she not grabbed the railing.

Oh, God, no!

Clutching the wooden post, she waited long minutes. The worst seemed past. She inched her way to the door, careful not to put too much weight on her left leg. Fumbling with the key, she made it inside, then leaned heavily against the outer door, giving herself a moment.

She'd seen Rosemary's car parked out front and felt a rush of relief that her roommate was home. A little massage therapy and this would pass, Pam felt certain. She wouldn't bother with trying for the key, but would knock instead.

Carefully, Pam stepped to the door, knocked twice, then, to her horror went down onto the polished wood floor with a thud. Biting her lower lip, she lay there in a crumpled heap, unable to get back up. She fought back the panic, the tears, and shifted to bang her fist at the bottom panel of the door. At last it swung open.

"Oh, my God!" Rosemary exclaimed. Quickly and expertly, she reached under Pam's arms and pulled her awkwardly upright. Bearing most of her weight, Rosemary got her inside and onto the couch, then went back to shut the door.

Pam lay still, letting her heartbeat normalize, grateful that Rosemary was a strong woman and that she'd been here for her. She looked up to find her therapist friend looking at her with a worried expression.

"I'll be all right in a minute," Pam said, her voice a little breathy.

"Sure you will." Rosemary helped Pam remove her jacket and angle her legs more comfortably up on the couch. Sitting down near Pam's feet, she pulled off her heavy shoes and ran her hands along her chilled legs. "Can you feel my fingers?"

"Yes. The numbness is passing."

Rosemary began rubbing and kneading beneath the fleece-lined fabric of Pam's sweatpants. "I warned you only last week that you were headed for this. Why must you push so hard, Pam?"

"I have a job to do. I'll be fine, really." But as she tried to push herself upright, she noticed that her hands were shaking. Though she clasped them together, they continued to tremble quite badly. Just then, a coughing spasm shook her. With fear in her eyes, she looked up at Rosemary. "Maybe you'd better phone Dr. Phelps."

Rosemary nodded and rose. "I'll get you a blanket first."

She would be all right. She absolutely had to be all right. Pam closed her eyes, blocking out the fear that threatened to overpower her. She had only a few weeks to go. She couldn't let her boys down, nor the town. Nor Miss Mackie, who'd put so much faith in her. She'd licked this before and she would again.

Rosemary settled a bright green afghan over Pam's legs and tucked it in at her waist. "I'll go call. Is there anyone else you want me to notify?"

"No."

"Are you sure? How about Patrick? I think he'd want to be here."

Pam knew that Rosemary had watched her relationship with Patrick grow deeper by the day. But this was her decision to make. "No, please." She watched Rosemary's quick frown of disapproval as she walked to the kitchen phone.

Feeling helpless, Pam stuffed her shaking hands under the afghan and hoped Dr. Phelps was in.

PATRICK THUMBED through the book on his lap thoughtfully. He'd read the contents carefully over the past two weeks and now was reviewing a few of the more important sections. There were over thirty different varieties of MS, he'd learned. Pam had said hers was benign progressive, which meant that each year— each time she was out of remission—the disease would get a tiny bit worse.

The symptoms she could experience ranged from double vision, difficulty in walking and topical numbness all the way to an eventual possibility of blindness, loss of bowel control and, for the most severe cases, ending up in a wheelchair. Symptoms that persisted for more than six months would indicate permanent damage in that area.

There was no way to predict the length of remission periods, or when they would occur. The governing factor seemed to be stress, as well as extreme temperatures and fatigue. Some patients developed all symptoms, some merely a few. And during pregnancy, all symptoms usually disappeared.

MS was not contagious, not hereditary and not fatal, just limiting. Patients could lead relatively normal lives much of the time, Patrick read. He closed the book and closed his eyes, leaning his head back on the couch. A loving relationship and a positive mental attitude could not only extend periods of remission, but could actually slow the progression of the disease.

A loving relationship. He felt ready, willing and able to give Pam that. The question was, would she accept his love?

Nothing he'd read, no prospect he'd seen forecast, had deterred him from one basic thought: he loved Pam. While it was true that loving and living with an MS patient would present certain problems, Patrick felt certain that together they could handle whatever came their way. After all, it wasn't as if he had a choice. He loved her, whether she had MS or not, just as he'd love her if she had red hair or brown. The choice wasn't his to make, nor hers. It simply was.

He sat up straighter, rubbing his chin, which was rough with a day's growth of beard. Damn stubborn woman, that's what Pam Casals was. He'd done as she'd asked—backed away, educated himself about her disease and taken a long look at his feelings. He'd even discussed the matter with his parents, needing their opinions, and had come away reinforced in his own thinking.

Anna and Johnny Kelsey respected him enough to not try to influence his decision. They'd left him with a single, straightforward thought. If he loved Pam—truly loved her—then that was all there was to it. Now all he had to do was convince Pam.

No time like the present, he thought, checking his watch as he walked to the phone. It was early, not yet six. He would ask her out to dinner, a nice quiet place, and they'd talk. Feeling better at having come to a decision, he dialed her number.

Rosemary heard the phone ringing and left Dr. Phelps alone with Pam to complete his examination. When she recognized Patrick's voice, she moved farther into the kitchen, out of hearing of the two in the living room.

"She can't come to the phone right now, Patrick," Rosemary said quietly.

"Oh?" He paused a moment, wondering at Rosemary's hushed tone. She usually was quite exuberant. "Is anything wrong?"

"Pam's a little under the weather. George Phelps is here."

Patrick's mind leaped ahead. "Rosemary, I know about her MS. Is it that?"

Rosemary hesitated, then came to a decision. "Yes."

"I'll be right over." Patrick hung up.

Hoping she'd done the right thing, Rosemary set down the phone and went back to where George was closing his bag.

"It's a warning," George told Pam, "a serious warning. You must not ignore this. You could very easily slip out of remission if you do."

Pam frowned, clearly unhappy with his answer. "But look," she said, holding her hands out. "The shaking's stopped, the tingling's gone and—" she stuck out her legs and wiggled them "—there's no more numbness."

George seated himself across from her. "Yes, for now. It could return momentrily, or not for a week. If you rest, if you keep free of stress, you may not experience more symptoms for a longer period. And I'm still worried about a possible respiratory infection. If you push yourself, if you catch a bad cold, get tired and run-down...well..." He let the implication hang in the air.

"Pam," Rosemary said, coming alongside, "let me tell Miss Mackie. Patrick can finish out the football season for you. He's certainly experienced enough to—"

"No!" Regretting her harsh tone, she reached for her friend's hand. "I'll be careful. I promise. Please."

Rosemary sent George a discouraged look. "She won't, you know."

"I will. Dr. Phelps, if I'm careful, do you feel I could hang in there another couple of weeks without collapsing? I need to see the boys through until the play-off game on Thanksgiving Day."

He sent her a critical look oddly tinged with admiration. "Maybe. If you work from a wheelchair, perhaps."

Pam groaned inwardly, but nodded. "I'll do it. But we tell the boys that I—I tore a ligament in my leg and that's why I'm in the chair. I was moving around a lot at practice today, so they'll believe that." She looked from one dubious face to the other. "Please, I've got to do this."

George Phelps stood. "You're a difficult woman, Pam Casals. And a gutsy one." He stretched out his hand to shake hers. "Just remember, it's against my advice, though I know you'll do it your way anyhow."

Pam gave him her first genuine smile of the day. "Thank you, Dr. Phelps."

Rosemary saw George out, then returned to glower down at her friend. "You're crazy to do this, you know. No job is worth it."

"It's not for the job. It's for those boys. I believe they need me. And . . . and I think I need them."

Rosemary looked suddenly sheepish. "Speaking of needing people, I have to tell you something." Just then, they heard two loud, impatient knocks on the door. "I think I'm a little late," Rosemary said.

Puzzled, Pam frowned. "Who?" Suddenly it dawned on her. "You didn't."

"I didn't call him, honest. He called here and I—I couldn't lie to him." She jumped as the pounding resumed, louder and more insistent.

"Pam. Rosemary. Someone open this door."

Pam looked over her shoulder at the door as Rosemary swung it open. Patrick, his face like thunder, stomped in. Stopping in front of Pam, he glared down at her.

"I met George Phelps outside. Pam, I've had about enough of this. You're going to marry me, and I mean *now*."

CHAPTER TEN

"I THINK that may be my exit cue," Rosemary said, looking from Patrick's stormy face to Pam's suddenly calm one. Then, as if she'd spoken too hastily, she laid a hand on Pam's shoulder. "Will you be all right?"

Her eyes not wavering from Patrick's, Pam nodded. "I'll be fine, Rosemary. And thanks." She reached to squeeze her friend's hand reassuringly.

Rosemary shrugged into her coat, then grabbed her purse. "I'm meeting some friends for dinner. I could leave a number in case you need me...."

"We'll manage," Patrick said curtly. He wasn't in the mood to be polite. His concern for Pam had had him racing over like a madman. His talk with George on the porch had turned that anxiety into anger. Pam's unruffled manner wasn't helping him simmer down. He wished Rosemary would leave quickly so he could talk some sense into her.

As Rosemary closed the door behind her, Patrick tossed his corduroy jacket onto the chair. Pulling the ottoman close to the couch where Pam lay quietly watching him, he straddled it and met her dark eyes.

"We're alone now, so you can continue yelling at me," she said.

He had the decency to look chagrined. "I'm sorry, but you scared the hell out of me. Why is it that you don't take better care of yourself, when you know it's so dangerous not to?"

"I got a chill and had a little setback. It's not that serious."

"The hell it isn't! George told me that if you keep this up, you could wind up in the hospital."

"But I'm not going to keep it up. I've agreed to work from a wheelchair for a while, to get lots of rest, stay warm—all that good stuff." Suddenly discouraged at his critical expression, she crossed her arms over her chest. "George Phelps had no business telling you anything."

"No business? He knows how I feel about you and—"

That pulled her up short. "And just how does he know that? Did you take out a billboard ad on the town square? Look, Patrick, I've already played this scene with my father, and I left home because of his constant concern. I can't handle hovering, so back off. It's *my* life."

Patrick ran out of steam. He leaned forward and took her hand, uncurling her rigid fingers and lacing them with his own. "Your life is very much entangled with my life."

"Not yet, it isn't." Pam tried desperately to compose herself, knowing all this was pretty new to him. "This is one of the reasons I wanted you to think carefully about getting further involved with me. I've known about my MS for two years now. At first, I sat in a wheelchair—stunned, angry, unable to accept my situation. I got weaker, more pitiful. Then I met Rosemary, and she made me see that I could give in and give up, or I could fight back. I chose to fight back.''

She wound her fingers through his and held on, her eyes narrowing in her desire to make him see. ''It wasn't easy. It took me a very long year of therapy, of learning how to develop a positive mental attitude. PMA, Dr. Black, the staff psychiatrist in Chicago, used to call it. Without an upbeat outlook, you might as well crawl into bed and vegetate, he told me. He's right.''

''Okay, I see that you can't do that. But you don't have to take foolish risks, either.''

''Foolish to you, maybe, but necessary to me. There's such a thing as quality of life, Patrick. I've got to fight to live as normal a life as possible, or it's no life at all. I'm not that delicate and I'm not a hot-house flower. I'm also a grown woman who knows better than most my own limitations. I won't have someone telling me what I can and can't do. If that's your plan—and I know you have this unbelievable compulsion to protect—then you'd better find some-one who wants that. I don't.''

He softened, because she was so lovely when she was debating an issue she believed in, and because she was right. He wanted badly to protect her, just as she'd said—to keep her out of harm's way, to ease her life. But she wouldn't allow it, didn't even want to hear about it. He didn't know whether to admire her or shake her until her teeth rattled. ''All right,'' he said quietly. ''You win.''

Pam looked at him skeptically. "All right, just like that? That was too easy, and I don't trust anything easy."

Patrick's eyebrows rose questioningly. "Easy? You think you're easy? Lady, I've got news for you."

"I'm not likely to get any easier, either. Are you prepared for that?" Maybe it was time to lay all their cards on the table. "Did you read the books?"

"Every word." At her hesitant expression, he went on, "Did you think you'd scare me away with those books?"

She removed her hand from his and threaded her fingers through the folds of the afghan. "If you had any sense, you'd run."

"I must not have any, then. I'm staying."

The words she'd wanted to hear. Why did she have trouble believing them when she so desperately wanted to? "Probably not terribly wise of you." What perversity was pushing her to try to dissuade him?

"Wisdom is highly overrated, don't you think?" Patrick cupped her stubborn chin so she'd look at him. "Of course, maybe you don't want me to stay. Maybe my personality doesn't blend well with yours."

"Your personality's not at issue here."

"Then maybe I'm not handsome enough and you'd prefer a blond, all-American type?" He kissed the tip of her nose. "Maybe I'm not ambitious enough, a small-town high school basketball coach with no great aspirations to become rich and famous."

"You're fishing. You know you're very attractive and you know you're bright enough to be anything you want to be."

"Okay, that's not it then." He removed the afghan from her and shifted to sit beside her, close beside her, his hand curling around her neck. "Maybe I don't turn you on then. Maybe my kisses leave you cold." He dipped his head and covered her mouth with his.

He found her lips soft and warm, but hesitant. He sent the tip of his tongue on a tasting journey, from one corner of her mouth to the other, teasing lightly. He increased the pressure, his movements gentle yet determined, and swallowed her breathy sigh. When her hand fluttered to his shoulder, he deepened the kiss, his tongue plunging into her, and felt her meet him thrust for thrust.

His breathing unsteady, Patrick pulled back and watched her eyes open slowly, smoky with the beginning of passion.

Pam had a little trouble finding her voice. "I wouldn't say they leave me cold exactly." He was doing it again, making her forget her concerns, making her dismiss their differences, making her aware of this incredible need she had for him.

He smiled at her answer, then shifted until he was lying alongside her on the narrow couch, his hard body pressed closely to hers. "Ah, but maybe I don't really thrill you the way you do me." His hand was under her sweatshirt now. He inched around front and closed his fingers over the fullness of her breast, and felt her quiver.

His thumb brushing over the sensitive peak caused an eruption deep inside her that was like a sharp, exquisite pain. Pam moaned softly and dragged him closer. Hungry for him now, she searched for his mouth with her own. Her suddenly eager hands fumbled with the buttons of his shirt, the need to touch his bare flesh overwhelming her. The confines of the couch and the awkward position limited her ability to explore him and she groaned with frustration.

Patrick was intent on making her burn for him, making her crazy with the same need that had him throbbing. Lifting her for better access, he buried his face against the side of her neck and feasted there a long moment. "Maybe my touch doesn't set you on fire the way yours does me. Maybe your nights the past couple of weeks haven't been as filled with thoughts and dreams as mine."

That was highly doubtful, but she didn't have the energy to answer him. Eyes half-closed, Pam let him lead her along this sensual journey, her breathing erratic, her blood heating and racing through her veins. She'd known need before, but not like this. Never like this.

Patrick's hand traveled downward now as his mouth moved to sample the sweet line of her throat. Under the waistband of her sweatpants he inched, inside the satin swatch that covered her. She trembled as he roamed lower, arching into him as his fingers found her wet and warm.

"Maybe you don't want me as much as I want you," Patrick breathed into her ear, seeing her face flush with desire.

"I want you," Pam whispered as she struggled against the restrictions of their position. "Oh, how I want you." Wild from his fingers, which aroused her beyond belief, Pam moved with him and against him, rising, then cresting in a fiery explosion of feeling.

Patrick held her trapped in his arms, feeling her heart pound in rhythm with his, watching her face, her beautiful face. Needing more, he drove her to the heights again, until she shuddered violently, then collapsed against him.

She was his. Lying with him bathed in unrivaled sensations, Pam knew she was his as she'd been no one else's. Her mind floated free as her body adjusted to the slowing pace, and she wondered if he knew, if he could feel how completely she was his.

Patrick felt the subtle change in her, saw the glow on her face and the knowledge in her eyes as she looked into his. There was magic in their being together, in the special feelings they shared. No one else had ever known what they experienced locked together. No one else was capable of reaching such heights, of knowing each other so thoroughly. No one.

He touched her cheek, saw the tears of understanding in her eyes. "Now do you know what it's like for me with you?" he asked.

She did know. For the first time in her life, she felt as if she truly belonged to someone. "I love you, Patrick."

Her admission tore at the last of his control. He had to be one with her, to be a part of her. In a near frenzy, he tore off his clothes. Sensing his need to hurry, Pam tussled with her own, tossing them aside. Then he had her beneath him, melding with him, as eager as he.

Patrick took her then, in a burst of passion that told her all she needed to know about the strength of his love for her.

STANDING UNOBTRUSIVELY on the sidelines, Patrick watched Pam drill her boys. They'd readily accepted her explanation of a torn ligament, as they accepted her instructions delivered from a wheelchair. She was no less authoritative confined to her seat than she had been charging up and down the line. It was heart-warming to see how far the team had come in respecting and trusting their diminutive coach.

Maybe it was because she never wavered in her beliefs. Ricky was still sullenly sitting out the games on the bench, unaware that his punishment would end if only he'd alter his attitude. Pam had left the door open a crack, but Ricky would have to walk through on his own. And teaching him the lesson hadn't been easy for her, Patrick knew.

Easing down on the nearest bleacher bench, he absently rubbed his knee, the one that had gone under the knife four times and left him with an aching joint. The cold November weather didn't help any. He wondered how Pam was faring, seated in that cold chair, unable to move around as much as he could. But she hadn't complained, and she'd stayed in her chair for the most part, though he could see she hated every minute of her confinement.

As he watched, she left her chair and walked out onto the field, evidently annoyed at something by the look of her slow but determined strides. This was the team's last practice before tomorrow's game, and he knew she was under a lot of pressure.

The Titans had lost last Saturday's game, and once again the Booster Club members, several parents and even Miss Mackie felt she should reinstate Ricky Travis. They wanted something closer to a sure thing, and B.J. was inconsistent. Sometimes he played his heart out; other times it was as if he were distracted or uninterested.

He saw Pam signal Ricky to take over as quarterback, then she walked off the field with B.J. in tow. Ricky was still required to attend practices and, to his credit, he hadn't missed one since his benching. Leaning forward, Patrick wondered what had caused Pam to remove B.J. and what she was saying to him with such a serious face as they sat down together on a lone bench across the field.

"ALL RIGHT, B.J.," Pam said. "Let's have it. What's wrong?" His timing was off, his aim was wild and his mind definitely wasn't on football. There were no onlookers today to distract him—except for Patrick across the field, whose presence was hardly intrusive—and yet B.J.'s concentration was off. The game tomorrow was important. She had to find out what was bothering the boy.

B.J. whipped off his helmet and set it down on the cold ground, then ran a hand over his face in such a world-weary way that Pam almost smiled. Seventeen and feeling the strain. She well remembered her teen years, which had never been the carefree time many thought them to be. Reaching for patience, she waited.

"I don't know," he finally mumbled.

"Are you feeling the pressure of quarterbacking?" Certainly his was the pivotal position. Perhaps the responsibility weighed heavily on him. The boy was more important than the game. "Would you like me to ready someone else to take your place?"

B.J. shook his head. "It has nothing to do with football." He looked up the wintry afternoon sky. "Well, maybe it does, a little."

He did know what was wrong. She'd thought so. She touched his arm. "Can you tell me?"

It took B.J. a long minute to gather his thoughts. "You ever care about somebody a lot and have them disappoint you, Coach?"

She should have guessed. B.J. had naturally caught some flak for last week's loss, and Cindy hadn't been around all week during practice sessions. Pam sighed. He'd certainly picked the right person to ask his question of. "Yes, I have cared for someone who let me down badly. It hurts, I know."

Keeping his eyes on the sky, B.J. nodded. "I wish I'd never met her."

She knew how that felt, too. The whole idea of it being better to have loved and lost than never to have loved at all was a lot of nonsense. "I remember thinking the same thing at the time."

He turned to look at her, studying her face, obviously trying to determine whether she spoke from experience or if she was just humoring him. "How'd you get over it?"

"I didn't for a long while. Then, with the help of a friend, I decided that walking away from me was *his* loss, and I set out to be the best person I could be. At first I think I worked really hard to prove to him that he'd lost something pretty terrific. Then I realized I was doing it for me, not for him. A good feeling, B.J."

"I kind of felt like that, too. I mean, I wanted to be first-string quarterback and all. But I wanted to show Cindy what I could do, you know?"

"She seemed very aware of your success. Did something happen recently?" Pam was pretty sure she knew what that something was.

B.J. looked down at the ground. "She broke our date last Saturday night. I heard she went out with Bruce Watkins, who's on the basketball team. The only time she wants to be with me is when we win. I got to thinking. No team can win every week. And what happens after football season?"

Cindy would probably hang around Bruce as long as he was the star basketball player, Pam thought. But that wasn't what B.J. needed to hear. "Some people are more interested in a person's accomplishments than what that person is inside. A fair-weather friend, so to speak. Most of us are better off without that kind of person."

"Yeah, I know." B.J. scuffed at a clump of dry grass with his shoe. "But it hurts anyhow." He turned back to her. "How'd you get over that guy?"

"Something occurred that made me realize that his leaving was the best thing that could have happened to me." Her eyes drifted across the field to where Patrick sat watching, as he did nearly every practice session. Available but not intruding. She felt a warm glow inside. "And later, I was fortunate enough to find a very special man who cares for me exactly as I am, not as he wishes I were."

B.J. followed her gaze and actually smiled. "Think that'll happen to me, too?"

Pam looked into his eyes. "I'm absolutely certain it will. Let go of the hurtful relationship, B.J., and be the best you can be out on that field. The rest will fall into place, just wait and see."

He nodded, a look of determination returning to his young face. "I'm sorry if my game's been off. I'm going to try harder."

Pam stood. "I'd appreciate that. The Titans need you."

B.J. eased his helmet onto his head. "Thanks, Coach."

"Go on out there now and tell Ricky I'm sending you in to replace him. I want to see that strong arm of yours in action."

"You got it." He grinned as he began to run.

Pam strolled back toward the fifty-yard line. Young love wasn't so very different from more mature love. Always doubts, always problems.

She winced as she touched the cold metal of the hated wheelchair. Sitting down, she sent her mind back to the night she and Patrick had made love on her living room couch, certain the memory would warm her. And it did.

The loving they'd shared had been so beautiful. He'd wanted to talk more that night, about the marriage proposal he'd barked out at her when he'd first walked in. She'd firmly and patiently explained to him that she wanted badly to get through football season and through this slight relapse with MS before seriously discussing their future. Reluctantly, he'd agreed, and he'd kept his word.

He'd kept his hovering to a minimum, too. But always he was around, in the background, giving her her space but adding his support. She was beginning to get very used to his presence in her life. Maybe their marriage could work. Still, they'd known each other only three months. A little more time wouldn't hurt.

She glanced over again and caught him looking at her, that slow smile changing his face as he captured her attention. Again she thought how much she loved him. Loved looking at him, talking with him, lying beside him while the night winds whistled outside the windows and he made her feel safe and warm.

Needing to touch him, Pam jumped up to cross the field, but sat down heavily as a spasm jerked her left leg. She took a deep breath, hoping no one had noticed. As the tingling eased, she looked up and saw Patrick walking toward her, a frown wrinkling his brow. Someone had noticed.

Quickly she put on a smile. Retrieving her clipboard, she pretended great interest in the top page.

"Are you all right?" Patrick asked, stooping in front of her.

"Of course." She smiled at him. "I'm glad you came over."

He tried to choose his words carefully. "You seemed to be having a little difficulty."

"No, I just stood too quickly." She peered around him. "Look at Moose. When that boy tackles them, they stay down."

But Patrick didn't turn around to look at Moose's tackle. He kept his eyes on Pam and his frown deepened. She'd grown thinner during the past two weeks, her face even paler. Beneath the bulk of her heavy jacket, she appeared small and frail. He fervently wished she'd allow him to finish out the season for her so she could recuperate indoors, stay warm and rest more. He knew better than to mention it.

Instead, he checked his watch. Half an hour of practice left. He gave his most persuasive smile. "I've got a surprise for you after you're finished here."

Pam tugged her attention away from the somewhat awkward play she'd been watching. "Oh? And what might that be?"

"A special dinner at my house prepared by a special cook. Me."

She knew the scenario, for they'd played it frequently over the past two weeks. He'd take her to his home, build a fire, tuck a blanket around her on the couch and fix their dinner. She was fairly certain he'd never cooked so often or so elaborately as he had been lately. And she loved him for it.

Pam smiled up at him. "It just so happens I'm free."

"How nice. And afterward, I need you to test a new product I bought earlier this week. Think you could help me out?"

"Possibly. What's the product?"

He leaned down close to her. "Blue satin sheets. Very sexy, I'm told. But I really should have a second opinion."

She felt the heat from his smile spread. "Definitely."

"LET'S GO! Let's win! Let's go! Let's win!" The cheerleaders had the crowd chanting loudly, urging the Titans on.

Pam was on the Titans' bench, for she refused to use her wheelchair during the games. Her mouth was a grim line as she heard the buzzer signaling the end of the third quarter. So, at the beginning of the fourth, the Tyler Titans and the Adrian All-Stars were tied, 14–14. She released a ragged sigh as the boys changed goalposts.

This was a vital game, one they had to win. If they did, they'd be facing the Wildcats next in a play-off for the district championship. The Titans hadn't been this close to the number-one spot in years, and once again, football was the talk of the town. But "close" counted only in horseshoes and hand grenades, Pam reminded herself. And they'd have to put this one away first.

Rubbing her chilled hands together, she watched the next play, tension rippling along her shoulder muscles. Damn. A loss on that play, not a gain. Now it was thirteen to first down. Terrific. Pam rubbed a spot above her left eye and consulted her notes.

Making a decision, she signaled to Aaron. "I want you to take in a different play to B.J. Tell him to try Reverse 16, Sweep on 3. Got it?" Aaron nodded and ran onto the field. As the loudspeaker announcement about the manpower switch came on, Pam stood and moved to the chalk line.

The play didn't work and the Titans had to punt the ball away. Dejectedly, the offense jogged off the field as the defense took over. Shaking her head, Pam walked back to the bench. She saw B.J. rubbing his throwing arm and nearly groaned aloud. That was all they needed, an injury to the quarterback.

Finally a hopeful moment came with only four minutes remaining. The All-Stars fumbled and the Titans fell on the ball at the forty-five-yard line. A ways to go, but a chance. Again Pam stood, as a player approached her from behind.

"Let me go in, Coach," a voice at her side said.

She turned to look up at Ricky Travis. He had both hands planted on his hips, his stance challenging. She didn't need this right now. "You're benched, remember?"

"Come on, Coach. I can make a difference. Hasn't this gone on long enough? The team's going to lose without me." He gestured back toward the stands, where it seemed every eye was suddenly on the two of them. "They all think so, too."

It was his arrogance, his insolent attitude that did it. Had he come to her offering to help, honestly caring about the team and not his own performance, she might have given in. She certainly didn't want her own stubbornness to keep the Titans from victory.

But staring up into his overconfident blue eyes, she reminded herself that she was here to teach these boys more than merely how to play football. And it would seem that Ricky was a slow learner.

Impatiently, he shuffled his feet. "You need me out there, Coach."

He made her decision easier. "You're out of here. Go to the showers."

Heat rose in his face and his eyes narrowed. "You can't do this to me."

"I just did."

"My dad's got a lot of friends. I'm taking this to the school board."

"You do that. Meanwhile, step aside. We've got a game to play." She turned her back to Ricky and found B.J. a dozen yards away, watching her nervously. She motioned him over. When he reached her, she put her arm on his shoulder. "I want you to take it slow, no wild tosses. Play a ground game and get us close enough for Jamie to kick a field goal. No theatrics, understand?"

Obviously thrilled at not being replaced, B.J. nodded, then ran onto the field.

Pam walked back to the bench, hearing the murmurs of the crowd. Many guessed what had happened, especially after Ricky tramped off in a huff, heading for the locker room. She could sense disapproval of her decision, but she couldn't let it get to her. She was right, dammit.

Her legs felt frozen and she was trembling with nerves. She sat down gingerly, praying for strength. The whistle blew and she watched the next play. A gain of four. Not bad.

Glancing over her shoulder, her eyes searched for Patrick. At last she found him. He nodded to her and gave her a thumbs-up gesture. He'd long since stopped trying to persuade her to change her mind about Ricky's suspension. He also knew what she was trying to bring about with B.J., and heartily approved. She hadn't known until quite recently how much his approval meant to her.

Her eyes on the clock, she returned her attention to the game. This time they'd managed to make a first down. A field goal from the thirty-five was risky for Jamie. A gain of five more would be comfortable, ten would be perfect. The two-minute warning sounded and B.J. came running to her side. Pam shut out the sounds of the crowd around her and concentrated on her quarterback.

"How we doing, Coach?" B.J. asked, reaching for the drink offered by one of the assistants.

"Fine, just fine," Pam told him. "Just don't get careless or cocky now. A little closer, that's all we need." Jamie ambled over, and she gestured with her arm to include him in their conversation. "How's your leg—loose and limber?"

"You bet," Jamie answered.

"B.J.'s going to get you another five at least, right, B.J.?"

He adjusted his helmet. "We're going to try."

"Two plays, B.J.," she reminded him, "easy handoffs. Use your time-outs and watch the clock. Then we kick."

"Right." He ran on out and Pam resumed her seat.

Two quick plays and they were six yards closer. Not impossible, Pam thought as the boys went into field-goal position. Absently, she rubbed her hands, tingling with cold and moving toward numbness. Less than a minute remaining. She coughed, feeling the heaviness deep in her chest. She could also feel the tension in the air as Jamie lined up. Watching intently, Pam held her breath.

Nice handoff; the kick steady and straight. And good! The referee signaled the field goal and the score shifted to Titans 17 and All-Stars 14. The Tyler fans roared their approval.

Pam let her shoulders sag with relief. Thirty seconds remained in the game, but the All-Stars had lost their drive. When the gunshot sounded, the Titan fans erupted in a huge cheer. They would be in next week's play-offs.

Feeling more tired than she could remember in a long while, Pam nonetheless stood congratulating her boys as they drifted in past her, their smiles broad. Some of the guys had taken to hugging her lately, even lifting her off the ground in their exuberance, a show of affection that warmed her. She saw Patrick trying to make his way through the crowd to her and waited.

B.J. came over to Pam, his face pleased but serious. "I want to thank you for not replacing me, Coach," he said.

"I knew you were the best man for the job, B.J. You've earned your position. No thanks are necessary."

"Still, I want to thank you. No matter what happens on Thanksgiving Day in the play-offs, I owe you."

Pam felt a rush of tears and blinked them away. Her emotions had been entirely too close to the surface lately. "Thank you for saying that. It means a lot to me."

B.J. turned and nearly bumped into Cindy Crane. The cute little cheerleader, seemingly confident of her charms, rushed to give him a big hug.

"You were wonderful, B.J.," she drawled. "Are we going out tonight?"

Standing somewhat stiffly, B.J. removed her hands from his waist. "I think you'd better go find Bruce. I've got another date." His face set, he watched hers fall. Angrily, she turned and flounced away. B.J. watched her walk off, then swung back to Pam, who'd witnessed the whole scene.

Suddenly, he grinned. "You know, you were right. It does feel good."

Smiling back at him, she nodded. B.J. ran after his teammates as Pam gathered up her things.

"Where's your chair, lady?" Patrick asked, coming alongside.

"It's around. How'd you like the game?"

"Pretty terrific, like the Titans' coach. The play-offs, right?"

"Looks like it." She rubbed the back of her neck wearily. "We have our work cut out for us this coming week."

"I can help, if you like."

"We'll see. You want to wait here while I go change?"

"Sure. Don't take too long. I'm hungry."

Straddling the bench, he watched her move toward the locker room. She was limping slightly, but trying to hide it. And her shoulders seemed to droop with fatigue. Thanksgiving was next Thursday, just short of a week away. He prayed she'd get through without further problems.

Waving to people he knew, Patrick watched the stadium slowly empty. Pam was one determined woman. Her determination alone had carried her this far. After next week, he would absolutely insist she do nothing but rest and eat and rest some more.

He stared up at the clear night sky. It was cold enough to see his breath, but at least it was dry. They'd had no rain and only a smattering of snow, which hadn't lasted long. He was glad of that, for Pam's sake. He worried about her being outside so much. But he'd refrained from hovering, one of the hardest restraints he'd ever put on himself. Thank goodness, her job was nearly over for this year.

Basketball season was just beginning, and he was busier than ever. However, perhaps during Christmas vacation, he'd take Pam away for a week. Someplace sunny and warm where they could spend long lazy days on the beach and long loving nights in the same bed without one of them having to rush off in the early-morning hours. He was mighty tired of that.

And he thought of the ring he'd bought for her. He hadn't mentioned marriage again, but it had never been far from his mind. Soon, when her mind was free of football, he'd be able to pin her down as to a date. Then they'd—

"Hey, Coach! Coach, come quick!"

Patrick swung around and saw Moose, wearing only his football pants and shoes, at the arch leading to the lockers. Jumping up, he began to run. "What's the matter?"

"It's Coach Casals," Moose called out. "She's collapsed."

CHAPTER ELEVEN

SHE LOOKED so pale lying on the cumbersome hospital bed, her small frame covered with a crisp white sheet. Seated in a chair nearby, Patrick kept watch over Pam as she slept, wishing there was something more he could do.

But there wasn't.

Dr. Phelps had left minutes ago. The disturbing conversation they'd had still rang in Patrick's ears. She'd pushed herself too hard, George had said. He'd warned her this could happen. She'd had the predicted relapse and was suffering from exhaustion and a respiratory infection. How long it would last was anyone's guess.

He'd put her on antibiotics and anti-inflammatory medication, and had given her something so she'd rest. Something quite mild, George had explained. She'd been so agitated when Patrick brought her in, after that fearful moment when he'd rushed to the Titans' locker room and found her on the floor, unable to rise on her own. She hadn't wanted to be taken to the hospital, but he'd insisted. She'd been frighteningly still on the drive in, which had increased Patrick's anxiety. Usually Pam was so active, so animated.

He picked up her hand, and bent his head as he clasped her cool, dry fingers with his. The prayer he sent up was heartfelt and filled with fear and uneasiness. She had to be all right. She simply had to be.

Odd how he'd read all the information he could gather on MS recently and had felt himself as knowledgeable as any layman could be. Yet seeing Pam like this had still hit him hard. Not nearly as hard as the boys on the football team. There'd been no hiding the truth after her collapse. Many had insisted on going along to the hospital. Once there, once George had taken over, Patrick had explained Pam's disease to the players the best way he knew how—honestly and simply. He'd also told them how much she'd hate their sympathy, but that she could use their moral support. To a man, they'd been shocked, but in total agreement.

When the doctor came out and explained that Pam was resting comfortably and not in immediate danger, they'd finally left. Patrick was certain that by now half of Tyler knew about Pam's condition, and the other half would know by morning. She would be upset about that, but she would have to accept it, as she'd had to accept so many other unpleasant things.

A nurse walked in on silent rubber soles and Patrick moved aside. She took Pam's pulse, then marked the information on a chart. Her movements brisk and efficient, she inserted a thermometer under Pam's arm, waited for the reading, then made note of that as well.

"How long will the sedative keep her asleep?" he asked.

The nurse checked a chart for medicinal information. "She's not really deeply under. She'll be groggy and probably sliding in and out of sleep for most of the night."

Thanking her, he watched her leave, then resumed his vigil.

George had said Pam's vital signs were strong and that as far as he could see, there'd been no permanent damage as yet. Of course, she'd have to remain for a while in the hospital, for several reasons—for the complete bed rest she needed, to clear up her infection and so they could monitor her closely. She was not going to take that news well, Patrick was certain.

On the drive in, he'd asked if he should phone her father, and she'd been adamant that he not contact her family. This was temporary, she'd insisted, and to be expected from time to time. There was no point in alarming her father, when she'd be out and about in no time. Patrick had listened and followed her wishes, but he'd privately wondered just how fast she'd pull out of this.

Again he took her hand, and this time felt a response as her fingers gripped his lightly. But she didn't open her eyes; the drug was still working on her. He wished she would so he could talk with her, if only briefly. He knew she needed the rest, but he wanted to reassure her that he was here, that there was no need to worry. Worry, he was certain, had contributed greatly to her relapse.

The profile in one of the books he'd read of a typical MS patient had described Pam perfectly: usually a very bright person, an overachiever, Type A personality with a tendency toward independence and perfectionism. Patrick wondered idly if he could persuade Pam to slow down, to hand over some of her concerns and let him take care of them. Then he remembered what she'd told him about quality of life and hating to compromise, and realized she wouldn't likely want to change.

Perhaps he could ease her mind if he assured her he loved her as she was, and that, though he hated seeing her have a setback, he also understood her need to live as normal a life as possible. And for Pam, pushing herself to achieve and excel was normal. He was the one who'd had to change his thinking and adjust. He had no choice. If he didn't, he'd lose her.

Patrick heard a soft sound from the bed. Her head had moved on the pillow slightly, as if she were fighting to come back to him. He squeezed her fingers and waited.

Pam struggled to lift her heavy eyelids. She blinked to clear her vision, recognizing that she was in a hospital bed. Slowly she shifted her gaze and found Patrick close beside her, holding her hand and looking worried. "Hi," she managed and tried for a smile.

"Hi, yourself. Feeling any better?"

"I feel a little floaty, like I've had too much to drink."

"George gave you a mild sedative, mostly because you didn't want to let him admit you, and you need the rest."

She licked her dry lips. "I remember." And she did. She remembered falling in the locker room, the frightened expressions on the faces of the boys who'd tried to help her up, only to find she couldn't stand. Then Patrick's anxious face and the mad dash to the hospital. "How long have I been here?"

"Couple of hours."

"Does everyone . . . did you tell them . . ."

"Yes. I had to, Pam. But it's all right. The boys understand."

She turned her head, closing her eyes, fighting a groan of frustration. Exactly what she hadn't wanted. Why couldn't she have held this off just one more week?

Patrick saw a lone tear escape from the corner of her eye, and he raised his hand to brush it away. "They're not censuring you. They're only concerned about you."

"What about Miss Mackie?"

"I haven't talked with her yet. But I plan to." It was important that Pam know there was no hiding the truth now. "Please understand that their knowing won't be a problem. You have the respect and admiration of the whole school board. The whole town, for that matter."

Pam turned back to look at him. "I wanted to finish out the season. I would have told them then. What about the play-offs? I've let everyone down."

He squeezed her hand. "You haven't. You've taken a fourth-rate team and made them into championship contenders. The Titans at this time next week will be number one. And you did it."

She shook her head. "No. *They* did it."

"With your help and guidance."

"But they need work before Thursday and I—"

"And you're going to stay right here until George says it's okay for you to leave. I want your permission to let me supervise the team's practice next week."

What choice did she have? Pam nodded, hating the fact that she needed him, needed anyone. But the team was the important factor here. And Patrick could handle them.

He knew how hard it was for her to relinquish control. Perching on the edge of her bed, he leaned down and smiled into her unhappy eyes. "I promise you I'll do everything just as I know you'd want it done."

Pam took an unsteady breath. "I know you will."

"I wish I could get in this bed with you, just hold you."

She almost smiled at that. "I wish you could, too."

He brushed his lips across hers, gently at first, then almost fiercely. She'd given him one hell of a scare and he wasn't over it yet. He pulled back reluctantly. "I love you," Patrick told her.

"Still, after all this?"

"After all this and more. I told you before, it's not easy shaking a Kelsey loose once one gets a grip on you."

"I'm beginning to believe you."

"That's good, because I'm with you to stay." He kissed her again. "Now, you get some rest and I'll be back in the morning."

Her eyelids threatened to close, but she had one more question. "You didn't call my father, did you?"

"No. I did call Rosemary, but she wasn't home. I'll call her again when I leave."

"Thank you, Patrick."

He leaned down again, nearly nose to nose with her. "Say it."

"I love you," Pam whispered.

"Keep saying it, because I need to hear it a lot. And keep remembering it."

She smiled as her eyes drifted shut. "I will."

Patrick stayed a few moments longer, until he was sure she was asleep. Then he quietly left the room.

Walking briskly toward the elevator, he remembered the bottle of wine he'd had chilling for their private little after-game dinner by the fire. Well, Pam would be home soon, if he had anything to say about it. The wine would keep.

PATRICK STOOD in the weak sunshine, a brisk wintry breeze ruffling his hair, and waited for the boys to gather around him before the week's first practice session. They had only three days to get into top form. They'd had questions about Pam and he'd answered them vaguely. Now he needed to get more specific, to relieve their anxiety and to inspire them to play the best ball they'd ever played.

He swung his gaze around the loosely formed semicircle and began. "Most everyone here knows by now that Coach Casals is in Tyler General and that she has MS. As I've told many of you, she's had a relapse and is out of remission. She needs lots of rest and no worries. I was with her this morning, and she's coming along fine. And now, *I* need your help."

He let his words sink in before continuing. "There isn't a man on this team who hasn't been helped by her coaching. She's worked very hard and so have all of you. You're facing a championship game Thursday. She knows you can win and so do I. You need to believe it, too."

Patrick cleared his throat around a sudden lump of emotion. "Coach Casals brought you along carefully and helped turn you into champs." He looked at B.J. "She saw your insecurities, taught you how to overcome them and showed you how to believe in yourself." He saw B.J. nod.

"Her training methods aren't all that unusual, but they're better because she genuinely cares, for each one of you." His gaze moved to settle on Ricky Travis. "Even for those of you too stubborn, too selfish and too insensitive to realize she was teaching you more than how to play football, more than how to win." Patrick saw Ricky flush and drop his gaze, and wondered if his remarks had hit home.

"You see, she was trying to teach you how to survive and be a winner in the game of life, which is a much tougher game than football. And she was also teaching by example, because not only did she work hard, overcoming all kinds of odds to become an Olympic champion, but she's fought hard to beat her MS, to not let the disease get her down."

He saw he had their total attention, so he moved in for the last word he would say on the subject. "I'm not here to replace her. I'm only here to supervise in her absence. I want you to practice exactly as if she were present. But there is something I want you to do. I want you to remember all she taught you and go out there on Thanksgiving Day and win. And then I'd like you to present her with the game ball. I can't think of anything that would make her get well faster.''

Several of the boys' faces registered determination, while others nodded their heads. Patrick felt proud of the Titans at the moment. ''Okay, let's get out on the field and go to work.''

He watched them put on their helmets and jog away. Studying Pam's clipboard of notes, he walked over to the bench on the sidelines, hoping he'd said the right things, the things that would inspire them to win.

His visit to Pam this morning had been encouraging. She was undergoing physical therapy for her legs, and doing hand exercises as well. Her cough was still with her, but not as persistent. She was cooperative and was getting lots of rest, even eating better. Her spirits were up, he could tell, because she was pestering him, Dr. Phelps and anyone she could pin down as to when she would be released. George was maddeningly evasive, she'd complained to Patrick, and he'd smiled to himself. Still, he was aware that Pam couldn't be held down too long.

She'd been scared to death of the school's reaction and that of the townspeople. When he told her she was the number-one topic all over town—at his folks' boardinghouse, at the Hair Affair and at Tyler High—she'd moaned aloud. But when he'd explained that she had the wholehearted support of everyone, from her players' parents all the way to Judson Ingalls, she could scarcely believe it.

Miss Mackie had been to see her on Sunday and had reassured her that her job was not in jeopardy, that all anyone wanted was for her to get well quickly. Pam had brightened considerably after that visit.

And there'd been others. Rosemary, of course, was practically her personal therapist, popping in frequently to chat as well. Tisha had brought her a huge blue-and-gold Go Titans! button, which she'd laughingly pinned on Pam's hospital gown. Marge from the diner had brought her a whole carrot cake, Pam's favorite, which she'd shared with the nurses. The cheerleaders had dropped in to show her pom-poms they'd made for Thursday's game, and the room was filled with flowers from half a dozen families of students. And Patrick's grandmother had walked in with several of her quilting ladies for a chatty visit. Martha had confided that she had a special quilt for Pam.

A private person by nature, Pam had been surprised yet pleased by the outpouring of affection. Through it all, Patrick had stood to one side watching over her, not letting her get too tired. And each evening, he'd stayed until she fell asleep. Yawning into his fist, Patrick decided he, too, would be glad when she was released.

Looking up at the sound of loud, angry voices, he saw Ricky Travis, B.J. and one of the linebackers in a tussle. Emotions and tempers were running high, he knew, and the pressure to win wasn't easy for the boys to handle.

Jumping up, Patrick went out onto the field to try to settle the dispute. "Okay, fellows, break it up."

Though the three had already been pulled apart by their teammates, B.J. still glared at Ricky, who stood with both fists clenched.

"What's this all about?" Patrick asked.

No one spoke, until finally Ricky dropped his angry stance. "Nothing, Coach," he said, turning away. "Just a friendly shoving match."

"Is that right, B.J.?" Patrick wanted to know.

"Yeah, it's okay, Coach."

Patrick watched the two boys walk off, wondering just what had caused their confrontation. Deciding to let it go for now, he called out the next play and stood back to watch.

PAM LAY RESTLESSLY in bed. The sun outside her window shone brightly, though she knew it was probably a cold day. Wednesday, the afternoon before the big game, and here she was still confined to her hospital bed. Patrick was probably out on the field right now, putting the team through their paces, doing everything possible to get them ready for the play-offs.

Oh, how she wished she could be there.

She was better. She knew she was. Not back in remission yet, but well on her way. But George Phelps was stubbornly keeping her here. For her own good, Pam knew, but that didn't make it any easier to bear. She just might be released by the weekend, he'd tossed out to her this morning, provided she behaved until then. Fat chance she had of misbehaving.

Picking up her rubber ball, she exercised her fingers slowly, the way she'd been taught by Rosemary. Her coordination was good, the tingling and numbing sensations minimal, her vision rarely clouding. And her speech had lost that vague slurring quality. Her cough was nearly gone. She'd probably recover even faster if George would allow her to practice walking more. But he was a firm believer in easy as you go, in slow progress rather than swift. Pam wished she didn't have such an impatient nature.

Wishing also that the hours would pass more quickly, she closed her eyes and willed herself to take a nap, hoping that she'd awaken to find Patrick in her room, fresh from practice and eager to tell her all about the boys. But before she could fall asleep, she heard the door open.

It wasn't Patrick coming in with a gentle smile, but rather his mother. Anna Kelsey, one hand in the pocket of the white lab coat she wore as Dr. Phelp's receptionist, walked over and bent down to give Pam a hug.

"You're looking wonderful," Anna said, her blue eyes shining from behind her gold-rimmed glasses. "George tells me you're making great progress."

"That's more than George tells me," Pam said, pushing the button that elevated the head of her bed.

Anna dismissed George's reticence with a wave of her hand. "He's the cautious type, like most doctors." She held out a paper bag. "I wanted to bring you something and Patrick told me you love chocolate-covered raisins. It seemed an odd gift, but..."

"It's a terrific gift," Pam said with a smile. "They're my favorites. Thank you."

Anna pulled the lone chair closer to the bed. "Hospital food isn't much, I know. I hope you're eating it anyway."

"I am. I figure the only way I'm going to get George to let me out of here is to do everything he says." Her hand shook a little, Pam noticed as she set her gift aside. They'd about run out of small talk and she was uncomfortable, wondering what Patrick's mother was going to say now that she knew about her illness. Perhaps the best defense was to take the offense. "I suppose it was a shock, learning I had MS."

"Patrick told Johnny and me several weeks ago."

"He did?"

"Yes. In practically the same breath, he told us he loved you and wanted to marry you."

That, she hadn't even considered. Nervously Pam pleated the edge of the sheet with her fingers. "I told Patrick that his family, loving him the way you all do, would naturally want someone for him who is healthy and whole. And I understand that."

Anna reached over and took hold of her hand, stopping the restive movements. Squeezing her fingers, she waited until Pam looked at her. "Do you remember the afternoon we talked on our back porch?"

"The day I'd fallen, yes."

"Then perhaps you'll remember what I told you about Patrick—that even when he was a youngster people noticed him, because whatever he did, he did with such intensity. When he played ball, he gave it all he had. When he studied, he put everything into his efforts. I always knew that when he fell in love—and he's thirty-four, you know, so he's taken his sweet time about it—he'd love that woman with the same intensity, the same wholehearted approach. When a man like that waits until his mid-thirties to find the right person, I don't for a moment think he could be persuaded to change his mind. Nor would his father or I try to do that."

Pam's heart began to hope, but she was so afraid to trust that fluttering feeling. "I know you must have your misgivings...."

Again, Anna made a dismissive gesture. "Nothing is certain in this world, Pam. Adjusting your life to living with another person can be difficult, and marriages really aren't made in heaven. But when two mature people decide to marry, the odds are better. When we married, I was nineteen and Johnny barely twenty. Our families had lots of misgivings. And yet, here we are."

She had to say it, had to get it out. "But we have an additional obstacle. My health will always have to be a consideration, and at times it will be a real problem for both of us."

Anna nodded. "Yes, I know. Patrick loaned me the books you'd given him and I read them all. Despite my working in the medical field all these years, I didn't know that much specifically about MS. I do now. I certainly don't discount the seriousness of your illness, and yes, some aspects of your lives will be restricted. But I'm going to tell you what Johnny and I told Patrick. If you really love each other, whether you have five years together or fifty, you need to be together."

There was no way Pam could have stopped the tears that flowed freely as she clutched Anna's hand. "Thank you. I want you to know I do love Patrick, more than I ever thought I could love someone. I'm going to try very hard to make him happy."

Anna blinked back a rush of her own tears as she handed Pam a tissue. "I have no doubt you will." She watched Pam blot her face dry and decided to change the subject, to allow Pam to regain her control. "Has my mother been to see you yet?"

Pam smiled. "Yes. She came on Sunday with several of her lady friends. She told me she had a special quilt for me. I've seen her work and it's beautiful."

"Actually, the gift is for both of you. Mother's been waiting patiently to present Patrick with his wedding-ring quilt for years."

"But how..."

"How did she know? We all knew, long before Patrick told us." Anna reached to grip Pam's hand again. "Since you've come into his life, Patrick's changed. He's more patient, less critical, happier, more loving. It wasn't hard to guess that he was in love." Glancing at her watch, Anna stood. "I ran over to visit you on my break—George's office is really busy, but I wanted to see you. I have to get back now. I'm awfully glad you're doing so well."

"Mrs. Kelsey, you can't know how much your visit means to me. I've been so worried...."

Anna bent to kiss her future daughter-in-law's cheek. "Don't be. Worry's bad for MS. And we want you out of here just as quickly as possible."

"Thank you."

At the door, Anna paused and looked back. "Patrick mentioned that he likes the idea of a Christmas wedding. What do you think?" Noticing that she'd caught Pam totally off guard, she smiled. "Think about it, and I'll see you soon." She closed the door behind her.

Stunned, Pam stared at the spot where Anna Kelsey had stood, wondering if she'd dreamed the whole visit. To be so openly accepted by Patrick's family surprised and thrilled her. In her wildest dreams, she hadn't expected such warmth.

Perhaps the future held more than she'd dared hope.

SHE SLEPT then, a dreamless sleep that helped heal her body and quiet her mind. She probably would have slept longer except sounds started seeping through—the opening of a door and heavy footsteps. Pam blinked and found herself staring up into the hesitant blue eyes of Ricky Travis.

Clearing her throat, she gave him a smile as she hit the button to raise her bed. "Hello, Ricky."

"Hi, Coach." He shuffled his big feet restlessly. "How you doing?"

"I'm doing much better. How'd practice go today?"

"Okay." With one hand, he grabbed the chair, swung it around and straddled it, leaning his arms on the back. "I wanted to come see you. Alone without the others."

"Yes?" Their last exchange hadn't been pleasant, and Pam couldn't help wondering what was on Ricky's mind.

"I've been wrong . . . and—and selfish. A couple of the guys, they talked with me today." Self-consciously, he touched a dark bruise on his left cheek. "They made me see I've only been hurting myself. I want to tell you I'm sorry."

Pam knew how difficult this admission must be for Ricky. "I'm glad you came, Ricky, and I accept your apology. You did hurt yourself, and the team."

"I know. I've learned my lesson, Coach." He met her eyes finally. "I want to ask a favor of you."

No, she wouldn't reinstate him despite his apology. Not now, not this late in the season, after he'd held out all this time. It wouldn't be fair to B.J. She braced herself for his request. "Yes, what is it?"

"I want to play backup for B.J. I think he's going to be all right, and so does Coach Kelsey. We talked a while ago. But just in case B.J. gets hurt, I want your permission to go in."

A piece of humble pie. She was surprised, and pleased. "Yes, Ricky. We'd be happy to have you as backup. And I want you to know, I'm proud of your decision to make the offer."

The boy nodded, somewhat embarrassed, but nonetheless pleased. He stood then, having run out of things to say. He replaced the chair and shoved both hands into his pockets. "I wish you could be there tomorrow. It won't be the same."

"Thanks. I wish I could, too. I'll be listening to the radio and pulling for all of you."

"We'll be thinking about you, too." He shuffled toward the door, obviously uncomfortable being in a hospital atmosphere. "Bye."

Pam smiled at him. "Bye, Ricky." She let out a sigh. Would wonders never cease? She was naturally curious how Ricky's change of heart had come about, though she thought she knew. That bruise on his cheek looked fresh and tender. Perhaps a couple of the boys had decided it was time Ricky grew up. They knew that at play-off time especially, it was vital everyone pull together, and Ricky hadn't done that in quite a while.

Whatever had caused his capitulation, she was glad he'd come around. Now they had a backup quarterback, though she hoped it wouldn't be necessary for Patrick to send Ricky in. B.J. deserved to play the game out.

A quick knock on the door was followed by a deep voice announcing dinnertime. Recognizing the owner, Pam began to smile.

Patrick came in, carrying a large white bag. "Ready for dinner?" he asked, removing his jacket and tossing it onto the chair.

"Junk food," Pam said, recognizing the aroma and sitting upright. "I love it. Did you get permission or must we duck under the covers to eat?" Her mouth watered just thinking of something other than the bland hospital food.

Patrick leaned down and kissed her soundly. "I asked George if you had any dietary restrictions and he said no, so here you go." He pulled over her tray table, spread a napkin and set the fat sandwich out for her. Next came the fries and a double chocolate milk shake.

"Are you trying to fatten me up, sir?"

"You bet I am." He sat down on the end of her bed and spread his own dinner in his lap. "I might as well get fat with you."

Chewing, Pam studied his flat stomach. "Not much danger there. So what's happening in the outside world? I feel so out of touch in here."

Patrick shrugged. "I talked with my friend, Brick Bauer, earlier."

"The police sergeant?"

"Right. It seems they found a man's gold wedding ring with the mysterious body. The date inscribed on it is 1941."

"Whoops! There goes your Indian theory. So they think it's a man then?"

Patrick shook his head. "Not necessarily. Brick says the bones are fairly small."

"Is there some significance to the year 1941?"

"Grandma tells me it's the year Judson and Margaret Ingalls were married."

"Oh, no."

"Of course, the police haven't released all their findings yet. It's taking so long because the body's been buried all these years."

Pam shuddered at the thought. "Let's talk about something more pleasant. How'd the practice go today?"

"Good." He sipped his milk shake. "The boys are all keyed up and ready for the Wildcats."

"Tell me, did we have any little skirmishes on the field today, any testy little punching bouts?"

"Yeah. How'd you know?"

Between bites, Pam told him about Ricky's visit, his apology and his offer to play backup.

"So he came to apologize. Looks like you're back to performing miracles, Coach." He paused to munch on a fry. "Ricky's not a bad kid. I think it's a case of everyone telling him what a great football player he is. After a while, he began to believe the team couldn't get along without him, and that everyone would put up with his inconsiderate behavior just as long as he played well. It took you to show him that football games—and life—don't work that way."

She shrugged off the compliment. "He'd have probably learned it sooner or later. What surprised me was that the boys sort of dented his face to drive the point home."

"Why should that surprise you? Those guys are nuts about you."

Pam set down the last third of her sandwich, realizing her eyes had been bigger than her stomach. "I'm pretty nuts about them, too. I'd give anything to be there tomorrow."

Patrick glanced out the window. "They predict a sunny day, but very cold. I doubt if George'll let you go." He met her eyes, hating to dash her hopes. "You don't want another setback, right?"

Pam sighed deeply. "No. But I'm sure getting anxious to leave this place. Everyone's been nice, but enough already. I talked with Rosemary today. She's working on George to let me go home if I promise to stay in bed. And she'll do therapy right there at the house."

Finishing, Patrick gathered up the containers and napkins, stuffed them inside the sack and tossed the remains in the wastebasket. Returning to her bedside, he sat on the bed and leaned close to her. "How are you feeling today?"

"Right now? Full, contented and happy to see you. But I think I need a kiss."

He smiled, then obliged her, his lips lingering long and lovingly over hers. He brushed a strand of hair from her face, then plunged into the subject very much on his mind. "We need to talk."

"Yes, we do. Your mother was here today."

"Really? What did she have to say?"

"Oh, not much. Something about love and marriage and a wedding-ring quilt."

His slow grin lit up his face. "So Mom did my work for me. Good. How about a Christmas wedding?"

Pam took his hand, her eyes serious. "Patrick, are you sure? This hospital scene, my fall, the drive here, all of it would become a part of your life. You could get awfully weary of caring for someone who—"

"Someone I love. No, I won't, and yes, I'm sure. I want you, only you. And I don't want you thinking it's a sacrifice on my part to marry you. It would be a privilege, an honor. Because without you, I'd be only going through the motions. Playacting, not living. *You* are the one who makes my life worth living." He saw her eyes fill and moved closer. "Pam, marry me. I love you so much."

Because she was too moved to speak, she shifted in his arms, burying her face in his neck. Her soft mumble was muffled in his throat.

"What did you say?" Patrick asked.

Trembling, Pam eased back and met his eyes. "I said yes."

He grinned then, the happiness bubbling forth. Pulling her back into his arms, he held her tightly to him, rocking her while he smoothed her hair. "You won't be sorry. I'm going to make you so happy you won't know what hit you."

"I just hope *you* won't be sorry."

"I won't be. I read in one of those books that the happier an MS patient is, the more loving a relationship she has, the longer her periods of remission last. And then, there's something else: no symptoms while you're pregnant. You do want children, don't you, Pam?"

Everything was happening awfully fast, almost overwhelming her. Yet a foolish smile kept forming on her face, and her heart beat with something resembling joy. "Do I want your children? Oh, yes. I very much do."

He kissed her then, and the kiss was filled with promise, with commitment and love. Winding her arms around Patrick, Pam let him transport her, let the sweet magic make the world go away, let her love for him shine through.

The kiss went on and on, so long that they heard nothing, saw nothing but each other. Until they heard a wild burst of applause that seemed very near. Breaking apart, Patrick pulled back and Pam peered around him.

Almost the entire football squad of Tyler High School stood at the foot of her bed—grinning, applauding and whistling their approval.

CHAPTER TWELVE

"HEY, COACH KELSEY," Moose called out. "This what you mean by moral support?" He got the expected laugh and more applause.

Patrick felt himself turning a dusty shade of rose as he got to his feet and stepped back from the bed. "Nice of you to drop in, fellows."

Pam was feeling too good to be annoyed. "Hi." She waved them closer and waited while they gathered around, a couple easing onto the foot of her bed, several more leaning on the bed railing while the rest lined up along the sides. "It's good to see you guys."

"You, too, Coach," B.J. said. From behind his back, he brought out a cellophane-wrapped bouquet of pink carnations. "These are from all of us." Shyly he handed them to her.

"How lovely." Pam took the flowers and laid them in the crook of her arm. "I'll get the nurse to put them in water."

"First time a football coach ever got flowers, I'll bet," Jamie said, grinning.

"Nah, I get them all the time," Patrick couldn't resist adding. Again, everyone laughed.

"So, you ready for tomorrow?" Pam looked into each of their young faces in turn, hoping they were.

"That hamstring okay, Moose? B.J., is your arm in shape?"

"You bet, Coach."

"We're going to cream those guys."

"I'm sure you will," she told them.

"Did Ricky stop in, by any chance?" B.J. asked hesitantly.

"Yes," Pam answered. "He was here. He asked to play backup, just in case. What do you think of that?"

B.J. glanced over his shoulder at a couple of the guys and saw them nod. "Yeah, we heard."

"Thanks for helping straighten out his thinking," she added, and saw their knowing grins.

"He couldn't come tonight on account of he's taking piano lessons," Moose said. Several of the guys snickered.

"Piano lessons?" Patrick interjected. "Ricky Travis?"

"Yeah," Moose went on. "Ricky's mom wants him to be well-rounded, she said. Nora Gates, the lady from Gates Department Store, also gives piano lessons, so that's where he is. If he doesn't show up for his lessons, he can't play sports, his mom told him. Ricky's *not* happy."

"Ricky used to take lessons years ago, I remember," Patrick went on. "You know, fellows, it's good to have interests other than sports."

"Yeah, Coach," Bubba chimed in. "I'm going to take up the flute." At that, everyone laughed heartily, considering Bubba's huge hands.

"I sure wish I could be there with you tomorrow," Pam said wistfully, bringing their thoughts back to tomorrow's game. "I hope you know I'll be glued to the radio."

"They're not even going to let you out for a Thanksgiving dinner, Coach?" Moose asked incredulously. "That stinks. Want us to sneak you in some turkey after the game?"

"I'll take care of her dinner, Moose," Patrick told him, moving closer to Pam's side and taking her hand. "But thanks."

They stayed a few minutes longer; then, as if by prior arrangement, they each moved to the bed and gave her a hug before filing out.

"Thanks again for the flowers." Pam watched them go, blinking back the tears. "They deserve to win," she told Patrick unnecessarily. "They've worked so hard."

"Don't worry," he said, moving to take her in his arms. "They will. Now then, where were we when we were so rudely interrupted?" And he touched his mouth to hers again.

PAM FIDDLED with the dials of the radio Rosemary had set up for her on her bedside stand. It was an hour before kickoff and the pregame interviews were going on, the announcer talking with the Wildcats' coach, who was predicting their victory, naturally.

Bunching her pillow more comfortably behind her back, Pam gazed out the window at the clear blue sky. A sellout crowd would watch the game, and those who were home putting the finishing touches on Thanksgiving dinner were likely tuned to the radio. It seemed the whole town of Tyler was riveted on the play-off game. Pam wished with all her heart that she could be there with her Titans.

She had much to be grateful for, she reminded herself, and she shouldn't keep asking for more. Leaning closer to the radio, she heard the sportscaster begin to interview the Wildcats' quarterback, just as the door to her room swung open.

Her face lit up as she saw Patrick enter, then it registered surprise. "Why aren't you on the field?" she asked.

"Because I've come to get you first." He tossed her blue slacks and gold shirt onto the foot of the bed. "Get dressed, Coach. Your team's waiting for you."

"You're serious? I can go to the game?" Pam threw aside her covers, excited at the thought.

"Yes, ma'am. I talked with George and he said I could take you provided you stayed warm and remained on the bench. You promise?"

"I promise." Testing her footing to be sure she experienced no sign of numbness as she walked, Pam smiled up at him. "I'll just be a minute." Grabbing her clothes, she went into the bathroom.

Patrick drew in a large, satisfied breath. It had taken some doing to convince George, but with Rosemary's help, he'd done it. What he hadn't yet told Pam was that he also had permission to take her to the boardinghouse for the usual huge Kelsey Thanksgiving Day dinner afterward. He'd promised her doctor he'd have her back in her hospital bed by eight. And if all went well, she'd be released Monday.

Removing her heavy corduroy jacket from the closet, Patrick waited impatiently. He hadn't yet told the team, and he could hardly wait to see their faces when he and Pam arrived.

UNWILLING TO TAKE a chance, Patrick wouldn't allow her to walk. But Pam didn't mind, not this time. It meant too much to her to be able to attend the game. Besides, being carried in his powerful arms wasn't exactly a hardship.

The boys were already on the field when they arrived at the top of the ramp. Patrick walked with her straight to the Titan's bench and, as soon as the first player spotted them, the word quickly spread. They turned then, one by one, and began to applaud Pam's arrival.

As Patrick set her down on her feet, they kept on cheering. The Titan fans picked it up and began applauding and whistling. Pam's eyes were suspiciously bright, but her smile was firmly in place as she waved to the crowd, then thanked her team. Finally she sat down on the bench with Patrick beside her.

Pam squeezed his hand. "Win, lose or draw, I'll never forget this. Thank you."

They all stood for the national anthem, followed by the toss of the coin. The Titans elected to receive and the game began.

By all standards, it was hardly a thrilling game, Patrick thought. But then, as many radio listeners

were later to comment, few one-sided football games
are. The thrill in this play-off game lay in the fact that
it was the first time in sixteen years that the Titans had
won the championship and been first in their division. It lay in the fact that a team that last year had
finished near the bottom, finished soundly at the top.
And it lay in the fact that a female coach had pulled
off the miracle of the year, as far as Tyler was concerned.

When the final shot was fired, the score was Titans
34, Wildcats 14. Feeling incredibly proud, Patrick
watched the boys on the field jump and pound one
another, hardly able to believe the scoreboard. Their
teammates on the bench ran out to meet them as they
returned, hand-slapping and back-patting one another.

And the fans exploded with delight. Miss Mackie,
in an uncharacteristic burst of exuberance, threw her
black felt hat into the air, as did dozens of other onlookers. Judson Ingalls, setting his dignity aside and
wearing a huge Go Titans! button, gleefully pulled the
smiling Tisha Olsen into his arms. Marge Peterson,
looking pleased to have a day off, hugged her companion, George Phelps, who seemed happier than
most folks ever remembered seeing him. Martha Bauer
and her quilting ladies waved blue and gold pom-poms
and cheered like teenagers. The two busloads of
Wildcat fans who'd journeyed to Tyler for the game
and the Wildcat players and coach seemed the only
people in the stadium with glum faces.

Folded in Patrick's arms, Pam couldn't stop smiling as he spun her into a bear hug. "You did it, lady," he said in a loud voice. But even that sound was drowned out as the band at the end of the field broke into the Titans' fight song.

Then there were large, callused hands reaching for Pam, and suddenly she was hoisted with great care onto the shoulders of the two Titan quarterbacks. Her arms around the necks of Ricky and B.J., Pam grinned back at Patrick as the boys carried her off. The whole team joined with them as they marched around the field, the boys chanting in unison. "We're number one! We're number one!"

Clutching the game ball in one hand, Pam waved with the other to the cheering crowd as the boys rounded the bend and headed back. When they finally returned her to the smiling Patrick, she fell into his arms.

As the boys ran for the showers, he searched her face. "You're all right, aren't you?"

"Better than all right. I feel terrific."

"I just don't want you to overdo."

She sent him a warning frown. "Don't start. I haven't felt as good about anything involving my career since... since the gold medal. Those boys are really something."

Nose to nose with her, he zeroed in. "How about personally? When was the last time you felt terrific personally?"

She gave him a womanly smile. "That evening, on my couch."

"Want a repeat?"

"Mmm, you know I do. When?"

"Soon, if you follow doctor's orders. That means coming along with me to the boardinghouse, where Mom has cooked this huge turkey and enough pumpkin pies to feed half of Tyler. Then back to your hospital bed. *But* if everything checks out, Monday you can go home."

Music to her ears. Pam hugged him to her. "Have I told you lately that I love you?"

"Not nearly often enough," Patrick said as he picked her up and carried her to his truck.

THE WEEK before Christmas found Tyler experiencing unseasonably warm weather. Instead of a predicted snowfall, it rained on December 18, which didn't sit well with Pam. For the first time since her relapse, she'd planned to get up early and go running with Samson on their favorite country road.

Sitting curled up on the couch, she sipped her morning coffee and stared out at the light drizzle. No, she wouldn't go running in rain, something she might have been tempted to do before her setback. Though the temperature hovered around fifty and actually threatened to reach sixty by midafternoon—almost unheard of for southern Wisconsin—she couldn't take a chance on catching another cold. Especially not since she was to be married on Christmas Eve morning.

She smiled at Samson as she slipped him the last of her toast and caught him looking at her oddly before he snapped up the expected treat. She'd been doing that a lot, smiling for seemingly no reason, confusing her dog and perhaps most people she ran into. But she simply couldn't help herself.

Patrick had won, convincing her that a Christmas wedding was perfect—not that she'd fought him much on the date. After the Thanksgiving game and dinner, she'd returned to the hospital for the weekend, then had been released. She'd been recovering since. She was coming along beautifully; even cautious George Phelps had been pleased. Back in remission, she'd been able to go off the antibiotics and anti-inflammatory medicine, though the doctor had advised her to keep up the massage therapy to strengthen her muscles. Since she lived with Rosemary, that had presented no problem. Just yesterday, Dr. Phelps had examined her again and pronounced her well enough to continue her normal activities.

So Saturday stretched ahead of her deliciously. Samson at the back door barked for her attention, and she got up to let him out into the yard. She was on leave of absence from school to allow time for her full recovery, but planned to return sometime in January to complete her paperwork and continue her regular girls' gym classes. That had been Patrick's recommendation and Miss Mackie had been all for it. She'd also been over yesterday to deliver Pam's new contract, for the next football season.

Last week, Pam had driven into Milwaukee with Kathleen Kelsey and found the perfect wedding dress. Patrick had hinted at a special honeymoon destination he was planning to surprise her with. And her father and brothers and their families had all been duly notified and were planning to attend the wedding. Pam had never been happier. Glancing out the window, she saw that even the rain had stopped. With a sigh, she paused in the kitchen for more coffee.

Moments later, the honking of a horn had her looking out the front window. When she saw Patrick's truck, she smiled and rushed to open the outer door.

Patrick bounded up the steps and kissed her soundly. His face buried in her hair, he inhaled deeply. "Good morning, lovely lady. Get your coat. I want to show you something."

"I'm not dressed," she said, indicating her blue jogging suit and gray running shoes.

"You're fine. Come on."

Shrugging into her tan corduroy jacket, Pam hurried after him. Inside the truck, she belted herself in before turning to him. "Where are we going?"

"It's a surprise." Taking her hand, he smiled over at the morning-fresh look of her, then concentrated on his driving. "I had an errand to run and drove back by way of a winding road. When I saw this, I had to come get you. I only hope it's still there."

Curious, she knew better than to prod him. Besides, in minutes they were on the outskirts of Tyler, bouncing along the same road she'd driven in on from Chicago that Saturday months ago when she first arrived in town. So much had happened since August,

Pam thought, lacing her fingers through Patrick's strong ones.

She'd found friends, a job she enjoyed and a love of her own. And she'd found a home.

As Patrick pulled the truck to a stop, she saw it. "A rainbow," Pam whispered. Getting out, she walked to the wooden fence, and felt Patrick's arm slide around her waist as he joined her. The arch was high, wide and handsome, spanning the pale blue sky after the rain. The fields had turned brown and the cows ambling around in them seemed surprised not to be as cold as yesterday. In the distance, a fidgety rooster crowed and a dog barked in reply. Pam moved closer to Patrick, leaning her head on his shoulder.

"Do you know how rare rainbows in December are around here?" he asked. "I don't think I've ever seen one before. I had to show you."

"It's beautiful. I drove along this very road when I came to Tyler, and I saw a rainbow then, too. I remember making a wish before I drove into town."

He turned her to face him. "And what was your wish?"

"That I'd find happiness here in the Tyler community."

Knowing the answer, he still asked. "And have you?"

"More than I'd dreamed possible." Easing up on tiptoe, she touched her mouth to his, letting the magic wash over her. The kiss was long and thorough.

Slipping his arms around her, Patrick studied her soft brown eyes. "It won't be long now and you'll be my wife. I can hardly wait."

"Nor can I. Santa Claus is arriving twice this year for me."

"For me, too."

"Miss Mackie came to see me yesterday. She brought over my contract for next year's football season."

"So now you have everything you wanted within reach."

"Yes. I'm thrilled to be asked to stay on. The boys have come to mean a great deal to me. But the football season is fairly short, and I want to do a couple of other things as well."

"Like what?"

"The MS Foundation needs fund-raisers, and they say I'm something of a name." She looked at him, a bit embarrassed.

He didn't bother to hide the pride he felt. "You called them?"

"Yes. I want to help raise money so they can find a cure. And I want to give hope to other MS patients, if I can, that they needn't look on their future as empty, but rather as limited. And perhaps one day, even that will improve."

"This is Pam Casals, the lady who wanted to live just for today?" he teased.

"I think that Pam Casals is retiring. Pam Kelsey wants to live every moment to the fullest. Life is for the living, Patrick, and none of us know how long we have left. I don't want to miss a thing, to wind up wishing I'd done this or that. I want to do it all. You taught me that."

"And you're a good pupil. What else did you have in mind to do?"

"Well, I'm nearly thirty-one and I'd like to start a family. That is, if you—"

"No problem." Patrick bent his head to kiss her again, knowing he held the world in his arms. "We can get started on that anytime."

Clinging to him, Pam sighed. "What a beautiful rainbow!"

"What say we go home?"

Home. What a beautiful word. Taking his hand, Pam nodded. "I'm ready."

And now,
an exciting preview of

WISCONSIN WEDDING

by Carla Neggers

the third installment of the
Tyler series

Nora Gates, the independent-minded owner of Tyler's first and only department store, finds her life—and her heart—in turmoil when blueblood Easterner Byron Forrester visits her beloved hometown to attend his brother's wedding. They'd once had a brief, passionate affair. Could Byron convince Nora that the love they'd shared deserved a second chance?

CHAPTER ONE

WITHIN THE SEDATE, mahogany-paneled president's office of Pierce & Rothchilde, Publishers, Byron Forrester pitched a dart at the arrogant face of his latest traitorous author. The dart nailed Henry V. Murrow smack in the middle of his neatly clipped beard. Byron grinned. He was getting pretty good at this! Now if Henry had been in his office in person instead of in the form an eight-by-ten glossy publicity photo, Byron would have been a happy man. Only that morning Henry had called to notify him that he'd just signed a mega-deal with a big New York publisher.

"For what?" Byron had demanded.

"A technothriller."

"What, do you have a dastardly villain threatening to blow up the world with a toaster? You don't know anything about advanced technology. Henry, for God's sake, you haven't even figured out the telegraph yet."

"Research, my boy. Research."

Pierce & Rothchilde didn't publish technothrillers. Its specialties were expensive-to-produce coffee table books, mostly about art, geography and history, and so-called literary fiction. Some of the latter was deadly stuff. Byron found Henry's books depressing as hell.

Technothrillers. From a man who'd been utterly defeated by the locks on Byron's sports car. "How does one exit from this contraption?" he'd asked.

Now he was calling himself Hank Murrow and planning to make a bloody fortune. Probably had shaved his beard, burned his tweeds, packed his pipe away in mothballs and taken his golden retriever to the pound.

"I wonder how much the fink's really getting."

Byron aimed another dart. Henry—*Hank*—had said seven figures, but Byron didn't believe him. He'd yet to meet a writer who didn't lie about money.

A quiet tap on his solid mahogany door forced him to fold his fingers around the stem of the dart and not throw it. He really wanted to. Henry had offered to send him a copy of his completed manuscript. Byron had declined. "It'll be more fun," Henry had said, "than anything that'll cross your desk this year." A comment all the more irritating for its probable truth. Byron had wished the turncoat well and gotten out his darts.

Without so much as a by-your-leave from him, Fanny Redbacker strode into his office. Trying to catch him throwing darts, no doubt. She regularly made it clear that she didn't think her new boss was any match for her old boss, the venerable Thorton Pierce. Byron considered that good news. His grandfather, whose father had cofounded Pierce & Rothchilde in 1894, had been a brilliant, scrawny old snob of a workaholic. He'd vowed never to retire and hadn't. He'd died in that very office, behind that very desk, five years ago. Byron, although just thirty-eight, had no intention of suffering a similar fate.

"Yes, Mrs. Redbacker?" he said, trying to sound like the head of one of the country's most prestigious publishing houses.

Mrs. Redbacker, of course, knew better. Stepping forward, she placed an envelope on his desk. Byron saw her eyes cut over to Henry Murrow's dart-riddled face and her mouth drew into a straight line of disapproval.

"It's tacked to a cork dartboard," Byron said. "I didn't get a mark on the wood paneling."

"What if you'd missed?"

"I never miss."

She inhaled. "The letter's a personal one addressed to you and Mrs. Forrester." Meaning his mother. Byron wasn't married. Mrs. Redbacker added pointedly, "The postmark is Tyler, Wisconsin."

Byron almost stabbed his hand with the dart, so completely did her words catch him off guard. Regaining his composure, he set the thing on his desk. Fanny Redbacker sighed, but didn't say anything. She didn't have to. It had been three months, and Byron still wasn't Thorton Pierce. He didn't even look like him. Where his cultured, imperious grandfather had been sandy-haired and blue-eyed and somewhat washed out in appearance, Byron took after the Forresters. He was tall, if not as tall as the Pierces, and thick-boned and dark, his hair and eyes as dark as his

father's had been. For a while everyone had thought
that despite his rough-and-ready looks Byron would
step neatly into his grandfather's hand-tooled ox-
fords.

But that was before he'd ventured to Tyler, Wisconsin, three years ago. After that trip, all bets were
off.

"Thank you, Mrs. Redbacker."

She retreated without comment.

Byron had forgotten his annoyance with Henry
Murrow. Now all he could think about was the letter
on his desk. It was addressed to Mr. Byron Forrester
and Mrs. Anne Forrester, c/o Pierce & Rothchilde,
Publishers. At a guess, the handwriting looked feminine. It certainly wasn't Cliff's.

"Oh, God," Byron breathed.

Something had happened to Cliff, and now here was
the letter informing his younger brother and mother
of the bad news.

Nora... Nora Gates had found out who Byron was
and had decided to write.

Not a chance. The letter wasn't big enough to hold
a bomb. And the scrawl was too undisciplined for
precise, would-be spinster Eleanora Gates, owner of
Gates Department Store in downtown Tyler, Wisconsin. She was the *last* person Byron wanted to think
about now.

He tore open the envelope.

Inside was a simple printed card inviting him and his
mother to the wedding of Clifton Pierce Forrester and
Liza Baron the Saturday after this in Tyler.

A letter bomb would have surprised Byron less.
There was a note attached.

Cliff's doing great and I know he wants to see you
both. Please come. I think it would be best if you
just showed up, don't you?

                                                    Liza

A hoax? This Liza character had neglected to leave
a return address or a phone number, and the invitation didn't request a reply. The wedding was to take
place at the Tyler Lutheran church. To find out more,
presumably, Byron would have to head to Wisconsin.

Was that what Liza Baron wanted?

Who the hell was she?

Was Cliff getting married?

At a guess, Byron thought, his brother didn't know
that Miss Liza Baron had fired off an invitation to the
sedate Providence offices of Pierce & Rothchilde,
Publishers.

Byron leaned back in his leather chair and closed his
eyes.

Tyler, Wisconsin.

A thousand miles away and three years later and he
could still feel the warm sun of Midwest August on his
face. He could see the corn standing tall in the rolling
fields outside Tyler and the crowd gathered in the town
square for a summer band concert. He could hear old
Ellie Gates calling out the winner of the quilt raffle, to
raise money for repairing the town clock. First prize
was a hand-stitched quilt of intersecting circles. By-

ron later learned that its design was called Wisconsin Wedding, a variation on the traditional wedding ring design created by Tyler's own quilting ladies.

And he could hear her laugh. Nora's laugh. It wasn't her fake spinsterish laugh he heard, but the laugh that was soft and free, unrestrained by the peculiar myths that dominated her life.

He'd gone to Tyler once and had almost destroyed Nora Gates. He'd almost destroyed himself. And his brother. How could he go back?

Please come....

Byron had waited for years to be invited back into his older brother's life. There'd been Vietnam, Cambodia, a hospital in the Philippines, sporadic attempts at normality. And then nothing. For five years, nothing.

Now this strange invitation—out of the blue—to his brother's wedding.

An Alyssa Baron had intervened on Cliff's behalf and helped the burned-out recluse make a home at an abandoned lodge on a lake outside town. Was Liza Baron her daughter?

So many questions, Byron thought.

And so many dangers. Too many, perhaps.

He picked up his last dart. If he or his mother—or both—just showed up in Tyler after all these years, what would Cliff do? What if their presence sent him back over the edge? Liza Baron might have good intentions, but did she know what she was doing in making this gesture to her fiancé's estranged family?

But upsetting Cliff wasn't Byron's biggest fear. They were brothers. Cliff had gone away because of his love for and his loyalty to his family. That much Byron understood.

No, his biggest fear was of a slim, tawny-haired Tylerite who'd fancied herself a grand Victorian old maid at thirty, in an era when nobody believed in old maids. What would proper, pretty Nora Gates do if he showed up in her hometown again?

Byron sat up straight. "She'd come after you, my man." He fired his dart. "With a blowtorch."

The pointed tip of the dart penetrated the polished mahogany paneling with a loud *thwack,* missing Henry Murrow's nose by a good eight inches.

The Nora Gates effect.

He was probably the only man on earth who knew that she wasn't anything like the refined, soft-spoken spinster lady she pretended she was. For that, she hated his guts. Her parting words to him three years ago had been, "Then leave, you despicable cad."

Only Nora.

But even worse, he suspected he was the only man who'd ever lied to her and gotten away with it. At least so far. When he'd left Tyler three years ago, Nora hadn't realized he'd lied. And since she hadn't come after him with a bucket of hot tar, he assumed she still didn't realize he had.

If he returned to Tyler, however, she'd know for sure.

And then what?

"MISS GATES?"

Nora recognized the voice on the telephone—it was that of Mrs. Mickelson in china and housewares, around the corner from her office on the third floor. For a few months after Aunt Ellie's death three years ago, the staff at Gates Department Store hadn't quite known how to address the young Eleanora Gates. Most had been calling her Nora for years, but now that she was their boss that just wouldn't do. And "Ms. Gates" simply didn't sound right. So they settled, without any discussion that Nora knew about, on Miss Gates—the same thing they'd called her aunt. It was as if nothing had changed. And in many ways, nothing had.

"I have Liza Baron here," Mrs. Mickelson said.

Nora settled back in the rosewood chair Aunt Ellie had bought in Milwaukee in 1925. "Oh?"

"She's here to fill out her bridal registry, but...well, you know Miss Baron. She's grumbling about feudalistic rituals. I'm afraid I just don't know what to say."

"Send her into my office," Nora said, stifling a laugh. Despite her years away from Tyler, Liza Baron obviously hadn't changed. "I'll be glad to handle this one for you."

Claudia Mickelson made no secret of her relief as she hung up. It wasn't that Nora was any better equipped for the task of keeping Liza Baron happy. It was, simply, that should Liza screech out of town in a blue funk and get Cliff Forrester to elope with her, thus denying Tyler its grandest wedding since Chicago socialite Margaret Lindstrom married Tyler's own Judson Ingalls some fifty years before, it would be on Nora's head.

Five minutes later, Mrs. Mickelson and the unlikely bride burst into Nora's sedate office. Mrs. Mickelson surrendered catalogs and the bridal registry book, wished Liza well and retreated. Liza plopped down on the caned chair in front of the elegant but functional rosewood desk. Wearing a multicolored serape over a bright orange oversize top and skinny black leggings, Liza Baron was as stunning and outrageous and completely herself as Nora remembered. That she'd fallen head over heels in love for the town's recluse didn't surprise Nora in the least. Liza Baron had always had a mind of her own. Anyway, love was like that. It was an emotion Nora didn't necessarily trust.

"This was all my mother's idea," Liza announced.

"It usually is." Nora, a veteran calmer of bridal jitters, smiled. "A bridal register makes life much easier for the mother of the bride. Otherwise, people continually call and ask her for suggestions of what to buy as a wedding gift. It gets tiresome, and if she gives the wrong advice, it's all too easy for her to be blamed."

Liza scowled. There was talk around town—not that Nora was one to give credence to talk—that Liza just might hop into her hot little white car and blow out of town as fast and suddenly as she'd blown in. Not because she didn't love Cliff Forrester, but because she obviously did. Only this morning Nora had overheard two members of her staff speculating on the potential effects on Liza's unusual fiancé of a big wedding and marrying into one of Tyler's first families. Would he be able tolerate all the attention? Would he bolt? Would he go off the deep end?

"Well," Liza said, "the whole thing strikes me as sexist and mercenary."

Liza Baron had always been one to speak her mind, something Nora admired. She herself also valued directness, even if her own manner was somewhat more diplomatic. "You have a point, but I don't think that's the intent."

"You don't see anybody dragging *Cliff* down here to pick out china patterns, do you?"

"No, that wouldn't be the custom."

It was enough of a shock, Nora thought, to see Liza Baron with a catalog of Wedgwood designs in front of her. But if Liza was somewhat nontraditional, Cliff Forrester— Well, for years townspeople had wondered if they ought to fetch an expert in posttraumatic stress disorder from Milwaukee to have a look at him, make sure his gray matter was what it should be. He'd lived alone at Timberlake Lodge for at least five years, maybe longer. He'd kept to himself for the most part and, as far as anyone knew, had never hurt anyone. Nora had long ago decided that most of the talk about him was just that: talk. She figured he was a modern-day hermit pretty much as she was a modern-day spinster—by choice. It didn't mean either of them had a screw loose. Cliff, of course, had met Liza Baron and chosen to end his isolation. Nora had no intention of ending hers.

"If I were in your place," she went on, "I'd consider this a matter of practicality. Do you want to end up with three silver tea services?"

Liza shuddered. "I don't want *one* silver tea service."

Nora marked that down. "When people don't know what the bride and groom want, they tend to buy what *they* would want. It's human nature. It's to be a big wedding, isn't it?"

"Mother's doing. She's got half of Tyler coming. Cliff and I would have been happy getting married by a justice of the peace without any fanfare."

That, Nora felt, wasn't entirely true. Cliff no doubt dreaded facing a crowd, but would do it for Liza—and for her mother, too, who'd been his only real friend for years. But in Nora's estimation, Liza Baron relished being the center of attention again in Tyler. It wasn't that she was spoiled or snobby; she was still getting used to having finally come home to Tyler at all, never mind planning to marry and stay there. It was more that she wasn't sure how she was supposed to act now that she was home again. She needed to find a way to weave herself into the fabric of the community on her own terms. The wedding was, in part, beautiful vivacious Liza's way of welcoming the people of her small hometown back into her life. As far as Nora was concerned, it was perfectly natural that occasionally Liza would seem ambivalent, even hostile. In addition to the stress of a big church wedding, she was also coping with her once-tattered relationship with her mother, and all the gossip about the Ingalls and Baron families.

And that included the body that had turned up at the lake. But Nora wasn't about to bring up that particular tidbit.

She discreetly glanced at the antique grandfather clock that occupied the corner behind Liza. Of the office furnishings, only the calendar, featuring birds of Wisconsin, had changed since Aunt Ellie's day.

"Oh, all right," Liza said with great drama, "I'm here. Let's do this thing. The prospect of coping with stacks of plastic place mats with scenes of Wisconsin and a dozen gravy boats does give one pause."

Gates carried both items Liza considered offensive. Nora herself owned a set of Wisconsin place mats. She used them for picnics and when the neighborhood children wandered into her kitchen for milk and cookies. Her favorite was the one featuring Tyler's historic library. She didn't tell Liza that she was bound to get at least one set of Wisconsin place mats. Inger Hansen, one of the quilting ladies, had bought Wisconsin place mats for every wedding she'd attended since they first came on the market in 1972. Nora had been in high school then, working at Gates part-time.

They got down to business. "Now," Nora explained to her reluctant customer, "here's how a bridal register works. You list your china, silverware and glassware patterns, any small appliances you want, sheets, towels, table linens. There are any number of variables, depending on what you and Cliff want."

Liza wrinkled up her pretty face. She was, Nora saw, a terribly attractive woman. She herself was of average height and build, with a tendency to cuteness that she did her best to disguise with sophisticated—but not too chic—business clothes and makeup. She didn't own a single article of clothing in pink, no flowered or heart-shaped anything, no polka dots, no T-shirts with pithy sayings, damned little lace. No serapes, no bright orange tops, no skinny black leggings. She preferred cool, subdued colors to offset her pale gray eyes and ash-blond hair, which she kept in a classic bob. Liza Baron, on the other hand, would look wild in anything. Cast them each in a commercial, and Judson Ingalls's rebellious granddaughter would sell beer, Ellie Gate's grandniece life insurance.

"Nora, Cliff doesn't want anything. He'd be happy living in a damned cave."

But, as Nora had anticipated, in the quiet and privacy of the third floor office, with its window overlooking the Tyler town square, Liza Baron warmed to her task. She briskly dismissed anything too cute or too simple and resisted the most expensive patterns Gates carried. She finally settled on an elegant and dramatic china pattern from England, American silver-plate flatware, a couple of small appliances, white linens all around, Brazilian knives and a special request to please discourage electric can openers. The stemware gave her the worst fits. Finally she admitted it was Waterford or nothing.

"Go for it," Nora said, amused. She tried to picture Cliff Forrester drinking from a Waterford goblet and found—strangely—that she could. Had someone said he was from a prominent East Coast family? Like most people in Tyler, Nora knew next to nothing about the mysterious, quiet man who lived at rundown Timberlake Lodge.

Liza slumped back in the delicate caned chair. "Is it too late to elope?"

"People would still buy you gifts."

Their work done, a silence fell between the two women. Despite her busy schedule, Nora was in no hurry to rush Liza out. The younger woman had gone through a lot in the past weeks, and if the rumors circulating in the shops, restaurants and streets of Tyler were even remotely on target, she had more to endure. Falling in love with an outsider had certainly been enough to stimulate gossip, even undermine Liza's beliefs about what she wanted out of life. In Nora's view, that right there was enough reason to steer clear of men: romance caused change.

It was as if Liza had read her mind. "You've never been married, have you, Nora?"

"No, I haven't. I like my life just the way it is."

Liza smiled. "Good for you. Have you ever been tempted?"

Nora's hesitation, she was sure, was noticeable only to herself. "Nope."

"Well, I certainly don't believe a woman has to be married to be happy or complete."

"But you're happy with Cliff."

"Yes." Her smile broadened. "Yes, I am."

Indeed, falling so completely in love with Cliff Forrester had already had an unmistakable effect on one of Tyler's most rebellious citizens. Liza Baron, however, seemed much more willing to embrace change than Nora was. She seemed more at peace with herself than she had when she'd first blown back into town, if a little rattled at the prospect of a big Tyler wedding.

Nora shrugged. "Romance doesn't have a positive effect on me, I'm afraid. It makes me crazy and silly... I lose control."

Liza's eyes widened in surprise, as if she'd never imagined Nora Gates having had anything approaching a romance, and she grinned. "Isn't that the whole idea?"

"I suppose for some, but I—" Nora stopped herself in the nick of time. What was she saying? "Well, I'm speaking theoretically, of course. I've never... I'm not one for romantic notions." A fast change of subject was in order. "How're the renovations at the lodge coming?"

"Fabulously well. Better than I expected, really, given all that's gone on. You should come out and take a look."

"I'd love to," Nora said, meaning it. As if marriage and her return to Tyler weren't stressful enough, Liza had also come up with the idea of renovating Timberlake Lodge, a monumental project Nora personally found exciting. Unfortunately, the work had led to discovery of a human skeleton on the premises.

Not the sort of thing one wanted percolating on the back burner while planning one's wedding.

"Anytime. And thank you, Nora."

"Oh, you don't need to thank me—"

Liza shook her head. "No, I've been acting like a big baby and you've been so nice about it. The store looks great, by the way. Your aunt would be proud, I'm sure. You've added your own touches, but retained the flavor and spirit everyone always remembers about Gates. When I think I'm living in the boondocks, I just walk past your windows and realize there is indeed taste and culture here in Tyler." She hesitated a moment, something uncharacteristic of Judson Ingalls's youngest grandchild. "Ellie Gates was quite a character. She's still missed around here."

"She is," Nora agreed simply.

"Well, I should be off." Liza rose with a sudden burst of energy. "I guess I'll go through with this big fancy wedding. If nothing else, Tyler could use a good party right now."

Now Liza Baron was sounding like herself. Nora swept to her feet. "You're probably right about that. I suppose you haven't heard anything more from the police?"

Liza shook her head. "Not a word."

Without saying so outright, they both knew they were talking about what Nora had begun to refer to as the Body at the Lake. The *Tyler Citizen* reported every new and not-so-new development in the case, but the rumors were far more speculative. Given her ownership of Tyler's only department store, her membership on the town council and her circumspect nature, Nora was privy to considerable amounts of local gossip, which she never repeated. Certainly *anyone* could have been buried at the long-abandoned lodge. Someone from out of town or out of state could have driven up, plucked a body out of the trunk, dug a hole and dropped it in. But townspeople's imaginations were fired by the idea that the body was that of Tyler's most famous—actually, its only—missing person, Margaret Alyssa Lindstrom Ingalls. People said Liza was a lot like her flamboyant grandmother. Bad enough, Nora thought, that Liza had to cope with having a dead body dug up in her yard. Worse that it could be that of her long-lost grandmother.

"I'll continue to hope for the best," Nora said diplomatically.

Liza's smile this time was feeble. "Thank you."

But before she left, she spun around one more time, scrape flying. "Oh, I almost forgot. Cliff specifically wanted me to ask if you were coming to the wedding. You are, aren't you?"

"Well, yes, I'd love to, but I've never even met Cliff—"

"Oh, he's seen you around town and admires your devotion to Tyler and . . . how did he put it? Your balance, I think he said. He says if he has to endure a huge wedding, he should at least have a few people around who won't make him feel uncomfortable." Liza's eyes misted, her expression softening. She looked like a woman in love. "God knows he's trying. He's still uneasy around people—I guess you could call this wedding a trial by fire. Not only will half of Tyler be there, but there's a chance his family'll come, too."

"I didn't realize he had any family."

"A mother and a brother." Liza bit the corner of her mouth, suddenly unsure of herself. "They're from Providence."

"Providence, Rhode Island?" Nora asked, her knees weakening.

"Umm. Real East Coast mucky-mucks."

Byron Sanders, the one man who'd penetrated Nora's defenses, had been from Providence, Rhode Island. But that had to be a coincidence. That wretched cad couldn't have anything to do with a man like Cliff Forrester.

"Are they coming?" Nora asked.

Liza cleared her throat hesitantly. "Haven't heard. From what I gather, our wedding's pretty quick for a Forrester, so who knows?"

"Cliff must be anxious—"

"Oh, no, I don't think so. He hasn't had much to do with his family since he moved out here. Nothing at all, in fact. He takes all the blame, but I don't think that's fair. He didn't tell them where he was for a couple of years, but when he did finally let them know, he told them to leave him alone. But they could have bulldozed their way back into his life if they'd really wanted to." She grinned. "Just like I did."

"But Cliff did invite them?"

"Well, not exactly."

Nora didn't need a sledgehammer to get the point. "You mean *you* did? Without his knowledge?"

"Yep."

Now that, Nora thought, could get interesting.

"I guess we'll just have to wait to see how it goes," Liza added.

With a polite, dismissive comment, Nora promised Liza that she and her staff would steer people in the right direction when they came to Gates hunting for an appropriate wedding gift. Liza looked so relieved and happy when she left that Nora felt much better. Why on earth was she worrying about Byron Sanders just because he and Cliff Forrester were from the same state? Rhode Island wasn't *that* small. No, that weasel was just a black, secret chapter in her life.

She tucked the bridal register under her arm to return to Claudia Mickelson. She did love a wedding—as long as it wasn't her own.